AIR TIME

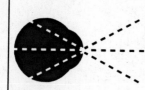

This Large Print Book carries the
Seal of Approval of N.A.V.H.

A CHARLOTTE McNALLY MYSTERY,
BOOK 2

AIR TIME

HANK PHILLIPPI RYAN

KENNEBEC LARGE PRINT
A part of Gale, Cengage Learning

GALE
CENGAGE Learning

Detroit • New York • San Francisco • New Haven, Conn • Waterville, Maine • London

GALE
CENGAGE Learning

LIBRARY OF CONGRESS CATALOGING-IN-PUBLICATION DATA

Ryan, Hank Phillippi.
  Air time : a Charlotte McNally novel / by Hank Phillippi Ryan.
  — Large print ed.
    p. cm. — (Kennebec large print superior collection)
  ISBN-13: 978-1-4104-3021-2
  ISBN-10: 1-4104-3021-9
  1. Women television journalists—Fiction. 2. Investigative reporting—Fiction. 3. Large type books. I. Title.
PS3618.Y333.A47 2010
813'.6—dc22   2010036632

Published in 2010 in arrangement with Harlequin Books S.A.

Printed in the United States of America
  1 2 3 4 5   14 13 12 11 10
ED320

ACKNOWLEDGMENTS

Unending gratitude to

Ann Leslie Tuttle, my brilliant, wise and gracious editor; Charles Griemsman, patient and droll, king of deadlines. To the remarkable team at MIRA Books, Tara Gavin, Margaret O'Neill Marbury and Valerie Gray. The inspirational Donna Hayes. Your unerring judgment and unfailing support make this an extraordinary experience.

Kristin Nelson, the most remarkable agent.

Francesca Coltrera, my astonishingly skilled independent editor, who lets me believe all the good ideas are mine.

The artistry and savvy of Madeira James, Bonnie Katz, Judy Spagnola, Charlie Anctil, Jonathan Hall, Kurt Hartwell, Janet Koch and Nancy Berland.

The inside info and unique knowledge of intellectual property attorney Mark Schonfeld; a fashion expert I promised not to name; and the FBI Citizens' Academy.

The bravery, skill and patience of airline flight attendants.

The inspiration of David Morrell, Mary Jane Clark, Amy MacKinnon, Jim Huang, Marianne Mancusi, Norman Knight and Margaret Maron.

The posse at Sisters in Crime and Mystery Writers of America.

My amazing blog sisters. At Jungle Red Writers: Jan Brogan, Hallie Ephron, Roberta Isleib, Rosemary Harris and Rhys Bowen. At Femmes Fatales: Charlaine Harris, Dana Cameron, Elaine Viets, Kris Neri, Mary Saums, Toni Kelner and Donna Andrews.

My dear friends Amy Isaac, Mary Schwager and Katherine Hall Page; and my darling sister Nancy Landman.

Mom — Mrs. McNally is not you, except for the wonderful parts. Dad — who loves every moment of this.

And of course Jonathan, who never com-
plained about all the pizza.

CHAPTER ONE

It's never a good thing when the flight attendant is crying. Franklin, strapped into the seat beside me, his seat back and tray table in the full upright position, headphones on and deep into *Columbia Journalism Review,* doesn't notice her tears. But I do.

She's wearing a name tag that says Tracy, a navy blue pencil skirt, a bow-tied striped scarf, flat-heeled pumps and dripping mascara. We're sitting on the Baltimore airport tarmac, still attached to the jetway, a full fifteen minutes past our scheduled takeoff for Boston and home. And Tracy's crying.

I nudge Franklin with my elbow and tilt my head toward her. "Franko, check it out."

Only Franklin's eyes move as, with a sigh, he glances up from under his new wire-rimmed glasses. He looks like an owl. Then, without a word, he slowly closes his *CJR* and finally looks at me. I can see he's as unnerved as I am. His eyes question, and I have the only answer a television reporter can give.

"Get your cell," I whisper. "Turn it on."

"But, Charlotte —" he begins.

He's undoubtedly going to tell me some Federal Aviation Administration rule about not using cell phones in flight. Like any successful television producer, Franklin always knows all the rules. Like any successful television reporter, I'm more often about breaking them. If it could mean a good story.

"We're not in flight," I hiss. "We haven't budged on this runway. But one of us — you — is going to get video of whatever it is that's going on here. The other — me — is going to call the assignment desk back at Channel 3 and see if they know what the heck is happening at this airport."

I look out my window. Nothing. I look back up at Tracy, who's now huddling with her colleagues in the galley a few rows in front of us. Their coiffed heads are bent close together and one has a comforting arm around another's shoulders. The faces I can see look concerned. One looks up and catches me staring. She swipes a tapestry curtain across the aisle, blocking my view.

Part of me is, absurdly, relieved that our

takeoff is delayed. I hate takeoffs. I hate landings. I hate flying. And if something terrible has happened, all I can say is, I'm not surprised.

But I have to find out if there's a story here. Maybe Tracy just has some sort of a personal problem and I'm making breaking news out of a broken heart. I yank my bag from under the seat in front of me and slide out my own cell phone. Bending double so my phone is buried in my lap, I pretend to sneeze to cover the tim-tee-tum sound of it powering up, then sneeze again to make it more convincing. As I'm contemplating sneeze three, I hear my call to the assignment desk connect.

"It's me. Charlie," I whisper. I pause, closing my eyes in annoyance at the response. "Charlie McNally. The reporter? Is this an intern?" I pause again, picturing a newbie twentysomething in over her head. Me, twenty-two years ago. Twenty-three, maybe. I start again, calm. Taking the snark out of my voice. "It's Charlotte McNally, the investigative reporter? Give me Roger, please." I glance at the curtain to the galley. Still closed. "Right now."

Franklin's up and in the aisle, holding his cell phone as if it's off as he pretends to take a casual stroll toward the galley curtains. I know he's got video rolling. I know his phone has a ten-minute photo capacity, and he's done this so many times he can click it off and on without looking. Talk about a hidden camera. Our fellow passengers will only see an attractive thirty-something black guy in a preppy pink oxford shirt checking out the flight attendants. I see Franklin Brooks Parrish, my faithful producer, getting the shots we need. Whatever is happening — all caught on camera. Exclusive.

"Roger Zelinsky." The night assignment editor's Boston accent makes it Rah-jah. "What's up, C?"

"We're in Baltimore, on the way home from the National Journalism Convention," I say, still doubled over into my lap and whispering. Luckily Franklin and I had an empty seat between us. A hidden camera is one thing — a hidden forbidden conversation on a cell phone is another. "We're at the airport. In a plane. On the tarmac."

"So?" Roger replies.

"Exactly," I say. "That's what I'm trying to find out." I give him the short-version scoop on the tears, the delay, the closed curtain. Franklin's now made it to the galley, his phone camera nonchalantly pointed at the spot where the curtain would open.

But it hasn't opened. Maybe Tracy broke up with the pilot. Maybe they don't have enough packages of peanuts. Maybe someone decided to smoke in the bathroom.

Then, even through the fuzzy phone connection, I hear all hell break loose at Channel 3. Strapped in and surrounded by passengers and pillows and carry-on bags, on Flight 632 there's only the muted sounds of passengers muttering, speculating. But about five hundred miles away, in a Boston television newsroom, bells are ringing and alarms are going off. I know it's the breaking news signal. The Associated Press is banging out a hot story. I bet it's centered right here. And any second, I'm gonna know the scoop in Baltimore.

"Runway collision. Two planes. A 737 and some commuter jet. Cessna. I'm reading from the wires, hang on." Roger's voice is now urgent. I can picture him, eyes narrowed, racing through the information coming through on his computer. Bulletins appear one or two sentences at a time and with every new addition more alert bells ping. "No casualty count yet. One plane taxiing toward takeoff, one on the ground."

"The little plane," I begin. "How many — was it — which —"

"Don't know," Roger replies. Terse. The

bell pings again and our connection breaks up a bit. "Fire engines," he says.

I've got to get off this plane. I've got to get into the terminal. This story is big, it's breaking, and I'm ready to handle it.

"Call you asap," I whisper, interrupting. "I'm getting out of here." I snap my phone closed, tuck it into my bag, unclasp my seat belt and stand up. Franklin looks over, and I signal with widening eyes and a tilt of my head. *Come back.*

Franklin glances at the still motionless curtain. He points his phone backward and returns to our seats. Camera rolling. Just in case.

I grab his arm and yank him back into seat 18C. "Listen," I hiss. "There's been a collision on the runway here. Fire, Roger says." I pause, hoping no one can hear me. "I've got to get off this plane and into the airport."

Franklin wipes away imaginary creases from his still-perfect khakis. I know this means he's thinking. Calculating. Taking in the information.

"Listen, Charlotte. I know you're addicted to the news," he says, voice low. "But you've got to get to Boston. Our interview with the Prada P.I. is scheduled for tomorrow morning. She's meeting us at the airport. It's

14

between flights for her. It's tomorrow or never. That's her schedule." Franklin apparently has a BlackBerry implanted in his brain.

"She's got the specs and some inside scoop on counterfeit bags," he says. "She's giving us documents from the purse designers. Without her, our 'fabulous fakes' story may not be so fabulous."

He glances toward the galley curtain, so I do, too. Nothing.

"Local reporters can cover the runway incursion," Franklin continues. "They're probably already on the air with whatever the story is. And you're the big-time investigative reporter, remember? You don't do breaking news like this anymore. You've got to stay on this plane and get back to Boston."

I know I'm an aging Dalmatian. But when the fire bell rings, I can't stand to be out of the action. The secret to TV success is being at the right place at the right time. And recognizing it. I flip up the armrests between us, stand up again, and try to edge around Franklin and into the aisle. Luckily I have on flats, so I'll be able to run if I need to. And my black pants, white T-shirt and black leather jacket will look appropriately serious when I go on camera. I'm heading for significant airtime. And a big story.

"Piffle," I say. "I can cover this story, make Channel 3 look good, thrill Kevin by providing him with the news director's dream 'local reporter on the scene to cover national news' segment, hop the next plane to Boston and arrive in plenty of time for the meeting. It's at eleven, after all. You worry too much, Franko. Now, move it."

Franklin doesn't budge. "You don't worry enough, Charlotte. You're not going anywhere," he says. He points to seat 18A. "Sit."

I don't. But I can't get out unless Franklin moves. I twist toward him, my back crammed against the seat in front of me, my head bowed under the too-short-for-my-five-foot-seven-self curving plastic ceiling of the 737.

"Your suitcase," he says. "It's checked. And you ain't goin' nowhere without it. After September eleven? Nobody checks a bag, then gets off the plane. Forget about it."

"Nope," I say. I try my exit move again, but Franklin is still blocking me. "I got the lattes. You checked both bags, remember? They're both attached to your ticket. Far as this airline is concerned, I have no baggage. Which means you can pick them both up in

16

Boston and I'll get mine from you later. There is certainly a morning flight. Which means I'm free to go. And I'm going."

I see Franklin hesitate. I've won.

"Call Josh, okay?" I say, edging my way closer to the aisle. "Tell him . . ." I pause, one hand on the seat back, considering. It looks like yet another news story will keep me from my darling Josh Gelston. Maybe I should just stay on the plane. Go home. Let the locals cover the story. Have a life with the first man in twenty years who isn't interested in my celebrity. Or jealous of it. Who isn't intimidated by my job. Professor Josh Gelston is also the first man in twenty years who, I realize, makes me want to go home. Well, as soon as I can.

"Tell Josh what happened," I say. "Tell him I'll be back as soon as I can. Actually, he's at some school event tonight, so just leave a message. And ask him to call Amy to feed Botox. And I'll talk to him tomorrow." Josh will understand about the cat sitter. And my situation. I hope.

Franklin smoothes the wrinkles again, then shrugs. And this time, he slides his knees to one side, allowing me to squirm my way out into the aisle. "They'll never let you off this plane," he predicts.

■ ■ ■ ■

The unfamiliar airport blurs into a collage of gate numbers, flashing lights and rolling suitcases as I snake my way past luggage-toting passengers, blue-uniformed flight crews, maintenance carts and posses of stern-faced TSA officers. I'm focused on finding gate C-47. My cell phone is clamped to my ear, the line open to Channel 3, but no one is on the other end yet. I'm waiting for more updates from Roger. So far all I know is I'm supposed to meet the Baltimore station's crew — a camera-person and a live satellite van — from our local network affiliate. We'll go live as soon as the uplink is set. And as soon as someone tells me what's happened.

No one in the terminal is running, which seems strange. I don't see any emergency crews. That's strange, too. Maybe because it's all happening in a different terminal. They don't want to scare anyone.

I wonder if anyone is hurt. I wonder what went wrong. I wonder if there's a fire. I think about survivors. I think about families. I've covered too many plane crashes over the past twenty years. And part of me knows that's why I'm so unhappy about flying. I try not to admit it, because an investigative reporter is supposed to be tough and fearless. When it comes to air travel, I pretend a lot.

"Yup, I'm here," I answer the staticky voice now crackling in my ear. The block-lettered signs for Terminal C are pointing me to the left. Following the arrows, I trot through the crowded corridor, listening to Roger tell me the latest. I stop, suddenly, realizing what he's saying. A Disney-clad family divides in half to get by, throwing annoyed looks as they swarm back together in front of me. I barely notice.

"So, you're telling me there's nothing?" I reply. "You're telling me — no big collision? No casualties? No fire?"

"Yep. Nope," Roger says. "Apparently one wing tip of a regional jet just touched a 737. On the ground. No passengers in the smaller plane. But the pilot panicked, May-dayed the tower, they sent the alarm, fire crews powered in. Every pilot on the tarmac picked up the radio traffic — guess that's how your flight attendant got wind of it. And the Associated Press, of course. It was a close call. But no biggie."

"So . . ." My adrenaline is fading as I face reality. I plop into a leatherette seat along the wall, stare at my toes, and try to make journalism lemonade. "So, listen. Should we do a story about the close call? Should we do an investigation about crowded runways? Is there a pattern of collisions at the Baltimore airport?"

"Charlie, that's why we love you," Roger says with a chuckle. "Always looking for a good story. Does your brain ever turn off? Come home, kiddo. Thanks for being a team player."

It's the best possible outcome, of course, I tell myself as I slowly click my phone closed and tuck it back into my bag. And it's certainly proof of how a reporter's perspective gets warped by the quest for airtime. How can anyone be sorry there's not a plane crash? I smile, acknowledging journalism's ugliest secret. A huge fire? A string of victims? A multimillion dollar scam? Bad news is big news. Only a reporter can feel disappointed when the news is good.

But actually, there is good news that I'm happy about. Now I can go home. To Josh. My energy revs as I race to the nearest flight information screen and devour the numbers displayed on the televisions flickering above me. Arrivals. Departures. If I'm lucky, my plane is still hooked to that jetway, doors open. I can get back on board, into 18A, and get home for a late and luscious dinner

20

with Josh. I imagine his welcoming arms swooping me off the floor in a swirling hug. Our "don't stay-away-this-long-ever-again" kisses. I imagine skipping dinner.

I find what I'm looking for. Boston, Flight 632. I find what I'm not looking for. Status: Departed.

I drop my tote bag to the tiled floor. Then pick it up again so the airport police don't whisk it away as an unattended bag. There are no more flights to Boston tonight. I'm trapped in Baltimore.

Wandering back down the corridor and into the ladies' room, I'm trying to plan. I twist my hair up with a scrunchie. Take out my contacts. Put on my glasses. No one knows me here. Might as well be comfortable.

I have no story. I also have no clothes, I realize, as I stroll by the bustling baggage claim area. No toothbrush. No contact-lens solution to put my lenses back in tomorrow. No . . .

"Dammit!" A twentysomething girl, teetering on strappy, outrageously high platform sandals, is struggling to wrestle the world's largest suitcase from the moving conveyor belt. I watch as she tugs at the handle with one French-manicured hand, trotting alongside the moving conveyor. Her tawny hair swinging across her shoulders, she yanks on the bag's chocolate-brown leather strap again. And again. But the baggage doesn't budge, continuing its travel away from her. And almost out of reach. She stamps an impatient foot, then looks around, defeated and annoyed, her hair whirling like one of those girls in a shampoo ad. I look, too, but there are no skycaps in sight.

"Need some help?" I offer. The laws of physics will never allow her the leverage to yank that obviously pricey closet on wheels away from the flapping plastic baffles that cover the entrance to wherever unclaimed baggage goes. Fashion-victim shoes aside, this girl probably lives on diet soda and breath strips.

I put down my tote bag, grab her suitcase handle, and wrench her tan-and-brown monolith from the belt. It lands with a thud on one wheel. We both move to steady it before it topples to the floor.

"Oh, wow. Thank you," she says. Her voice has the trace of an accent, exotic, but I can't place it. "I practically live in airports, but usually there is someone to help."

"Yeah, well, that was clearly going to be a problem," I say, gesturing to her actually very elegant and certainly expensive designer suitcase. Unless — hmm. I wish the

Prada P.I. was here now to tell me if it's authentic. "I guess that's why they call it luggage."

She stares at me, uncomprehending.

"Lug?" I say. "Luggage?" I try to cover my failed attempt at humor by offering a compliment. "That's quite the gorgeous bag. Where did you —"

The girl compares her claim check with the one on the bag. It's tagged ATL, from Atlanta. Although there's hardly going to be a mistake about who it belongs to. This isn't one of the black wheelie clones circling the baggage claim.

"Ah, yes, it's from . . ." She pauses, putting one slim hand on one impossibly slim blue-jeaned hip, and looks me up and down. Assessing, somehow. "You've been so nice to me. Let me ask you. Do you like it?" She points to her suitcase.

She's not from Atlanta. Canadian? French, maybe? As if she needed to be even more attractive. And she's asking if I like her suitcase? Maybe it's a cultural thing. I shrug. "Well, sure."

The girl holds out a hand. "I'm Regine," she says. Ray-zheen.

"I'm . . ." I begin to introduce myself, shaking her hand. But she's still talking.

"If you are interested in designer bags?

Like this one?" She waits for my answer, head tilted, one eyebrow lifted.

"Well, of course, I . . ."

"Then here," she interrupts again. She digs into her recognizably logo-covered pouch of a purse, pulls out a cream-colored business card, and presents it to me with what looks like a conspiratorial smile.

I glance at it, then back at her. Her eyes are twinkling, as if she has a secret. And I guess she does. "Designer Doubles?" I read from the card. I look back at her suitcase. This day is getting a whole lot more interesting. And potentially a whole lot more valuable. Talk about the right place at the right time. Thank you, news gods.

"Designer Doubles? You mean, your suitcase is not really . . . ?" I pretend to be baffled.

"Not a bit," she replies. She pats her purse. "And neither is this one. But they are perfect, are they not? The Web site on that card will tell you where you can find a purse party. And there, you can buy one for yourself."

"Well, my goodness," I say, allowing my eyes to go wide. As if I'm considering some fabulously tempting offer. "I think I've heard about this in magazines."

"Exactly." Regine nods, as if the lust for

24

luxury somehow bonds us. She twirls her bag on one wheel, ready to join the swirl of departing passengers heading for the exit. "My pleasure."

And she's gone.

Buy one for myself, she'd suggested. What a very lovely idea.

Tucking the card safely into a zippered pocket of my tote bag, I'm already reworking our story. Talk about the right place at the right time. If this all goes as I hope, I am indeed going to buy one for myself. Perhaps several. But what Regine doesn't know is I'll be doing it in disguise. Undercover. And carrying a hidden camera. This glossy, expensive little business card could be my ticket to journalism glory.

If I don't get caught.

CHAPTER TWO

White wine from the minibar. And peanuts. Very glam. It's just past 11:30 p.m., according to the glowing green numbers of the hotel room clock. I bite a snip into the plastic peanut package and flap open the leatherette Guest Services loose-leaf binder on the dresser, considering whether it's worth it to expense dinner in the "world-class" Atrium Lounge.

Taking a sip of wine, I survey my home for the night. The Baltimore Airport Lodge. Could be anywhere, with its mass-produced faux masterpieces on the walls, fake leather ice bucket with a plastic liner. Heavily scented little soaps wrapped to look expensive. Everything pretending to be something it's not.

Folding suitcase rack, empty. At least I won't have to worry about packing in the morning.

Room service it is. Avoiding my lipstick, I

carefully peel off my white T-shirt, knowing it's all I have for tomorrow, then hang it and my wilted black pants in the otherwise empty closet. I'd be so bummed if it weren't for the purse-pushing Regine. I need to tell Franklin about that.

And that reminds me I have to call him. Chat with him about tomorrow's encounter with the Prada P.I. It kills me that designers hire private investigators to scout for knock-offs of their trademarked products. Working online and in stores, they're more like industrial spies, searching for the secret signs manufacturers use to mark an authentic item. Not a bad gig. Next life, I'm going to be a shopper.

I throw on the fluffy white bathrobe the hotel, thankfully, provided on the bathroom door hook and plop cross-legged on the bed. Alone.

Josh. I survey the empty king-size expanse surrounding me with emptiness, missing him. If anyplace is meant for two, this is it. Pillows. Chocolates. And if Josh were here, I wouldn't mind the no-clothes situation. I smile and hug my knees, remembering the last time there was a no-clothes situation. His daughter, Penny, was with her mother, so there was no threat of invasion by a nine-year-old. Just Josh and me on the couch,

Fred and Ginger on a DVD, port wine and apples. I have no idea how the movie ended.

We've only known each for — I think back, mentally counting on my fingers. And then my heart gives a tiny flutter. Almost exactly a year. Does it seem like longer than that? I know every inch of his body. And I bet he's just as familiar with mine.

I pull a downy white pillow from under the bedspread and hug it to my chest. I wonder what will happen with Josh. Whether this relationship will go the way of the others — interesting and exciting for a while, then slowly changing. Someone pulling away. Someone too demanding. Someone too dismissive. Someone too impatient. Someone too complacent. Someone's work too important.

Mine, usually.

Suddenly I feel — sad? Out of balance. I help people. I track down criminals and confront corrupt politicians. Make the world a better place. I've devoted the last twenty-some years to being a good guy.

But tonight I'm alone in a cookie-cutter hotel room. Josh is cozy at home with his beloved daughter. Is that where I should be? What would I be giving up? What would I be getting? How do I know if it's the real thing?

Back to reality. And I'm still holding the pillow. I plop it back in its place, shake off the memories. And the phone rings.

"That is the most ridiculous thing I have ever heard." All thoughts of Josh have vanished. Franklin, also at home, is spilling the latest from the newsroom. And the latest stinks. My voice rises to a squeak as I interrupt. "Susannah is changing our fake-purse story — to what?"

"Like I said, Charlotte. It's not about you. It's not about journalism. You know it's about the ratings. The all-important November sweeps. You're familiar with that, of course." Franklin is using his Charlotte-calm-down voice, even pulling out his Mississippi drawl, which he knows I think is irresistible. He only uses it when he's stressed. Or when he's trying to charm his partner, the adorable Stephen. Or when he's trying to get me to relax. It sometimes works on Stephen. It hardly ever works on me.

"Listen, Franko, Susannah's a glitz-addled, glam-loving, ratings-addicted Chanel-worshipping . . . um, um, um . . . consultant." I finally spit out the word. "Are we not reporters? Did we not go to journalism school in order to enrich, enlighten and inform? Would Edward R. Murrow do a story about how to tell if the purse you're buying is fake?"

"Technically, I was the only one of us who went to journalism school." Franklin's voice has a smile in it now. "You majored in Shakespeare, if I remember correctly. And as I said, we offered to give them the inside scoop about where the fake bags come from. A big investigation. But they want —"

"They want shopping!" I stand, phone in one hand, pacing back and forth on the fake oriental rug, pointing one finger accusingly at no one. "This summer we got an innocent woman out of prison. Last fall, we broke the story of a mammoth insider-trading conspiracy. And now they want us to follow those with a story on how to tell whether your Fendi is really a Fakey? It's pitiful."

"It's the demos," Franklin replies. "Women aged eighteen to forty-nine want —"

"I'm eighteen to forty-nine," I retort. For three more years, at least. Two, actually. I keep forgetting my intentionally ignored August birthday. "And what I want is a real story. So here's what we're going to do."

By the time the room-service cart arrives with my grilled chicken salad with no

30

onions or croutons and balsamic vinaigrette on the side, two Diet Cokes, a white wine and a pot of tea, Franklin and I have cooked up our scheme. We're going to pretend to do the story about counterfeit designer bags Susannah Smith-Bagley and news director Kevin O'Bannon want for the November ratings sweeps. But we're also going to work on a different story. The investigative story about phony bags *we* want to do. And then when our bigger and better story turns out to be an investigative blockbuster, they'll forget about their wimpy little feature. It's a gamble, we agree. And it could be somewhat professionally risky, we agree. But we both agree it must be done. And we have a month or so to pull it off.

"And, Franko, let me tell you what's going to make it all possible." I fill him in on Regine and her Designer Doubles luggage.

When I finish, he's silent.

"Franko?" I prod him. "Isn't that amazing? Isn't that just a gift from the journalism gods? I mean, if I hadn't gotten off the plane, I never would have met her. Never gotten the lead on the purse parties. And now all we have to do is check out the Web site on the Designer Doubles card, and then plan our next moves."

"Charlotte, one more thing," Franklin says.

I hear the drawl again, which makes me put down my Diet Coke. And frown. What does he have to calm me down about now? I wait.

"Speaking of suitcases. I went to baggage claim to pick up yours, you know? When I went to pick up mine?"

I knew it. "Yeah?"

"Well, yours . . . didn't arrive. It's lost."

I knew it. "What are the odds," I begin, clipping each word. Bitter. "What are the chances that Every. Single. Time. I take an airplane, my luggage gets lost?"

"Well, according to the latest Department of Transportation statistics I checked," Franklin replies, "on the airline we flew, an average of one out of every —"

Of course Franklin knows the real answer. I don't want the real answer. I want my suitcase. Which has my — I won't even think about what's in it. The airlines always lose my suitcases. But I always put my name inside and I always get them back. This time will be no different.

"What did you bring me, Charlie Mac?" Penny's scampering in front of me, then behind me, then trying to peer into my tote bag as we make our way up the walk to Josh's front door. The last of the fiery dahlias lining the path are struggling to flower, the ancient sugar maples in his yard beginning to promise their fall intensity. Tradition has it they were planted by the blue-blood Bexter family themselves when they founded their namesake academy just outside Boston more than a hundred years ago. Now faculty housing, which looks more like a cozy Cotswolds village, winds through the narrow streets. Josh, on the Bexter board and head of the English Department, lives at number 6. At Bexter, the lower the number, the higher the prestige.

"And how are you, Pen?" I ask with a smile. "I missed you, too."

Penny ignores my mild attempt at sarcasm. Or maybe nine-year-olds are immune to comments or criticism from the girlfriend-of-their-divorced-father. Penny and I had a rocky start. I was invisible for a while. Next she went through a phase of referring to me as "Um." As in, "Um, Mom always lets me stay up till ten." That was followed by a month or so of territory-marking, consisting of her jockeying for position next to Josh in restaurants and movies, as well as her insistence on wearing Josh's T-shirts as "dresses" at every possible moment. Then one day this summer, out of nowhere, she called me "Charlie Mac." And that's who I've been since then.

But although Penny now sees me, she doesn't always hear me.

"And Aunt Maysie says the baby's coming in three months. Like a Christmas present."

Penny's oversized Bexter sweatshirt, of course, belongs to Josh. The sleeves are rolled into doughnuts around her slender wrists. Her stick-straight brown hair is held back, unsuccessfully, with two pink butterfly barrettes. As always, she needs her bangs trimmed. She's still in her beloved pink-flowered flip-flops, hanging on to summer.

"And she says the baby can be like my sister, too. Like my pretend sister. So she'll be Molly's real sister, and my pretend sister. And she says you're going to do her radio show when she has the baby. It's so cool your best friend is on the radio. And on TV, too. Like you. Are you going to be on the radio? Can I be on the radio with you? Molly says . . ."

"My flight was fine, thanks." I continue my side of our separate conversations. "Crack of dawn. I came right here from the airport. Haven't even had breakfast. I've got to get to the station soon and then back to the airport, but your Dad left me a phone message, saying to come right over."

Then, I give up.

"And of course I brought you something," I say. Defeated by a nine-year-old. As we reach the front door, I put down my bag, and give Penny a hug, feeling her little head burrow into my chest, smelling the shampoo in her tangle of nut-brown hair. I also pick up a faint scent of . . . chocolate? Could this be my new life? A daughter to greet me? A house in a neighborhood?

The front door opens, as if by family magic or pheromone ESP. Josh, also in flip-flops and jeans and his favorite gray Bexter sweatshirt, takes the two front steps as one. His pepper-and-salt hair is still morning mussed. His greeting is muffled as his arms encircle me, strong but gentle, my face snuggling into its familiar place in his shoulder. My body remembers his every contour, fitting, settling, connecting. Talk about home.

I feel him sigh as he lets go. He steps back, keeping my hands in his, looking down at me.

"Hey, sweets. Welcome back," he says. "I — Penny and I —"

There's a look on his face, a flicker behind

35

his tortoise-shell glasses I don't quite recognize.

"Charlie Mac brought me something! Do you think she brought you something?" Penny's tugging at her father's arm, her standard tactic every time she thinks too much of Josh's attention is directed at me. After almost a year together, at least I finally learned I don't need to compete. There's room for both of us in Josh's life.

I'm still trying to read his expression. "What?" I ask.

Josh rakes a hand through his already-tousled pepper-and-salt hair, then puts one arm around each of us. "My girls," he says. "Let's go inside."

"But what were you saying?" I persist, as we crowd, still connected, into the front hallway. I can usually read him, know what he's thinking sometimes before he does. But now, no. "You and Penny — what?"

He glances at his daughter, who's hopping from one foot to the other. Just about out of patience. And perhaps, in the way. I get it.

"Hey, Penneroo," I say, pulling a crinkly plastic sack out of my tote bag. It's a package of Hello Kitty barrettes from the airport. And a do-it-yourself balsa wood plane. And a T-shirt from the journalism conference with the First Amendment printed on the front. Just covering all bases. "Take this up to your secret place and check it out."

The lure of loot overcomes her need to monitor her father's activities. She scoops up the bag and heads to her spot under the attic stairs.

Josh smiles and takes my hand again, leading me down the sunlit hall. Family photos once covered the walls here, as they do in my apartment. But the Gelston gallery is now checkered with empty places. Photos removed by divorce. Are they now hanging on Victoria's walls? Or maybe stored somewhere, the remnants of his ex-family. Memories fading with the images.

"Coffee?" Josh asks, as we arrive in the kitchen. An open box of Cocoa Puffs is on the counter, which probably explains Penny's chocolate aroma. "Food? Of some kind? I could make . . . eggs? Guess you don't want Cocoa Puffs." He closes the cereal box, and puts it in a cabinet. He looks at his watch. Josh is fidgeting. And he doesn't fidget. "Is it too early for lunch? It's too early for lunch. And I know you have to get back to the station."

I pull a green wrought iron stool up to the ivory-speckled Formica island in the center of the kitchen and perch on the wicker seat.

I nervously examine a clumsily raffia-wrapped container of pens and pencils, probably one of Penny's school projects. I suddenly remember I haven't changed clothes since yesterday. Maybe I should have gone to my apartment first. Maybe I should have showered? I feel one foot begin to jiggle. Josh has seen me look worse. But he's certainly distracted by something.

"Coffee, of course, you know me," I say. I'm wary, but maybe I'm wrong. I troll for info. And try to fill the unusual gully of silence between us. "But I can be here for a little while before they start hunting me down. So. What's up? Your message? You guys okay? Penny fine? Bexter fine? Victoria and what's-his-name fine?"

His name is Elliott, but Victoria's husband, Penny's stepfather, is the one who must not be named around here. Last time Josh looked like this, it was the "Victoria wants to dump what's-his-name and get back with me and Penny" trauma. Terrifying. But turned out that didn't happen.

Josh yanks the metal top from a new can of coffee, the air filling with that unmistakably tantalizing caffeinated perfume. He starts to scoop out a portion, then stops. He pours the coffee grounds back into the can. He turns back to me, leaning against the kitchen counter. Pushes up the sleeves of his sweatshirt. Crosses his arms.

Body language saying: here comes something bad.

He uncrosses his arms. Holds them out toward me, open.

Okay, maybe it's something good.

"I was in the bursar's office, yesterday. And you know Eleanor always has the television on in there. Sound off, pictures on." Josh crosses his arms again. And he looks serious. "She says since September 11, you've got to monitor for breaking news."

I open my mouth to make some sort of pro-television, thank goodness for viewers remark, but something in Josh's demeanor stops me. "Uh-huh, sure," I say.

"And I was in her office when the news of the plane crash in Baltimore came on. What they thought was the plane crash, at least."

"Uh-huh."

"And I almost lost it, Charlie. I almost lost it. That's why I was so unsettled in that phone message. There was a moment when I thought you might be gone. Forever."

"But it wasn't really — Franklin called you — and my plane wasn't —"

"I know, I know." Josh pulls up the kitchen stool across from me. "I'm not saying it was logical. And it was just, well, I thought of that shooting star we saw on our first date. How big the universe is. How small we are. How out of control." He takes my hand, examines my palm, turns it over, then back. Looks at me again. "And I thought — Charlie's gone. And I had just found her."

I realize I'm fingering my necklace, a star of pave diamonds Josh gave me in honor of our shooting-star evening almost a year ago. Our first date. After midnight, in the front seat of my Jeep. Neither of us wanting to say goodbye. We both saw a shooting star, and Josh insisted that required a kiss. Our first. I haven't kissed another man since.

I realize I thought of Josh, too, last night. And Penny. As I raced through the Baltimore airport to what was supposed to be my live shot, even in my panic for airtime and a big story I'd yearned to call them. To tell them I was okay. I'm the big-time crusading journalist. Independent. Free. It was the first time in years, decades, I'd even thought of letting someone know I was safe.

"And the thought of losing you," Josh continues. "It was galvanizing. I adore you, Charlie. I don't want to live without you. You must know that. You know that, right? And do you feel the same way? You do, don't you?"

"I — you — we —" I'm searching for answers to his questions. And I'm wondering, gradually, suddenly, whether there's a bigger one coming up.

Josh is patting the pockets of his jeans.

My heart stops. Races. Stops. Races.

"It all happened so fast," he's saying. "And I wish I had more time." He pauses. "But I don't." He pulls a piece of paper from his pocket, then takes a pen from Penny's raffia container. He begins to write, hiding the page from me with a cocked shoulder.

"What?" I'm confused. My heart's imagination had envisioned a little robin's-egg-blue box, tied with white satin ribbon, emerging from one of those pockets. But paper?

Josh twinkles at me, looking up from under his unfairly long eyelashes. "You're the genuine article, Miz McNally. The real thing. And I think we ought to have it in writing." He folds the paper in half, then half again, then holds it out to me. He's smiling, but his face has the second unreadable look of the day. "What do you say to this?"

I don't like surprises. But I do like Josh. Love Josh. Do I want to marry Josh? I do. I don't. I do. Seems like I'm going to have to answer that pretty damn soon. If this, um, unfolds as I predict — I'm going to have to answer it right now.

My foot is still jiggling as I accept the square of paper. Unfold it once. Twice.

It's a change of address form from the United States Postal Service. Josh has filled in the blanks. Under "new address," it now shows:

Charlotte Ann McNally
6 Bexter Drive
Brookline, MA

Josh is looking at me. Expectantly.

Dear Miss Manners. My boyfriend, who I crave and adore, has just asked me to marry him. Or maybe not. I'm a 47-year-old reporter and he's a 49-year-old English professor, so you'd think we'd be able to communicate with some clarity, and that's often true. But this time, I'm not sure I understand exactly what he's talking about. Should I just say yes, and then clarify what it is I'm agreeing to? Marriage? Or living — as my newlywed mother would pronounce it — in sin? Or do I risk ruining the potentially most romantic moment of my life by asking for clarification first?

And, Miss Manners, how do I know if it's the real thing?

"Charlie Mac! Duck!" Some unseen projectile swoops across the room, snags through my hair, then crashes into the pencil jar. Penny's not far behind, waving her arms, running, her flip-flops slapping on the linoleum. "Did you see that? Daddy? Daddy? Did you see that? I can fly my plane! It flew, just like real!"

The balsa wood plane I brought Penny has come to a landing, precariously tilt-winged, on the kitchen's Formica runway. Penny grabs it, pretending to fly it into her father. Apparently her daddy-time alarm signaled we've been alone too long.

Josh glances at me, then defends himself from Penny's invading air force. My future is at stake. And a little girl flies an airplane into the room. I hate flying.

"Watch it, kiddo," Josh says. "No airplanes in the house. That goes outside. Now."

Penny puts one foot on her bare knee, standing stork-like, apparently considering her options. "You come out with me, daddo. Charlie Mac can. . . . Can . . . Well how about if I fly it inside but I don't let go? That's perfectly okay, right?"

Nothing like an nine-year-old attempting to chaperone two adults. Penny's in full swing now, holding the plane in one hand and piloting it through the room.

Josh comes around beside me, takes my hand and keeps hold as he wraps his arm around me. "I don't want to push you, Charlie. But I'm not going to let go of this topic, either."

I look up at him, as confused as I've ever been. I always know what to say. That's my job. Now I'm as inarticulate as a newbie on a job interview. *Do it, McNally.* All you have to say is: are you asking me to marry you?

With a hoot and a roar of jet engine noise, Penny flies out the back door. The screen door slams, and we're alone. And then my cell phone rings. And then my beeper goes off.

"Your master's voice," Josh says. "I know you must obey." With a grin, he lifts me by the waist and perches me on the kitchen island, holding me there. He looks into my eyes. Challenging.

"Penny's headed back to Victoria's this afternoon. Do you, Charlotte Ann McNally, promise to come back here — tonight? Do you promise to think about me? Do you promise to consider what I've said?"

I'll figure this out somehow.

"I do," I reply.

CHAPTER THREE

"Welcome back to bad news, Charlotte. So you got my beep? The Prada P.I. postponed our meeting. So now we have to wait to hear from her." Franklin's at his desk, holding two brown-and-tan logo-covered purses, one in each hand. He holds them out to me. "So meantime, here's a quiz for you. Which one is the real thing and which is the copy?"

At first glance, it looks like both purses are Delleton-Marachelle hobo totes. If they're real, they're worth at least four thousand dollars each. I'm embarrassed to admit to myself that I'd love to have one. I'm working on dampening my lust to own a designer bag displaying those intertwined D-M initials. It's actually Mom's fault. She educated my little sister, Nora, and me using *Vogue* and *Harper's Bazaar* like textbooks for a course in acquisition. What to Want: 101. I know it's unworthy. But I'm guilty. I want it.

"You know how I feel about pop quizzes," I say, throwing my tote bag onto the extra chair in our office. I glare at my desk. "And you know how I feel about mail piled on my desk." I gather up the pile of letters, press releases and junk our current intern has unceremoniously delivered and deposit it on the floor. Swiveling into my chair, I put down my coffee and hold out my hand. "Let's see those bags again. What's the scoop? Is one a fake? Who do they belong to? Did you get them from the Prada P.I.? Today? I can't believe she canceled the meeting."

"Me, either. And no note about why she cancelled. Annoying. Someone in her office left a message on my voice mail, just saying 'Katie Harkins will have to reschedule.' I e-mailed her to set us up again, but I haven't heard back. I also talked to the special agent in charge of the FBI's counterfeit squad. Marren Lattimer? You know of him, right? He's new?"

I nod. My FBI pals told me he'd just been transferred to the Boston office from down south someplace. The new special agent in charge. "SAC" they call it. Like "sack." "So the new SAC's interested? He'll help us?" I ask.

46

"Yup. I explained what we're looking for," Franklin continues. "Lattimer says the bureau has started a whole operation targeting fakes — they've even named it. Operation Knockoff. Says he 'blew the lid off' a phony purse ring in Atlanta, so the 'brass' sent him here. We've got an appointment at headquarters tomorrow."

Franklin picks up the bags again, offering them to me. "Anyway. Speaking of knockoffs. Which is real? Can you tell? And if so, how? Oh."

He stops, looking toward our office doorway, and puts the bags back down. "Hello, Susannah."

I can't believe I didn't smell the warning fragrance. A waft of her trademark Poison usually heralds the arrival of Susannah Smith-Bagley, the "news doctor" consultant Channel 3 management hired to "young up" the news. She actually says "young up." I think she's more about "the buzz" than "the news," all platinum hair and collagened face, a package of pretense straight from the coast. Even her shoes. The platforms of her patent leather pumps rival that girl in the airport. Regine. The belt artfully twisted over Susannah's bouclé jacket alternates chunky pearls and gold links. She might as well be wearing a T-shirt that says "I heart

Chanel." No one I know of hearts Susannah.

"Thanks for the teamwork in Baltimore,
Charlie. Too bad there wasn't a plane
crash," she says, eyeing me. A pause. A curl
of her plump lip. "You haven't been home
yet, I see."

Franklin risks giving me a surreptitious
eye-roll as Susannah attempts to raise one
waxed brow at my tote that's occupying our
extra chair. I grab the bag and stash it under
my desk, balancing it atop my collection of
backup shoes.

She descends into the throne, one silky
leg swishing over the other. Queen bee and
the drones.

"Anyway, you two. Just checking on your
'It's in the Bag' story for November," she
says. "Do you love it?" She looks at us, back
and forth, as if she's expecting we'll applaud
yet another cliché of a title ripped from the
news-consultant handbook. We don't.

I smile noncommittally. Change direction.
"Well, we were just looking at some purses,
matter of fact. From the Prada P.I.? She's
the private investigator who scouts for the
fakes. Franklin found her mentioned in
some newspaper article and tracked her
down. She's been giving us the scoop via
e-mail on the secret signs manufacturers

use to designate the genuine article. And she's arranging for us to visit the actual Delleton-Marachelle design studio in Georgia."

"Well, in fact, I found her through a reporter pal who had used her as a source in Atlanta. Gave me her e-mail. And she didn't —" Franklin begins.

I'm realizing it might actually be a good thing old Susannah showed up. This creates the perfect opportunity for us to make her think we're really working on the story she thinks we are. I can't let Franklin interrupt my flow. "See the two Delleton-Marachelles Franklin has? One of them is —"

"Stand by," Susannah interrupts. She flips open a leather-bound portfolio and pulls a calendar out of a pocket, checking the dates with a chunky black ballpoint. She holds up the calendar, her pen pointing to one square. "We're thinking — first week of November? Thursday? We'll have a solid lead-in from that new 'top model' reality show. Models at ten, then you're all about fashion at eleven. Perfectamundo. So, Frank? Charlie? Do you love it? I mean, do you love it?"

My turn for a furtive eye-roll. No one calls him Frank. And I don't love it. Not one bit.

"No problem," I say. "Can do." I'm performing my dependable reliable worker-bee act. Then I take the two bags from Franklin's desk and offer them, one in each hand, to Susannah. Big smile.

"Up for a pop quiz?" I ask. "Think you can pick out the authentic D-M? Franklin just asked me if I can — but maybe you should try."

"Let's see if Charlotte can do it," Franklin says, interrupting. He pushes the two purses back toward me, smiling like a ten-year-old trying to taunt his big sister. "Just for fun."

"Sure," I say. I look at Susannah, and try for some wiggle room. "I just got back from Baltimore, though, remember? Franklin's had more time."

"Chicken," Franklin says.

"You're on." I wish I could stick my tongue out at him, but I know that's unprofessional. And it would let him know he's won.

Okay. How do I tell the real thing? At first, the bags look identical. I choose one, and turn it over, examining, remembering the research Franklin and I have already done. I check the stitching, the leather piping around the edges, the metal d-rings that hold the camel leather handle. The brown-and-tan logo pattern matches at the side seams. That's a point for authentic. The zipper sticks. Possible fake. The lining is flat and the stitches are even. I open an inner pocket. There's a tiny brown leather rectangle, stamped in gold with the D-M logo. Good. A tiny label says: made in China. Hmm.

The second bag. This one's handle is wrapped in protective plastic. When I zip it open, the zipper sticks. There's no "made in China" label. I zip open an inner pocket. Inside is an identical tiny dark brown leather rectangle, letters on it stamped in gold: Delleton-Marachelle. Below the name, it says: Made in Paris.

"Aha!" I say, pointing a finger to the ceiling in triumph. I attempt a French accent. "I have deescovaired ze secrette. Eeet ess —" I can see Susannah is not amused. To her, humor is as alien a concept as compassion. I hold out the bag marked "made in China" and talk like myself again. "This one."

Susannah deflates, her shoulders drooping and her lined lips pursed in disapproval. "Made in China? That's how you tell it's fake?" Her voice gets more brittle with each word. She taps her folder with that pen. Considering. "I'm thinking we may have to re-slot this story. Maybe hold it for after the sweeps. I mean," she pauses, closing her eyes as if we're just too, too ridiculous. "China?"

"No, wait, Susannah," I say. "You've got it wrong." Almost always, I don't add.

Franklin's turn to pantomime applause. "You're good, McNally," he says with a double thumbs-up. "How'd you know?"

"Well, it's the label of origin," I explain. "Isn't that it? This one says Paris. And we know —"

"Right," Franklin interrupts. "Most people think D-M bags are made in France. But we know —"

I turn to Susannah, picking up Franklin's train of thought. "Their main office is in Paris. Their fabric is made in France. Their hardware is stamped in France. Their brand-new design headquarters are in Atlanta. But these babies are actually put together . . ."

I pause just long enough for Franklin to know it's a cue.

"In China." We say it together.

"Sensational." Susannah says. She flips her notebook closed with a snap. "Four weeks until airtime. 'It's In The Bag.' Do you love it? I mean, do you love it?"

"Black. With wheels. From Baltimore. It had a name tag." I should not have come to the airport. I should not be leaning on Logan

52

Airport's lost luggage counter, at what should be dinnertime, discussing my missing possessions with an overpierced and overworked clerk. The name tag on his wilting blue polyester shirt says Todd. And I predict Todd is just pretending to talk on the phone and check his computer records until I agree to go away. And I do want to go away. But I also want my stuff. And I can't believe it's not here somewhere.

"Excuse me?" I say, entreating. I point to the expanse of unclaimed luggage covering the floor. "Could I just look through the misdirected bags you're holding?"

Todd is talking through a headphone, and covers the tiny mouthpiece with one hand. "I can't hear you," he says, obsessively clicking a ballpoint open and closed. And goes back to his "conversation."

I scan the wretched moonscape of black wheelie bags, stranded and orphaned, a forlorn dumping ground surrounded by a sagging strip of webbing that's stretched between two stanchions. I shrug at Todd, then head into the forest of black canvas and plastic, picking my way through hundreds of astonishingly identical suitcases. Some with colorful bows, some with leather name tags. Some bigger, some smaller. So far, everyone's bag but mine.

"Passengers arriving on Flight . . ." A barely decipherable announcement crackles over the public address system. I squint my ears to understand. But all I get is ". . . now at Claim Station C."

Suddenly, a wave of travelers troops wearily past me toward the area ceiling signs designate Claim Station C. Carry-on bags slung over their shoulders, cell phones in their hands, kids in tow. They stand in clumps, staring dully at the still-empty black conveyor belt each one is hoping will hold their belongings. A few more passengers straggle in, also focused on the conveyor belt. With a flashing of red warning lights, the blare of the "luggage arriving" klaxon echoes through the baggage claim area. The segmented belt lurches mechanically into motion. The black plastic strips over the opening flap and flutter as the parade of suitcases begins.

I'm hypnotized, staring in amazement as the once-placid passengers power into fast forward, swarming the conveyor, grabbing bags, yanking them, tossing them onto carts and wheeling them away. Kids ignored, the travelers elbow and shoulder their way closer to the belt, manners and turn-taking forgotten. They're all talking at once, jockeying for position, and it's every man for himself. No person and no bag is safe.

And suddenly, it's clear what's happened to my suitcase. It's not lost. It's stolen.

Sidestepping and tiptoeing my way back through the maze of luggage leftovers, I stomp back to Todd, my realization swelling my tired brain into anger. Todd's still staring only at his computer screen, playing with his ridiculous pen. I slap both palms on his desk and lean toward him, almost hissing.

"You guys don't even compare claim checks," I say. I know it's not Todd's fault, exactly, but he's the only one here. And I'm tired and cranky and need a shower and the stupid airline has lost my suitcase. Again. And I'm sick of being nice about it. "It's outrageous. And it's probably why you guys have such a disastrous record of lost luggage. It's not the curbside check-in agents getting the tags wrong. It's not the weather. It's just open season around here. People could just come in and — I mean . . ."

I wave a disdainful hand at the bag-hungry crowd, shaking my head. I knew I shouldn't have come here. I'm making myself even crankier, heading toward full-out rant. "Look at them all! Anyone could just walk in and take a bag. Who would know? And they just hope they grab one with good stuff in it, and head for the door."

I pause for breath. Wondering who took home my bag with the only jeans that have ever fit me. Wondering who's wearing my had-to-have-them boots. I hate flying.

Todd furrows his forehead and flips the phone mouthpiece up over his spiky hair. "Aren't you Charlie McNally?" he asks. "On TV?"

Fine. Now he'll probably call the *Boston Herald*'s gossip columnist to say that I'm a complete bitch and describe how I lost it at Baggage Claim C.

"So how come your luggage is under someone else's name?" he continues, narrowing his already squinty eyes. "You're not supposed to do that."

"Who cares?" I say, hands in the air, newspaper threat forgotten. "Anyone could have picked it up and they probably did. It'll never get returned."

I turn my back on Todd, and lean against his desk, my arms crossed, frowning at the universe. Then, slowly, one click at a time, my brain shifts gears. What if there's a bigger story than phony purses?

CHAPTER FOUR

I'm starving. I'm exhausted. But my eye is on the prize. *Josh.* Grabbing the curlicued wrought iron railing with one hand and my keys with the other, I drag myself up my front steps. The motion detector flips a spotlight onto the red-lacquer front door, where someone's placed an elaborately twisted wreath of flaming orange bittersweet and a blaze of amber maple leaves over the brass lion knocker. Pots of tiny golden chrysanthemums in concrete urns flank the front stoop. In the entryway, a slender cherry table holds a crystal vase of red gladiolas. My condo fees at work. I clamber up the zigzag stairway, fueled by hunger, lust, my airport idea, and the knowledge that this day could possibly have a happily-ever-after ending. What was Josh getting at this morning? Am I almost — engaged? I pause on the second-floor landing, stopped in my tracks by the weight of my own question.

What if?

One way to find out. One more flight to go. Maysie will go bananas. Mom, too.

I can hear Botox before I even hit the landing. She's probably been in full-blown feline pout mode, clawing open paper pouches of cat food, knocking over wastebaskets and flipping kitty litter as far as she can. The meowing gets louder as she hears my key turn in the lock.

"Hey, baby cat," I say. I bend to pick her up, but after a baleful glare, she flips her calico tail at me and flounces into the kitchen.

"Fine, be like that," I call after her. Amy, the cat sitter, has piled the mail on the dining room table, an outrageously expensive mahogany antique cleverly converted to a staging area for my embarrassing stack of definitely-going-to-read-them-soon *Vogues* and *New Yorkers*. It's also a handy storage spot for to-be-paid bills. The curvy navy silk-upholstered dining room chairs are gorgeous, too. Those I use as coatracks.

Mom's wedding album — the new one — also currently lives on the dining room table. She and Ethan sent me my personal copy soon after they got home to Chicago last month, fresh from their honeymoon. With a note. "You next. Love, Mrs. Mom."

Honeymoon.

With a burst of energy, I sprint down the hallway, past my gallery of family photos, as always, saluting the framed shot of Dad in his cub reporter days, and head into the spare bedroom I've cleverly converted into a walk-in closet. I peel off my tired white T-shirt, now permanently infused with two days of stale airplane air. Pants, too, wrinkled beyond redemption, into the hamper. I can't even imagine wearing either of them again.

I'll shower. Twist my hair up and ignore my salon-needy brown roots. Throw on my good Levi's. No. Dammit. They're in my "lost" suitcase.

The blast of hot water and foaming grape-fruit shower gel erases my annoyance. I continue mapping out my unalterable plan. Shower. Clean clothes. My second-best jeans, high-heeled black boots, a black cashmere v-neck with a lacy come-hither camisole underneath. Grab a power bar. Sneak past Botox. And then, I'm going to Josh. After all. This morning I made a vow.

Just as I have my hand on the doorknob, finally headed for some potentially life-altering answers and a memory-making night, the phone rings.

Answer it. It might be Josh. The phone rings again.

Don't answer it. It's undoubtedly a telemarketer. It rings again. I can't stand it. And I can't resist.

Rule one in journalism, every phone call might bring a good story. Rule two, it most likely won't. Rule three, if you don't answer the phone, refer to rule one. Another ring. I dash to the kitchen and grab the receiver from the red wall-mounted phone.

"McNally. I mean, hello," I say. But I'm too late. My voice mail has started. I hear my recorded self saying "We're not here to take your call right now . . ." Now the machine and I are both talking, in a double-talk babble that must be annoyingly confusing to whoever is on the other end. "Sorry, hang on," I say, raising my real voice to compete with my recorded voice. "The message will be over in a second."

When there's just one of me, I continue. "Hello?"

"Charlie McNally, from Channel 3 News?"

The voice is low. Almost gruff. And unfamiliar. Which is strange, because I'm obsessive about keeping my home phone number private.

"May I ask who's calling?" I say. Don't

need to confirm who I am.

"You think you're on to something, don't you, hotshot? You and your hotshot buddy." The voice continues. There's a sound in the background, like a clicking? But I can't place it. "I'm going to warn you just once, hotshot. Knock it off. We saw you at the airport. Got me? And that's not all we know about you."

Clutching the phone, I look out my third-floor window, through the birch tree leaves and past the glare of the streetlight to the well-tended square of garden and sidewalk below. Scanning. Searching. Nothing.

I have to be smart. Keep whoever it is on the line. I can call 911 from my cell phone. If I can keep this guy talking, the police could trace the call.

I guess.

"Who is this? What do you want?" I ask. I try to sound afraid, which isn't actually that difficult, but I figure my "weakness" could convince whoever it is to keep threatening me. And buy me some time. Problem is, the tote bag with my cell is in the other room, still parked by the front door.

Of course I'm on my landline. Stretching the curly cord around the corner, pulling it to the limit, and then stretching out one arm as far as I possibly can . . . I still can't

61

get to my bag. "Just tell me what you want," I say. My voice is as taut as the phone cord.

"You know exactly what we want," the voice says. It's muffled and raspy, but definitely a man. And there's that sound again. "We want you and your hotshot pals to stay away from our business."

I stretch one leg backward toward the bag, manage to hook the heel of one boot around the loop of a handle, and drag the black canvas across the sisal rug toward me. Got it. Tucking the kitchen phone under my chin, I dig through the bag for my cell. Got it. I check the window. Now a dark-colored car is pulling up. My eyes widen, contemplating who that might be. And why they're here. I flatten myself against the pinstriped wallpaper, away from the window, out of sight.

"I'm so sorry, I just don't understand," I say. Suddenly I can't hold back the genuine tremor in my voice. Then I frown at myself, regrouping. This is just some jerk. I've handled worse. And I have a plan. Just keep this guy talking. "Your business? What's that, exactly?"

I get the cell open. Smash the green on button. Finally, finally, I hear tim-tee-tum of the power up music. And so does he.

"Smart," he says. "Cell phone." And the

line goes dead.

"Call the police," Josh demands. "Now."

I'd waited, staring out my window, waited until I saw his pale blue Volvo pull up under the streetlight. Watched him, holding my breath, as he opened the car door, got out, walked to my front door. For the brief moment he was out of sight, I know my heart stopped beating.

Then his footsteps, running up the carpeted stairs. His key in the lock. And then he was inside and I was melting into his arms, protected, relieved, safe.

And now. He's angry. After almost a year together, I've seen him tired, almost drunk, in bed with a fever, bored, passionate, cheering for the Red Sox, playing Twister with Penny. I've seen him annoyed, suspicious, and briefly unhappy. But I've never seen him this angry.

"If you don't call the police," Josh says, unwrapping his arm from around my shoulders and leaving me, longing, on my midnight-blue leather couch, "you're simply allowing yourself to be in danger. That's not 'intrepid tough reporter.' That's absurd."

He goes to the bay window overlooking Mt. Vernon Square, and pulls aside the delicate oatmeal muslin curtain. "You were planning to notify the cops when — whoever it was — was still on the phone, correct?"

He's holding the curtain open and facing out. Directing his questions to the window. "So what's the difference with calling them now?" His voice is arch, critical. The voice I've heard him use on the phone to Victoria.

I'm simmering a bit myself. Shouldn't he be comforting me? Isn't this the part where Prince Charming is supposed to draw his sword and protect me from evil-doers? Why do I have to defend myself and my actions? I'm the one who, apparently, just got threatened. I don't need Josh's advice. I don't need him to tell me what to do. I just need a reliable friend.

But maybe he needs something, too. Coming up behind him, I prop my chin on his shoulder. "I'm so glad you came over, sweetheart. I must say I had a few freaked-out moments. And I wasn't happy about going outside just then, so thank you for coming over. You're right, I was going to call the cops when the guy was on the phone.

"But now," I step back, turn his shoulder so he's facing me and take both his hands. I try a tentative smile. "But now, what could they do? Besides, if an investigative reporter gets flummoxed by a crank call — well, I've handled worse. Right? I've gotten dozens over the years. Nothing has ever come of them. It just means I'm on the right track. Of whatever it is. And that's a good thing. Right? Listen, I promise I'll tell the news director about it tomorrow. Kevin can notify the cops if he wants. Right?"

Josh is silent, so maybe I'm succeeding.

"And now you're here," I continue, "and now it's fine, and now let's finish our wine and maybe even finish the evening we were supposed to have when we were so rudely interrupted. This morning, you were saying?"

I scan his face, gauging my attempts at reconciliation.

"The last time you had a 'good story,' you were chased down the interstate by murdering thugs," Josh replies, ignoring my question. His voice is cold. "Then held at gunpoint. Twice. A 'good story' almost got your own mother killed, just two months ago, and now —"

"Well, no, that's not quite accurate." I take a step back, and I can feel a frown creasing my forehead.

"It is accurate." Josh shrugs, then looks down, slowly shaking his head. "I know you're devoted to your job. And getting the bad guys, as you always say. And that's

65

admirable. And scoring yet another Emmy."
He looks back up at me. "But if someone is
calling you at home, threatening you, how
can I protect you? How can I protect any of
us? And you're calling it a good thing?"

"Well, in TV news, you know, 'good' is
kind of relative, and —"

"Let me finish. If we're a team? You and
me and Penny? You can't be putting us all
in danger. If they know where you are,
they'd know where she is."

"But they're not going to —"

"Who are 'they'?" Josh says. "You have no
idea what 'they' would or wouldn't do,
because you have no idea who 'they' are.
And for you to just dismiss a threatening
phone call, not even report it to police,
seems irresponsible."

Josh steps away from the window. I see
him eyeing the front door.

He's going to bolt? Without even having a
real conversation?

"Honey?" Then I stop. He's displeased
because I'm not doing what he says? I'm
not one of his errant students, a kid who
disobeyed orders or passed notes in class or
whispered or cheated. I've been fine on my
own for all these years. Which used to worry
me. Now I see why being on my own might
have been much, much easier. But do I want

66

to be on my own anymore?

"Honey?" I say again. I'm teetering on angry, but trying to soften my voice. "Maybe we should really talk about this. Not fight. I mean, I give my opinion, then you give yours. And we discuss it. But if I give my opinion, and then you say I'm wrong, that's not a discussion. You know?"

"It's not just about calling the police," Josh says, ignoring my question. "Covering that plane crash was more important to you than coming home. To me. To Penny. She relies on you now. Her mother left us. She chose her job. And now, you —"

"I wasn't choosing my job in Baltimore," I interrupt. My hands are on my hips. I didn't decide to put them there. "I chose it twenty-five years ago."

Botox pads into the room, then stops. She eyes us, her tail waving. She hops onto the couch and begins daintily licking a paw. As if the entire world wasn't about to fall apart.

"I see," Josh says. In three controlled paces, he's in the dining room. He yanks his leather jacket from the back of a mahogany chair, thumbs it over one shoulder and marches toward the front door.

"Josh?" I say. My hands drop to my sides. My chest turns to ice and my eyes swim with tears of indecision. What do I do? What do people do? People disagree, don't they? Sometimes?

"Let's talk tomorrow," he says. In a voice I've never heard.

"Whatever," I say. In a voice I've never heard.

The front door opens. And closes. And Josh is gone.

I've lost my luggage. That I can handle. But now, what if I've lost the love of my life?

CHAPTER FIVE

My mother is going to kill me. Maysie will be so sad. They're both happily married. Maysie about to have kid number three. I'm apparently the only one who is unable to balance my personal life with my professional life. Mom's twenty years of fears and warnings are now confirmed. I'm raggedy and raw this morning, and my eyes sting whenever I think about Josh and Penny, which is all the time. I can't even imagine how Josh will explain to her what happened. I can't really explain it myself. I yank myself back into the real world. I can always count on work. And Franklin. *Right.* He and Stephen are also in a committed and fulfilling relationship. I'm the only loser.

A swirl of coffee-swilling subway commuters bustles around us as we stand on the sidewalk in the midst of the Government Center Station crowd. Our destination this morning is the curved stone facade of Two

Center Plaza, the Boston office of the FBI. We've got ten minutes until the meeting.

"The purse party's tomorrow, out in Great Barrington," Franklin says. "Four in the afternoon, the voice-mail message said. Like a tea party, I guess. Only without the tea. And with contraband." Franklin's eyeing a little map on his latest phone gizmo. "GB's about a three-hour drive from here."

"They certainly called back quickly," I say. I'd left our undercover phone number on Regine's Designer Doubles Web site just yesterday. It's our private line, not hooked in to the Channel 3 phone system, and it has caller ID blocking. We give it out whenever we need to stay anonymous.

Franklin and I ignore the crosswalk and scuttle through the middle of Cambridge Street traffic. "But why not, I guess, when it's all about the money," I continue. "So here's the plan. You put together the hidden camera equipment today. Tomorrow I'll hop on the Turnpike and pay a visit to the purse ladies. I'll come back with some knockout video and some knockout evidence."

"Charlotte —" Franklin briefly puts his hand on my arm as we step onto the sidewalk. "We need to talk this over. What are you going to do at this purse party, wear a paper bag over your head?"

My brain is so absorbed by my collapsing universe I'm barely keeping up with what Franklin is saying. I used more than my quota of under-eye concealer this morning. And I'm grateful that September has provided just enough sunshine so I can logically wear sunglasses. They'll at least prevent Franklin from focusing on my certainly still puffy-from-crying face. FBI Special Agent Marren Lattimer has never met me, so he'll just have to live with it.

"Wear what? A paper bag over my head?" I'm confused. Then I get his point. "Oh, come on, Franko, no way the women at the purse party are going to recognize me, way out in western Massachusetts."

We revolve through the front door of the anonymous-looking gray stone building and show our station ID cards to the front desk guard. Self-important in his blue blazer and packing a two-way radio, he shows us how conscientious he is, holding up each card briefly and matching our faces. He doesn't ask me to take off my Jackie O sunglasses, though. So I could be anyone.

"Channel 3's signal doesn't carry out to Great Barrington," I continue. "They get TV from Albany, New York, someplace like that. Not Boston."

Franklin and I sign the loose-leaf notebook, as instructed, struggling with a pen attached by a tangled and too-short strip of plastic. "I'll leave off all my makeup, pull my hair back, wear my glasses, some dumpy outfit. They won't suspect a thing."

I lower my voice, so the guard won't overhear. "They especially won't suspect that I'll be carrying a hidden camera."

Ignoring us, the guard is now comparing our sign-in signatures with the ones on our ID cards. My signature is illegible, so he's just matching scrawls.

"I still think, Charlotte, that you may be taking an unnecessary chance." Franklin says, shaking his head. "If you get recognized, you've blown our story. Maybe we should think of another way."

Somehow Franklin's tone clicks the "upset" button in my brain and tears well in my eyes again. Why is everyone suddenly criticizing everything I do?

"I hardly think I'd put our story in jeopardy," I say, hearing an unusual haughtiness creep into my own voice. "I have thought this through, you know. It's not like I'm some kind of novice."

The guard shoulders his way between us to slip a glossy white key card into a slot outside one chrome elevator. With a ping the door instantly slides open. Motioning us in, the guard taps a five-digit code on a number pad, then pushes the button marked sixteen. He holds the door in place, looking stern. "Someone will meet you on sixteen," he instructs. "Wait there until they arrive. Don't leave the sixteenth-floor lobby until they escort you."

He looks up at a corner of elevator, gestures with his head. "Surveillance cameras. They're watching you."

As the doors slide shut, I push my sunglasses onto the top of my head, which knocks the reading glasses I've perched there onto the elevator's carpeted floor. This is the last straw.

"Dammit," I hiss. I snatch up the glasses and stuff them, without putting them in a case, into my bag. I hear Franklin make some sort of sound of disapproval.

"What?" I look at him, challenging. They're *my* glasses. I can put them in my purse however I want. If everyone wants to fight, I'll fight.

Franklin's face evolves from surprise to concern. "Charlotte, are you okay?" he whispers. He reaches out and touches my shoulder. "The sunglasses? And you look, uh, tired. And as for the paper bag thing — we always discuss story strategy. I'm just brainstorming. You know? What's up with

73

you today?"

Leaning against the brass railing of the elevator, I try to figure out how to answer him. The car slowly carries us past floor 5 to 6, and then to 7. I press my lips together, realizing how close to tears I am. And Franklin's gesture, his offer of comfort, pushes me even closer. Glancing at the elevator buttons, I measure our progress to the top. Eight floors to pull myself together.

"Yeah, Franko, I'm sorry," I say softly. "Josh and I had a fight. A downright real fight. And he left, went home. At about one in the morning."

Seven, six floors to go.

"You'll see each other tonight, as usual, right?" Franklin interrupts, gently. "And you can talk it out."

Five, four.

I sigh, briefly considering whether he might be right. I feel a flutter of hope attempt to break through to the surface. Franklin and Stephen have what they call "tiffs," I know. They even joke about it later. But I fear this is different. The wisp of hope evaporates, destroyed by reality.

"I don't think so," I say. And with that, I recognize what I'm feeling. My heart is breaking.

Two, one.

And the door opens on the sixteenth floor. I struggle to manage a fragile smile, attempting to reassure Franklin that I'm tough. I'm a reporter. Don't have to worry about me. And then I remember I haven't even mentioned last night's anonymous phone call. Too late now.

I hitch my tote bag higher on my shoulder, but it catches on the shoulder flap of my new camel suede jacket and falls back into the crook of my elbow, yanking the sleeve out of shape. Now even my own purse is fighting me. I glare at it, then take a deep breath. Edward R. Murrow would not be defeated by a few emotional bumps in the road.

"Let's catch some bad guys, Franko," I say. "It's Emmy time."

"Profits? Two billion dollars a year. Maybe three." FBI Special Agent in Charge Marren Lattimer is spewing stats, staccato, almost faster than Franklin and I can write them in our spiral notepads. I've got three pages covered already and we've only been here two minutes. "Terrorists make more money selling counterfeit than selling dope."

Lattimer's as hard-nosed and craggy as a recruiting poster for the Marines. White shirt. Boring tie. His navy blazer falls open to reveal just a corner of under-the-shoulder holster.

"Recognize this?" he asks, pointing to a framed photo on the wall. "They haven't got all my stuff on the wall yet, just moved into the place of course. But I said, make sure this one goes up asap. Top priority. Keeps my eye on the target. So. Do you know where this is?"

I look up from my notebook, examining the black-and-white poster-sized photograph hanging beside an array of eight-by-tens. Lattimer piloting a helicopter. A younger Lattimer, before the gray hair, with a former president. An even younger Lattimer, tallest in a group of crew-cutted young men and determined women, all holding diplomas. Lattimer posing in a leather bomber jacket, tough guy, with a huge machine gun. A stack of framed pieces, probably more Lattimer nostalgia, leans against the wall.

"It's, um . . ." The shot isn't wide enough for instant context. Only the first floor is showing. I see smoke billowing from the front of a stone-and-glass building. Cops. TV cameras. I know it perfectly. But I hate pop quizzes.

"World Trade Center, 1993," Franklin answers.

"Correct," Lattimer says. "And how do you think those assholes — excuse me, Ms. McNally — how do you think that operation was financed? With the ill-gotten gains from counterfeit goods. Those women who think they're picking up a bargain deal on a knockoff Prada?" He taps on the poster again. "Think they realize they may have paid for this?"

"Brass brought me up here to clean up this mess." Lattimer leans toward us, palms down, over his expanse of government-issue, beige metal desk. "Organized crime. In on it, too. Guys with names like Billy the Animal. Kurt the Russian. That's who's selling this stuff. And that's what Susie Suburban doesn't know. She thinks having one purse party for the gals in her neighborhood won't hurt anyone."

Franklin and I exchange uneasy glances. I'm sure we've just thought of the same two things. And we should have thought of them earlier. One of them I'll bring up now.

"Is, uh, buying the purses illegal?" I ask.

"Time to call your congressman," Lattimer replies. Scornful. "Why? Because it's perfectly legal to buy the things. And to own them, just for personal use. Until they change the law, that's what we we're dealing with. What we'd like to do? Swoop down

77

on one of those unsuspecting housewives and cart her and her purse-happy friends off to the slammer." A brief look of conquest crosses his face. "That'd send a message."

"But you can't now? I mean, you'd think you could arrest at least the hostess," Franklin puts in. "Selling the stuff is illegal, right?"

I grimace, picturing that. And the complications that would ensue. "I guess the headlines might be pretty unpleasant, though: 'Fashion Police Feds Collar Neighborhood Moms.'"

"I get my orders from the top," Lattimer says. "Brass says, we're going after the big guns. The source. Cut off supply, you kill the demand."

Now he's talking. This is the kind of nitty gritty information we came here to get.

"So you see our situation," he continues. "We can't go to China, close down the big fish there. No jurisdiction. Our U. S. Customs teams intercept what they can at the border. But once these bags get into the States, that's what we're targeting. The distribution chain."

"So, just for background for our story, may I ask how you're tracing the products?" I turn to a new page in my notebook, hoping for some inside scoop. "You see these bags all over Canal Street in New York,

Downtown Crossing here in Boston, people selling them right out in the open. Where do they get them? Are there warehouses someplace, full of purses? Have you raided them? How do they get to the little fish? When? Where? Who?"

"Are there records of the raids?" Franklin adds. "If we could analyze, say, your database of searches and seizures . . ."

"Classified." Lattimer says, making a *no way* gesture with both hands. "No can do."

He lifts the World Trade Center photo from the wall, revealing what looks like a wall safe underneath, a number pad imbedded on the wall beside it. He plants himself in front of the pad, ostentatiously blocking our view as if there's some possibility we're going to come back into his office later and open the safe. I can tell he's entering in a code. He moves aside as the metal door clicks open, then reaches in and pulls out a purse. Then another and another and another. He piles them on his desk, a mound of designer logos, camel-and-red plaid fabric, elaborate initials adorned with painted pastel flowers. Susannah would drool over the sleek black quilted-leather pouches and their silver-embroidered interlinked *C*'s.

"All these?" says Lattimer, waving a hand

over the contraband. "All fakes. And all purchased at suburban purse parties. All in Massachusetts. Our undercover teams are — Well, stand by." He pushes a buzzer on his desk phone.

"Yes, sir," a voice instantly answers.

"Send in Agent Stone, please," Lattimer says.

"When the going gets tough, the tough go shopping." Agent Keresey Stone sweeps into the SAC's office, managing to look about as masculine as a centerfold in her FBI regulation man-centric dark blue trousers, white oxford button-down and navy blazer. Her leonine hair threatens, as always, to escape its taut chignon, and she wears her gold badge, encased in plastic and hanging from a government-issue aluminum chain, with the flair of a Tiffany necklace. She's pushing the limits with her sturdy shoes. They're not standard issue, but no one else in the Bureau will recognize Ferragamo.

"This is —" Lattimer begins. But Franklin and I are already on our feet.

"Hey, Keresey," I say. Even in this professional environment, I feel comfortable giving her a quick hug. "I didn't know you were on the —"

"Hey, Keresey," Franklin says, at the same

time. He holds out a hand, but I've gotten to our old friend first.

"I see you're already acquainted," Lattimer puts in. He frowns. "Agent Stone. I'm certain you haven't discussed Operation Knockoff with the media without going through the proper channels."

"No, sir, Chief. Charlie and I know each other from way back. When I was still in Firearms. I taught her how to shoot a Smith & Wesson —" she pats her hip holster as she continues her explanation "— for a story on illegal weapons and women's self-defense. Took her to the range at Fort Devens, in fact."

She points to me. "You been practicing? You were quite a prodigy."

Lattimer clears his throat, cutting off our nostalgia and reminding us he's the man in charge. He leans back in his cordovan vinyl leather swivel chair, and waves us to our seats. Keresey stands, looking more cover girl than cop, next to Lattimer's desk. "I brought Agent Stone in because she's the primary on our local undercover operations."

So Keresey's now with the counterfeit squad. That's promising. Maybe we can convince them to let me go undercover with her. Double team.

"You know, I'm wondering . . ." I stop myself, mid-sentence. If we tell them we're going undercover, what if they order us not to? I'm pretty sure they can't do that, but it's a legal tangle I'd rather avoid.

"Never mind, sorry. Go ahead." I smile apologetically at Lattimer. "Lost my train of thought." Maybe Keresey will tell me more, off the record.

"We have one squad targeting supply side," Lattimer continues. "Agent Stone and her crew target demand. We're laying groundwork now, seeing if we can follow the trail backward. See where these ladies are copping their product. Trace it back to the source."

"It's like dealing drugs," Keresey adds. "We know the big fish are hiding somewhere. They distribute to the street dealers regionally, and they in turn, distribute to Internet dealers, and of course, the house parties."

"Exactly like drugs, actually," I say. I pick up a Chanel knockoff, examining it. "Except those women are addicted to fashion. Addicted to labels."

"And these ass— sorry, these guys, provide a cheap fix," Lattimer agrees. "All the bag at half the price. That's what they say. And it's a gold mine. All cash."

"I'm still interested in your raids," Franklin says. "Where they were. What the results were. What you seized."

"Let me just say," I add, "if we make a public records request, even for redacted material, I think legally you'd have to give it to us."

"Negative. Exemption 7. Investigative sources and methods. Investigation's still underway." Lattimer's shaking his head, signaling subject closed.

I don't think so.

"How about if you just blacked out the specific places?" I persist, going for the "see, we're going to make you look successful so you should help us" gambit. "Just to show the public you're making some progress? Getting the goods?"

Lattimer's confident posture suddenly seems to sag. He leans forward, arms crossed on his desk. He's wearing a mammoth Rolex and a chunky ring with a square blue sapphire. "Kere— Agent Stone?" he says. His voice seems to sag, too. "As we discussed, this will be off the record."

"Off the — ?" I say.

"Off the — ?" Franklin repeats the dreaded words at the same time. We both know if we agree to "off the record" it means what's coming is something we'd love to know and that probably no one else knows. A news tidbit made frustratingly unusable because we're not allowed to put it in our story. We're dying to hear it because it's undoubtedly major-league info. Not being able to use it, however, is a major-league pain. Sometimes, there's a compromise.

"What if we go for modified off-the-record," I offer. "We could say: 'we have learned.' Or: 'sources close to the FBI say.' Something along those lines. Not reveal where we got the information, but still be able to use it." It's juggling bubbles to haggle over information we don't have. Make the wrong move and it all disappears.

"Sorry, Charlie," Keresey says.

Franklin hides a smile with what I know is a fake cough. He knows I hate the tuna-fish line from the old TV commercial.

"But —" I say. I still have more compromises in mind.

"Take it or leave it," Lattimer points to his watch. "I've got another meeting."

What is this, ultimatum week?

"Okay." I wave a hand. Defeated. I quickly confirm with Franklin. "Okay?"

He shrugs, and gives me the floor.

"Okay," I repeat. "Deal. We won't use it unless we can find out about it on our own." I mentally cross my fingers. At least that

84

will be easier now because we'll know what to look for.

"What we can tell you, and this is all we can tell you," Keresey begins, "is our focus is on the distribution system. The middle men. How the bags get to the parties and to the street dealers. And that's what we haven't cracked."

"Yet." Lattimer interrupts.

"Yet." Keresey agrees. "As of this date, there have been two E-As. Both based on CIs. Not in Massachusetts."

I nod. Enforcement actions. Confidential informants.

"They were both no-go's," Keresey continues. "Empty warehouses. Both times. Old barns. Nothing inside. The informant's info was bogus." She swallows, then her face goes uncharacteristically somber. She looks at Lattimer.

"We lost two of our agents," Lattimer says.

"One was killed. One was —"

"Classified." Lattimer brusquely interrupts her.

"Do you think you received counterfeit information?" I say. "You think someone was trying to lure your agents into a trap?"

"Your question is duly noted," the SAC replies. "But, I repeat, classified. But now you know Operation Knockoff is no walk in the park. It's deadly. We're following big money. International smuggling. Child labor. Legitimate companies ripped off for millions. These bags may be beautiful on the outside, but that's the ugly reality."

He picks up what looks like a Burberry shoulder bag with the trademark red-and-camel plaid. Holds it out with two fingers, as if the touch of it is poison. "Greed rules the world," he says. "It's a dirty business."

Franklin and I exchange silent glances as Lattimer turns back to his secret safe. I raise an eyebrow, and know Franklin understands. A dirty business is just what good journalists are looking for. We're the ones who can help clean it up.

Bring it on.

CHAPTER SIX

I spear a piece of lettuce, consider it, then reject it. I'm just not hungry. And I can't remember the last time that happened. Franklin and I are discussing our FBI info in the lunchtime bustle of the Kinsale Restaurant, a faux Irish burger and salad joint favored by clerks, lawyers and blue-uniformed officers from the New Chardon Street Courthouse around the corner. Walking here from FBI headquarters, the Josh-fight memory slithered unpleasantly back into my brain. Now I've got my sunglasses back on.

"We're in a window seat," I explained un-necessarily to Colleen, our server. As if she cared. "There's glare."

Franklin's focused on his usual double cheeseburger, squirting concentric circles of ketchup on his toasted bun. He arranges the tomato, then the lettuce, then carefully places the bun on top of the whole teetering stack. If I tried to eat that, rivulets of ketchup would drip onto my silk blouse, followed by splurting tomato seeds and oozing cheese hitting my pearl necklace then splattering down onto my just dry-cleaned black wool skirt.

Franklin picks up his creation and takes a bite. Nothing happens to his pristine yellow shirt. The charcoal cashmere sweater tied around his shoulders remains immaculate.

"Let's say, okay, we can doll you up — or doll you down, I suppose is more like it — so you won't be recognized," Franklin continues. "And I agree, Great Barrington is so far west, almost to the New York border, it's out of our viewing area. And that does make our odds of pulling this off even better. But, Charlotte, are we contributing to the problem? If we give them money?"

We're silent, considering this.

"What if I just don't buy anything? Just get the video?" I offer. "That's one solution."

I push the lettuce around on my plate, half my mind consumed with my impending attendance at tomorrow's purse party, the other half consumed with my impending lifetime of loneliness. I shake my head. Back to the present.

"Look, look, look," I say, waving off Franklin's concerns with my fork. "How many women do you know who have fake purses? I mean, it's everywhere. Walk down the halls at the station. Check out the women here at lunch."

I take off my sunglasses, and follow my own instructions, pointing as I pick each one out. "There's a fake Prada, there in the red booth. That bag doesn't even come in that color. That Fendi coming through the door? Look at the strap. No tassels. Phony as they come."

Franklin and I scan the room. I'm right. Counterfeit couture is as popular here as an afternoon cappuccino.

"Plus . . ." I'm warming to my own argument now ". . . the feds buy the purses. Right? Keresey must be handing over cash — taxpayers' money — to make her undercover buys. So if they're saying payments for fake bags are contributing to terrorism, which I must say I have my doubts about, doesn't that mean our own government is doing the same thing?"

"And they would answer, it's all about stopping the flow." Franklin nods, picking up a forkful of french fries. "Like Lattimer said. 'It's a dirty business.' "

I push my plate away and deposit my

napkin on top of it. "Wouldn't it be hilarious if Keresey were undercover at the same party I'm going to? Or someone else on her team? I mean, she'd recognize me. And I'd sure recognize her. I considered telling them our plans —"

"Me, too," Franklin says. "But —"

"Right," I interrupt. "They'd clearly try to stop us. Huge can of worms. And they don't need to know what we're doing."

"Still, though, Charlotte." Franklin looks uncertain. "A dead FBI agent."

"It's a purse party, not a raid," I reply. "You don't hear about suburban homemakers getting killed because they bought a fake Chanel tote bag. We'd hear about it, you know? It's perfectly safe. This is the little-fish level."

"I suppose you're right," Franklin agrees.

"As always," I say.

A few hours later, Franklin appears in my office with a miniature suitcase, aluminum with a black handle. He places it on the corner of my desk, and flips two snaps on the side. He opens the cover with a flourish.

"The new Sony HC-43," he says. "Tiny, silent, almost invisible. Your new best friend."

He takes out a thin metal rectangle, about

the size of a playing card, attached to a narrow black electrical cord. He points to a glass dot in the center of the card, smaller in circumference than a pencil eraser.

"See this dot? It's the lens," he says. "You tape it in position so it shows through, say, a buttonhole. Maybe wear a work shirt with a patch pocket? And we can tuck this card into the pocket. Then we'll make a little hole in the shirt behind it, and snake the cord down underneath."

He holds up the cord, and I see it's attached to a camera, miniature, no bigger than a paperback book. "You can wear the guts of the camera, the recorder, in a fanny pack or something," he says. "No one will ever see it."

"A fanny pack?" I snort, my eyebrows headed toward the ceiling. "A fanny pack? Oh, Franko, not a chance." I burst out laughing, and realize it's the first time today anything has seemed funny. "Next you'll want me to wear gaucho pants. Or tube socks with my strappy sandals."

Franklin winds the cord back around the lens card with a little more flourish than necessary, not amused.

"Oh, I'm not making fun of you," I hurry to apologize. "And the camera is great. Much better than the ones I've used before.

91

Much smaller. It's just that, you know, I'm going to a place where the focus is fashion. I can't slog in looking like a refugee from Geekland." I raise a one finger. "Wait a second."

Getting down on all fours, I peer under my desk, moving aside a recycled gift bag full of plastic silverware I keep just in case there's a spoon emergency, three pairs of rubber rain boots and about six umbrellas. With a yank that topples the boots, I pull out a black canvas purse, covered with D-rings and flap pockets on both sides, vintage 1995 or so. I figured I would need it someday. Right again.

I swipe the dust from my knees as I sit back in my chair, holding up my under-desk find. "This'll work. We'll put the guts of the camera in this bag, make a hole in one of the pockets."

I open the bag and confirm my hidden-camera hiding plan will work. I put the bag over one shoulder, and stand up, posing casually, one hand covering the place where the hole would be.

"See?" I lift my hand, demonstrating. "When I do this, the camera lens is open. I put my hand down, it's covered. Open, covered. Open, covered. See?"

Franklin shrugs. "Sure, that'll work. You

just can't ever put your purse down."

I hand him back the high-tech contraption. "Just make sure I have tapes and batteries. *Charged* batteries. Remember when the batts failed in the middle of that drug bust? Disaster."

"Not as bad as when you got caught with the camera at the cult church. When that phony minister hauled off and tried to hit you? And grab the camera? Now, that was unpleasant."

"Yeah, well, we got it all on tape," I reply. "Great video. All that matters."

Franklin puts the camera back in the case and snaps it closed. He puts it on his desk, not mine. "You sure you don't want me to go with you tomorrow?" he says. "I could be your cute gay purse consultant. Totally believable."

"You just want some new purses," I say, teasing. "Seriously Franko, I'll be fine."

The message machine is empty. No flashing message light, not even one. Maybe it's broken, I think when I get home that evening. I punch in my code, hoping.

"You have . . ." the mechanical voice pauses ". . . no new messages, and —"

I hit the off button, disappointed. But maybe Josh called and didn't leave a mes-

93

sage. Maybe I should call him.

I plop down on my bed, and pick up the receiver from the phone on my nightstand. Or maybe not.

I put the receiver back and lean into my pillows, stretched out on the puffy down comforter, not caring if I wrinkle my silk shirt, not caring if I wrinkle my just-dry-cleaned skirt. I kick off my suede slingbacks. One shoe tumbles, toe over heels, into the wastebasket. And there's the metaphor for the day.

Sighing in defeat, I get up to retrieve my shoe. I'll get through this, one step at a time. Wearily, my thoughts flailing and random, I peel off my work clothes and cuddle into my sweats.

My apartment has never felt so empty. My flip-flops echo down the hall toward the kitchen, where I pour a glass of Australian Shiraz. "Josh's favorite," pops into mind before I can prevent it. With Botox trailing after me into the dining room, I decide to torture myself.

Picking up Mom's wedding album from the dining room table, I curl up on the living room couch. "Where Josh and I sat" pops into mind.

The handsomely textured black album, thick metal-edged pages bound together, is the size of a Manhattan phone book. It opens with a creak, fragrant of leather, showing Mom and Ethan, smiling as only newlyweds can, on the first page. Her gossamer dove-gray dress, elegantly couture; Ethan, blissed out, one arm around his new bride. I turn the page, knowing what's next. Steeling myself to see it. Unable to resist.

An August breeze had lifted my layers of ice-pink chiffon, not as Pepto-Bismol as I'd feared, into a graceful flutter, and the photographer had caught just the moment when Josh and I had locked eyes, laughing.

I turn the heavy page with a sigh. Penny, her first time as flower girl, showing off the pearlized Mary Janes she'd refused to take off for days. My best friend Maysie, five months pregnant, watching her husband, Max, and the kids lead a rambunctious conga line at the reception.

Me, catching the bouquet.

The photograph taunts me. I look happy. Which suddenly now is the saddest thing I've ever seen.

Maybe this is payback from the universe. Maybe I've already gotten my happiness in my career and it's greedy to want more. A confident and blazingly attractive man, who respected my work and couldn't keep his hands off me. An adorable daughter, part of life I thought I'd missed. Instant family.

Maybe I wanted it too much. And so I misjudged Josh. Focused on fantasy instead of reality. Mom knew what she wanted. And Maysie.

I slam the album — and all it represents — closed. How do you know it's the real thing? Maybe if you have to ask, it isn't.

The last word I said to Josh was "whatever."

I feel one tear straggle down my cheek. And then, the doorbell rings.

I slide back the chain and open my front door. Slowly. With each click of a link, I wonder if I'm doing the right thing. Detective Christopher Yens of the Massachusetts State Police had introduced himself through the still-chained door. He keeps holding up his gold statie badge and ID card as he eases his lanky frame into my entryway. He's wearing a leather jacket, jeans, a tiny radio clipped to his shoulder, and what I read as an apologetic smile.

"Sorry, Miz McNally, to bother you so late," he says. He flips his badge wallet closed and tucks it into an inside pocket, then pulls out a tattered spiral notebook. He pats a pocket with his palm, then another, then brushes back a shock of almost-auburn hair. Another apologetic look. Adorable schoolboy who needs another hall pass and knows he'll get it. "May I bother you for a pen?"

"Sit here, I'll get one," I say. I turn down my CD of *Puccini for Lovers* and wave him to a dining room chair, pushing today's pile of mail to the other end of the table.

"May I bring you a glass of water?" I ask. I can get one for myself at the same time. It's probably more my fraying emotions than the glass of Shiraz that's making my brain fuzzy, but whatever. I'm uncomfortably aware I'm not at the top of my game. I sneak a peek at myself in the microwave glass, but it's impossible to tell the extent of the damage. Maybe it's better not to know how tear-stained I am.

I search the fridge for two unopened bottles of Poland Spring. It's possible I shouldn't have let this Detective Yens inside, but there's an iconic, unfakeable navy-and-gray car with Mass State Police decals on the top and sides parked on the street below. So I'm certain he's a real statie. I'm considering whether I should call Toni DuShane, the station's legal Amazon. Maybe I ought to get her over here before I say anything.

But it's late. And I'm too curious to be that time-consumingly careful. Yens told me

97

over the intercom it was about an investigation. Is someone dead? Or hurt? I'd blurted the question through the speaker, fearing a calamity of the worst kind. Josh killed. And our last words had been a battle. The whole bleak soap opera played out in my mind before the cop could even answer. But then he'd said no. So, it's nothing terrible. Plus, I can always end the interview if I get uncomfortable. Or I can lawyer up.

"What can I do for you, Officer . . ." Damn. There goes the short-term memory. I place two clear plastic bottles of water on the table, mine on the back of an old *New Yorker,* his on this week's J. Crew catalog.

"Yens," he says. "Detective Christopher Yens. I need to talk to you about Katherine Hockins. When was the last time you spoke to her?"

I cross my arms, pursing my lips, thinking. Botox hops onto the table, and I brush her back to the floor so Detective Yens won't think I allow my cat on the table. As if *"allow"* is in her vocabulary.

"Who?" I begin. "Hockins?" Then I get it. Boston accent. "Oh, Harkins. Katherine Harkins. Katie Harkins. The Prada P — I mean, does she work for Prada?"

Yens doesn't respond. "When was the last time you spoke to her? When was the last

98

time you saw her?"

"Well, never," I reply. "I've never spoken to her and I've never seen her. She's only —"

Yens is flipping through his notebook as I respond, glancing between me and his notes.

I stop talking. He stops flipping.

"Why?" I ask. "Why are you asking me about Katie Harkins?"

Yens, who I'm noticing is completely attractive in a good boy/bad boy kind of way, is suddenly completely bad boy. "I'll ask the questions if you don't mind, Miz McNally. Like I said, when was the last time you saw her?"

I do mind.

"Detective . . . Yens," I say. I can go bad boy, too. I put on my two-can-play-this-game face. Almost a smile. I lean back in my chair. My brain is unfogging nicely.

"I don't have to answer any questions, as you well know. And I'm kind of curious about your attitude. But if you'd like to start over, I'd be delighted to see if I can help you. I'm sure you understand, however, I have no problem bringing the station lawyer in on this meeting." I shrug. "Your call."

Yens scratches the back of his neck, then turns on a lazy smile. He flips his notebook closed.

"Look, Miz McNally . . ."

"Charlie. Is fine." Olive branch.

"Charlie," he nods, acquiescing to our impending teamwork. "Here's the situation. We got a call from . . ." He checks his notebook. "Well, it doesn't matter. It's not a missing persons yet, so I won't say she's disappeared. But we're tracking her activities, and according to our investigation, she kept to her schedule to the letter. She was supposed to be in Atlanta. And she was supposed to meet you in Boston."

"I never —" I begin.

He holds up a hand. "Which is why I am asking. When you saw her, did she seem worried? Nervous?"

"Detective —"

"Was she on time? Did she say where she was going?" His questions fire, machine-gun fast. "What was she wearing? How long was your meeting? Did she get any phone calls?"

I slap a palm onto the dining room table, a bit more loudly than needed. "Detective," I say, also a little more loudly than necessary. "I. Never. Saw. Her."

"But you're in her calendar."

"That may be," I say. "But just listen for a moment." I relate almost the whole story, editing out the parts about the undercover purse party and our discussion with Lattimer and Keresey. Leaving in the parts about our feature story. Mentioning the non-plane crash, and my unexpected overnight in Baltimore.

"The next day, Franklin, my producer, said he'd gotten a call from her office, saying she'd had to cancel and she'd call to reschedule."

"And did she?"

Huh. "No. No, she didn't. And Franklin hasn't been able to reach her."

My ringing phone interrupts the conversation. "Let the machine get it," I say. And then I realize what I'm saying. The phone is ringing. And it can only, *only* be Josh. I bite my bottom lip. Got to, *got to,* answer the phone.

"On the other hand," I say, getting up, "excuse me. It might be . . ."

The detective clamps a tanned hand on my arm, stopping me. "Katherine Harkins is missing. You were the last person who was supposed to see her. Is there anything else you can tell me? Someone's life could be at stake here."

Mine. The unworthy thought springs to mind before I can stop it. The phone is now on ring three. One more and the machine starts. But the detective is right.

I put my elbows on the table, chin in hands, mulling this over. "She had e-mailed Franklin she wanted to meet us at the airport because she was between planes. Had a flight to — to somewhere. Did she make that flight?"

The phone stops. And the silence is devastating. *Leave a message,* I mentally chant an imprecation to the goddesses of romance. Leave. A. Message. I've done the right thing here. You owe me.

"We can't find her name on any flight manifest," Yens says. "It's possible she may have taken a private plane. We have an APB out in her hometown, Washington, D.C., as well as Atlanta. But 'private plane.' Does that ring a bell?"

Which reminds me of the call I just missed. Which reminds me of the crank call I got last night. Now that Katie Harkins seems to be missing, I'm tentatively wondering whether my creepily anonymous caller may have been someone like — what did Lattimer call him? Billy the Animal?

With one determined leap, Botox jumps on the table again, crashing into my water bottle, sloshing the whole thing across the table and right into the detective's lap. She skitters away, embarrassed.

"Jeee . . . zus." Yens leaps from his chair,

brushing water from his jeans, his hands dripping and his little notebook soaked.

I race to the kitchen, yank a handful of paper towels from the stainless steel holder and lean over him, attempting to help him dry off. Suddenly, that's awkward. Touching him. I hold out the towels, apologizing.

"I'm so sorry," I say. The table is one big puddle, mail soaked, and my handful of towels is not terribly successful at drying it all. "The silly cat. Your notebook. I hope it's okay."

"No harm done, Charlie," he says, and seems to mean it. He blots his legs, then peels back each page of the notebook, dabbing off the water. "But I was asking you. You've never seen her, is that correct? Not even a photo? Did Ms. Harkins ever say where she was headed? Because . . ."

"I see where you're going with this. You think she may still be in Boston somewhere."

"Let me know if you hear from her," Yens says. He gives me back his soggy wad of towels. "And tell your cat she's on my list."

"You're sure you don't need any more towels?" I'm trying to be polite and solicitous as I guide the detective toward my front door. But there's only one thought in my mind. Leave, leave, leave, I silently chant. I have to check my phone messages. *Leave, leave, leave.*

CHAPTER SEVEN

There was no lovestruck message on the machine. But there's also no mystery. And, sadly, no good news in romance world.

It was Franklin.

"So the cop arrived at your house? Already? And he's gone? I called you as soon as we got home and I picked up his message on our machine. I figured that's why you didn't answer your phone."

"Yes, well, he wouldn't let —"

"So that means he's on the way here." Franklin ignores me. "He said he was going to you first, then me. Stephen thinks it's so *Law and Order,* having the police arrive. He's literally considering getting doughnuts."

"Bad plan," I say. "This guy's more about Red Bull, from what I see."

"So what did he say?"

I tell Franklin about the maybe-missing Katie Harkins. Her schedule, the police backtracking.

"And seems like we were the first appointment she missed. Like I told him though, obviously I've never talked to her. They seem somewhat concerned, you know? I mean, why not just wait until tomorrow?"

"Yeah, especially since I don't know any more about Katie Harkins than you do," Franklin says. "Well, except for maybe one thing."

"It's past eleven now," I check the clock on the microwave as I sip my second glass of Shiraz. "And this detective may be a little delayed. He may have to change clothes first."

"Change clothes?"

"I'll tell you tomorrow," I say. "And you can tell me about your tête-à-tête with Detective Yens." I hold up my glass of wine, examining the kitchen ceiling light through the ruby liquid. It should have been Josh on the phone. I'm suddenly bone-tired. My adrenaline's crashed and my reserves are gone. And tomorrow, I have to go under-cover.

"Fair warning, Franko. I'm going to be late coming in. I've got to be at that party at four. Got to leave Boston by, say, noon. So you know what? I'm going to sleep in. Turn on my computer so it looks like I'm there, okay? Everyone will just assume I'm

106

somewhere else. Then I'll come in and get the camera."

We're both silent for a moment. Franklin is probably deciding whether it's morally acceptable for him to dupe our coworkers by turning on my computer. I'm replaying our conversation.

"Except for what?" I ask.

"What?"

"You said a minute ago, you don't know any more about Katie Harkins than I do, except for — except for what?"

So the Prada P.I. used to be an FBI agent. Franklin said he'd Googled her name and came across a story about some cops busting a counterfeit purse ring in Georgia. It quoted officials as saying she had resigned from the Bureau and had pointed the police to the bad guys. He also found a couple of quotes from her in newspaper stories about the hunt for fake purses. But after that, he said, nothing. No television interviews, so that's the good news. We'll be the first. I wonder if she knew Lattimer. Or Keresey. Wonder if she's in trouble.

I punch the buttons on my Jeep's radio, trying to find a clear station as I head out the Mass Turnpike toward exit one. That's the beginning of the toll road that stretches

107

pinstripe straight across the state. I'm going as far away from Boston as you can get and still be in Massachusetts.

Past Framingham, past Worcester. The foliage intensifies as I head west, the lofty roadside maples and white birches giving me a preview of the autumn to come. Fall always arrives in Boston last, then disappears into months of dreary sleet and slush.

I flex my fingers on the steering wheel, then steal a high-speed glance at the camera on the seat beside me. Confirming, yet again, that my equipment is set for the job ahead of me. Of course I came into the station on time, couldn't possibly sleep late on the day of an undercover assignment. Couldn't possibly sleep at all, actually, my brain ping-ponging between missing Josh, the maybe-missing Katie Harkins, and my strategy for the pivotal first purse party.

This morning in our office, Franklin had the gear ready to go. I loaded it into my specially cut-out purse, then walked through the newsroom, practicing. He watched from the top of the stairs as I sauntered past the ceiling-high bank of flickering television sets, displayed like some electronics store on steroids, and into the warren of identical beige desks, a writer or producer on the computer at each one.

Acting like I was looking for the news director, I chatted with the arriving reporters, each with supersized coffee and briefcases bulging with lunches and extra shoes. I casually walked past the satellite feed room, waved at the weather team intent on their Doppler radar screens, and wound up focused on the assignment desk crew. Three worried twentysomethings wearing leftover-from-college khakis and new-to-TV frowns, each frenetically examining the *Boston Globe* for all the stories the night crew had missed.

Not one of those intrepid journalists noticed there was a camera in my purse recording their every move.

I walked out, oh so casually, getting it all on tape and gave Franklin a triumphant thumbs-up.

He and I checked the video upstairs, heads touching as we watched it through the tiny playback screen on the camera. I got great shots of a producer searching Facebook, the satellite guy doing a crossword puzzle, and the new morning reporter shopping online for red patent Louboutin pumps. If the camera were set to record audio, I could have also provided slam-dunk proof that our noon anchor was making comments to an intern that Nanette in Human Resources would certainly have frowned upon.

"She's totally coming on to that kid." I pointed to the miniature image flickering by. "Too bad state law says you can't secretly record audio. So what do you think?"

"Looks good, Charlotte." Franklin pursed his lips, nodding. "Watch that the lens doesn't become dislodged, and move, or tilt. You'll wind up with a bunch of shots of the ceiling. Or shoes."

I tucked the camera back into its metal case and checked the red buttons to confirm the batteries were fully charged.

"We need purses. Money changing hands. Women with bags. The faces of everyone there. Especially the hostess. And maybe, license plates, you know? I'll get all the license plates. And cars. Who knows what will matter when our story all comes together. So can't hurt to get it all."

"You've got half an hour, max," Franklin reminded me. "After that, tapes out. Batts out. You're done."

The computer voice from my GPS interrupts my thoughts, announcing exit seven, Ludlow, is next. I have four spare batteries, each the size of a triple pack of gum. If necessary, I can click in a new one in the ladies' room. That'll also be a good place to check my video. If the lens gets out of position, or the tape didn't roll, I'll be able to go back and pick up what I missed. Better to reshoot than to drive back to Boston with an hour's worth of shoes.

I nod my head, planning. Going undercover, carrying a hidden camera. It's risky. And intimidating. A lot can go wrong. But a lot can go right. I love it.

I look in the mirror. And a stranger looks back. I smile in approval. Even I don't recognize myself. My hair is scrunchied in a high slicked-back ponytail. My contacts are in, so I can see, but I found a pair of ultrahigh-fashion square black-rimmed glasses, very Manhattan chic. Also very fake, since the lenses are just glass. Blue eye shadow, so retro some magazines claim it's hip. And pink lipstick. A long skirt, vaguely Woodstock, and a vaguely peasant blouse. And, of course, my special purse. Not me at all. But now, I'm not me.

Luckily, I have some time alone in the ladies' room of the Plucky Chicken Restaurant. Luckily the place is somewhat empty, post-lunch hour, and no one will notice that the blue-jeaned blonde in the big sunglasses who hurried into the room marked "Hens" carrying a bulky tote bag walked out a short while later transformed into someone else.

Someone else. I instantly decide on the name I'll use. Elsa.

I study my counterfeit image in the full-length mirror. My fellow party-goers will either believe my story that I'm Elsa, an artist visiting the Berkshires from "the city," or write me off as a combination leaf-peeper and disastrous fashion victim. Either way, they'll figure I need a new purse.

Time for a little experiment. At this point on the Turnpike, I'm still in Channel 3's viewing area and I know we've got high ratings around here. On a typical day, I probably couldn't walk into this place without being recognized.

I open the door and pause, taking my first step into a new identity. Heading to the lunch counter, I perch on an old-fashioned black leather stool, the once-puffy seat cracking with age and years of heavyweight fried chicken eaters.

I wait for someone to ask if they can help me. As Charlie McNally, well-known reporter, maître d's hoping to woo a "famous" guest have offered me free appetizers, celebrated chefs have served complimentary amuse-bouches, attentive waitstaff have proffered arrays of desserts, all on the house. I enjoy the flattery, but have to explain I can't accept anything free. A good reporter can't be objective when beholden. But now, I note with some satisfaction, I'm not going to have to fight that battle.

The three counter women, one an unhealthy-looking should-be-in-college girl with random tattoos, and two plump-but-pleasant-looking mom types ignore me. I consider robbing the cash register, that's the extent of my invisibility. They may be Channel 10 fans and not know Charlie Mc-Nally from Charlie McCarthy. But I'm convinced my disguise will work. I'm no longer Charlie McNally. I'm someone — Elsa.

Chapter Eight

I've been worried most about this very moment. The crossroads between planning and reality. I'll walk through the already open door and face a roomful of strangers. What if someone stretches an accusing arm across the open doorway, blocking me, and says, "Excuse me, this is invitation only. And you don't have an invitation." Then I'm done. No story. Video of a door slamming in my face. The only thing that would be worse is being recognized. Then I get busted, my news director and old Susannah find out what we're really doing, and Franklin and I are toast.

Sitting in my Jeep, parked a block from my destination, I check the camera in my purse one final time. It's rolling. I check my watch. Ten after three. Which means I've got batteries until 3:40 p.m. I check the address once again. I'm in the right place. The message we got said just to arrive between three and four in the afternoon, knock, then open the door and come in. If that's how these things work, fine.

With one final adjustment to my "purse," I walk up the bluestone path toward the front door, head high and pointing the lens in front of me. I pause, briefly, to shoot a steady pan of the unassuming house at 57 Glendower Street. It's yellow vinyl siding with white trim around the door, black-and-white vinyl awnings over each window. Wrought iron window boxes filled with last-of-the-season geraniums telegraph someone struggling to make the best of a too-small home in a deteriorating neighborhood. It looks as if the houses on either side may be empty. One has a For Sale sign stuck into the browning grass of the careworn front lawn. I get the signs. I get the house. I get the license plates of the cars in the driveway.

I aim the camera lens to take a shot of my fist knocking on the door, then shifting the camera back beside me, open the door. There's hardly room for me to fit inside. The place is wall-to-wall women.

A zoo. Filled with the din of shopping animals seeking their prey. Maybe thirty? forty? women, from lanky-haired teenagers to gray-bouffanted grandmothers, in Levis and designer T-shirts, madras skirts and ladylike flats, tunic tops over cropped pants with chunky-heeled mules, all converging around tables set up in two rooms. Two rooms I can see, at least. It smells like leather and plastic. It smells like makeup. It smells like hair spray. And way, way, too much perfume.

I step inside and almost get knocked over.

Two women, each carrying an armload of leather and plastic loot, power across my path. I step back into the entryway, getting my bearings. On my left, through an archway of once-dark wood, what's probably a dining room table is covered with a jumble of more purses, umbrellas, tote bags, wallets and scarves than I've ever seen outside of a department store. I aim my camera in that direction, but I know I'll have to get closer. Right now all the lens will capture is a not-terribly-flattering shot of a row of women's rear ends, as shoppers scramble through the faux treasures piled in front of them.

Holding my camera steady as I can, I slowly turn to my right. The two shoppers who almost put me on the floor are now part of another pack of purse hunters surrounding two card tables set up in the center of the living room. Furniture is sparse. There are no photos, no knickknacks. Maybe it's all been hidden for today's extravaganza.

Wide shot of the dining room. Got it. Wide shot of the living room. Got it. Ready to go in for close-ups.

I hear a knock on the door behind me. I flatten myself against the wall as three more purse-stalking fashionistas flutter and yoo-hoo their way to the tables.

No one has acknowledged my existence. Happily, I don't see anyone who could be Keresey in disguise. And my time is ticking by.

Stepping into the living room, I smile my way confidently to a clear section of one of the card tables. Welcome to Burberry City. Shoulder bags, coin purses, umbrellas, tote bags, pouches and wallets, all with the well-known camel, black, red and white plaid. Placing my purse carefully on the table, lens aimed toward me, I choose a small shoulder bag and pretend to examine it. I'm actually checking for the Burberry tell — a distinctive and never-changing pattern in the plaid. With a glance to confirm no one is noticing and a secret smile of triumph, I casually hold the bag up in front of my hidden lens. These babies are fakes.

I put my camera purse on my shoulder again. Keeping my hand near the lens just in case I need to cover it, I aim for the table, recording the intently calculating faces of the bargain hunters, each focused on selecting from the still enormous assortment of designer doubles.

"Amazing, huh?" I put a little squeak in my voice, pitching it high and feminine. How Elsa talks. I've got to get some usable info, and my time is running out. I carefully tilt my purse in hopes of getting her face on camera, even though I'm not allowed to record her voice. "Have you been here before?"

The woman beside me, hair chopped in a bob and wearing a baby-blue twinset reaches her acrylic red fingernails toward a Gucci-looking leather bag decorated with interlocking G's.

I know the G's are in the wrong place.

Blue-twinset apparently doesn't. Or doesn't care. "Nope, friend told me about it. Perfect, huh?" She never takes her eyes off her catch, opening the not-really-gold-plated clasp and checking the inside with an appreciative nod. She snaps it closed, tucks it under her arm, and reaches into the pile again.

"My husband would die if he knew I was here," she says, scrutinizing a Chanel wannabe. "But I say, I can get five or six bags

118

like this for the price of one real one, you know? And wouldn't he be more upset if I bought the real one?"

"So, everyone here knows they're, um, copies?" I ask. Elsa is so naive.

"Well, of course." She still hasn't looked at me as she considers her choices, keeping up a stream of chat. "But I figure there's nothing wrong with it, as long as they don't say they're genuine. Right? Don't ask, don't tell. And it's all cash, of course. So I just take it out of the grocery money." She cocks her head. "You pay in the kitchen."

"Ah," I say. Putting my purse on the table again, I pretend to examine a Fendi clutch, holding it up as the camera — cross fingers — rolls. I'm oh-so-casual, hoping this next question won't set off any intruder alarms. Talking like Elsa. "Do you know our hostess? I'd love to meet her."

"Kitchen," she says.

"Thanks," I say. This is working. I'm pretty sure I'm getting good stuff. Franklin is going to be thrilled, and turns out he'd have been quite a sore thumb here. There's not a man in the place.

The table closer to the kitchen is all Delleton-Marachelle, from their iconic short-handled doctor's bag to their newest suede sling, sleek and oversized, dripping with fringe and tagged with a heavy brass *D*. Like the ones the Prada P.I. sent Franklin. I lift my hand from the lens and aim at the display. I can't even calculate how much this collection would cost if they were authentic. That might be a fun element for our story, putting a price tag on this shot.

"Charlie?"

The voice is coming from behind me. Friendly and welcoming. And devastating.

I carefully lower my hand over the lens and begin to turn around. This is going to be difficult to explain. This is, actually, going to be impossible to explain. This is going to be a mess.

Then I remember. I'm not Charlie. Someone named Elsa would not acknowledge a shout-out to someone named Charlie. Knees jelly and tingles of sweat forming across my upper lip, I summon my inner Elsa and continue shopping the phony bags. I don't budge. I don't respond. In about two seconds, either my cover is going to be blown. Or not. I race through my options. One: Leave. Two: Leave very quickly.

Three: Calm down. Even if someone recognizes me, they wouldn't know I have a camera in my bag. Probably. And if they ask whether I'm a TV reporter, I'll just say no. If they demand to see what's in my purse,

120

I'll just say goodbye. Option three it is.

"Charlie Sue Wanamaker? Is that you?" There's a hoot of greeting, "girlfriend!" and some other shopper named Charlie turns, arms wide, to embrace the woman who almost caused my heart attack. As they kiss the air, I whisper a silent thanks to the journalism gods.

I check my watch. Ten minutes, maybe, until I have to hit the bathroom and change batteries. Time to check out the kitchen. Follow the money.

Chest-high swinging doors, like in some John Wayne western, block the entrance to the kitchen. I take a Delleton-Marachelle suede tote from the table, the one with the fringe. The price tag says one hundred thirty-five dollars. By my calculation, if this honey is real, that would be an eighteen-hundred-dollar discount. I can tell it's a phony. The fringe is attached under a suede flap, as it should be. But it's not stitched, it's glued. Fake.

I carry my prize through the doors, digging in the pocket of my skirt for my wallet. This is the tricky part. And almost funny. Of course I can't open my hidden camera purse to pay for the counterfeit purse.

Okay, Elsa. You're on.

I pause at the door, risking a wide shot.

121

There's only the two of us in the room, so there's no one to distract her from my surreptitious photographic activity.

"Do I pay you for this?" Elsa-me squeaks, chirpy and chatty. I hold up the D-M, waving it a bit to draw her eye away from my camera-purse. "This is so wonderful. You have so many nice things."

The woman at the kitchen table has a gray metal box, shoebox size, in front of her. It's closed, and as I approach her, she puts her hand on top of it.

"That's all you found?" she asks. "Or would you like me to hold this for you? So you can keep shopping?" She takes the purse from me, putting it on top of the strongbox, and examines the price tag. Her lipstick is probably named Killer Copper, or Molten Metal, and her hyper-permed hair pretty much matches. Her tank top T-shirt, too skimpy for someone her age, proclaims "When the going gets tough . . ." on the front. I can predict the back.

Elsa is congenial. I hold out one hand, covering the lens with the other. "Elsa," I say, stepping into reporter waters. Let's see how she handles my first test question. "Thank you so much for inviting me." Did she invite me? And will she say her name?

"Just call me Sally," the woman says. "And

no problem, I have my little gatherings all the time. That's one hundred thirty five dollars. Cash only. Sure you don't want to keep shopping?"

I open my wallet, peel out three fifty dollar bills, and hand "Sally" the cash. "Just-call-me-Sally" means "Sally" is probably the only name that isn't hers. I carefully lift my hand away from the lens. "Sally" has opened her cash box and I need that shot.

"I, um, well," I give Elsa an embarrassed look and lean in closer to Sally as the purse proprietor adds the bills to her stash. The cash box is Fort Knox. The mint. Crammed with cash. I hope the camera stays in focus this close.

"Well, I'd adore to keep shopping of course. And thank you for offering to hold my darling bag, but I'm afraid first, I . . ." Elsa drops her voice to a whisper, scrunches up her shoulders, points the camera right at the boxful of bills ". . . have to go to the ladies. Could you point me?"

"The bathroom." Sally hands me my change, then closes her box and looks around the room. Almost scanning. Maybe she's wondering why people aren't arriving with more cash and purses. I suddenly wonder if there's some kind of security system out there. Making certain the desperate housewives don't abscond with their purses without paying. "Of course, it's, uh . . ." she brightens ". . . upstairs. Top of the stairs."

I click the bathroom door closed, and twist the little latch on the door handle. Just to make sure, I lean against the door, my back padded by a set of yellow towels hanging over a rack. I open my purse.

Come on, video. Show me the money. And the loot.

I push Rewind and watch a chaotically jerky mishmash of colors flash and flicker backward. That's all I needed to see. If I watched it forward, I know it would be pictures.

I click out the tape and search for a pen to mark the label tape one. Damn. I don't have a pen. This isn't my real purse. Inside is only a camera. I touch my finger to my pink lipstick, then touch the finger to the tape label. Tape one is pink.

Just in case someone is waiting outside, I flush the toilet, then turn on the water in the sink. I click off the almost dead battery and click on a new one. I insert a new cassette, push Play, and watch the tiny cassette start to reel forward. I'm back in business.

I turn off the water, pause a beat, and open the door.

And there's just-call-me-Sally. Standing, feet apart, hands on hips, three inches from me.

Rule one of carrying hidden camera. The person you are shooting does not know you have it. No matter what they say, no matter how they behave. The most ordinary remarks will sound suspicious and threatening. But they don't know. Rule one is banging through my brain as I size up the situation.

"Hi, Sally," I say, in my chirpy Elsa voice. "Need the bathroom? Hey, where's my beautiful new bag?"

"Looks like you already have a pretty nice bag," she replies, pointing. She makes no move to go inside.

Rule one, rule one.

"Oh, this old thing?" I reply. "I think my mother bought it for me. I use it to carry around my art supplies. That's why I think its time to splurge on a new one. Oh, don't tell me. The party's not over, is it?"

"How did you find out about our little get together?" she asks.

Rule one, rule one.

"Oh, golly, I met a lovely girl in the airport, gosh, I think maybe Baltimore?" I reel off the whole story of Regine, and her card, and the Web site. Gauging her reaction the whole time. She backs away a bit. Seems to relax.

Rule two of carrying a hidden camera. The best defense is a good offense.

"You have such a wonderful turnout today. Of course, you have all those wonderful purses. I can't believe they're so inexpensive," I say. Then I tilt my head as if I'd just had an offhand thought. "How does this all work? I mean . . ." I pause, and glance both ways down the hall, as if confirming the coast is clear and we're alone. I lower my voice. "Does your husband know about this?"

Sally laughs, quietly, and shakes her head. Her coppery curls don't budge. "My husband — my ex-husband — is God knows where. If he did know about my side business, he'd probably try to take back the alimony checks. Such as they are. Anyway, are you finished in the bathroom?"

Rule one rules. And has also provided me a way into Sally's confidence and into purse world. "Oh, don't I know it," I say. I hold out my left hand, showing it's ringless. "I'm in just the same boat. Men. The worst."

"I hear that, girlfriend," she says. She eyes me. Up. And down.

I don't even flinch.

"How does all this work, you wanted to

126

know," she says. "Why'd you want to know that?"

"Oh, you know." I try to make Elsa sound calculating but uncertain. "Money. You know. My guy left me with nothing. In fact, took most of what I had. You know."

"Poor thing," she says, nodding. "And you like purses, huh? Like I do."

I look up and down the hall again, then put on a conspiratorial face. Now that we're sisters in man-hating, perhaps she'll think we can also be sisters in crime. "Can I — talk to you briefly? Go for coffee, maybe? Somewhere? I'm thinking maybe you could help me get started on my own."

"Yes, she's meeting me here at the mall," I explain to Franklin. I'm holding my cell with one hand, and with the other, I'm trying to jam sugar packets under the annoyingly uneven table at the food court in the Lee Discount Mall. My disgusting faux-latte from Coffee King has already almost tipped over several times. They can copy a complicated purse for cheap. Why is perfectly simple coffee so tough?

"I told her I was interested in getting into the purse biz, and she seemed open to discussing it. So, we'll see." I sit back up and rescue my latte once again. Watching both ways down the halls of the bustling mall, I scout for Sally. She's almost late.

"I'll see if I can get some kind of a lead from her, you know? Find out her source. Listen, anything new on Katie Harkins? Have you heard from Detective Yens?"

"Nothing," Franklin replies. "Are you on your cell? You're breaking up. Just tell me, before I completely lose you. Did you get the shots? Purses?"

"Yup. Can you hear me now? I got a great D-M copy, just like the ones we have, and the fakest Burberry you've ever seen. The place was a madhouse. Money out the wazoo."

"Did you get the money shots?"

"Are you kidding me? You're talking to the undercover queen." Then, down by the entrance to Macy's, I spot an unmistakable copper mop of curls. "She's here," I whisper to Franklin. "Bingo."

By the time Sally arrives at my table, my cell is tucked into my bag. My bag is sitting on a chair. The lens is carefully pointed right where I hoped Sally would sit.

She yanks her chair to the right, right out of range. I scoot around, pretending to give her more room, moving my purse at the same time. She's already in full sales pitch, a nonstop, slang-heavy staccato. I can't record her audio of course, but this video could cover the part of our script that'll say "One woman who admitted she's made thousands of dollars selling counterfeit bags told us . . ."

"Legal? We don't even go there," Sally is saying. "We're talking purses, ya know? It's not like we're selling, I don't know, guns or something. This is harmless, right? What's a purse or two going to hurt?"

"Sure," I reply, playing along, remembering what Lattimer said. "That's what I thought, too. And you know how it is, money and all. Anyway, I'm so glad you could meet me. Because, you know I was wondering . . ."

I was actually wondering how one casually asks a person engaged in a criminal enterprise how you sign up to be part of it. Especially how you have that discussion in the center of a crowded discount mall, surrounded by bargain-hunting tourists and drooling babies and teenagers showing off their piercings. It seems outrageous. And, then, suddenly, I'm clutched by fear.

What if Sally's FBI? And they, of course, don't know anything about me, Charlie, being undercover. Sally thinks I'm Elsa. So wouldn't it be one for the books if I'm secretly taping her? And she's secretly taping me? And the real bad guys are getting away with it? Laughing all the way to the bank?

"We don't say outright the bags are fake." Sally's talking right over me. "So that makes it legal. Ya know? The way the law works, if you don't make a promise, you can't break a promise. And everyone is happy."

I mentally hold my nose and jump in. What Sally's saying of course, is absurd. And wrong.

"So, do you have more of the bags? Do you ever let — do you ever let anyone else sell them for you? Split the, um . . ." I pretend to be nervous, which isn't all that difficult, since I'm still not one hundred percent sure I'm not the one being set up.

I lean toward her, almost covering my mouth with one hand, speaking through my fingers. "Do you worry about being . . ." I look both ways, as if making sure we're not overheard ". . . arrested?" I whisper.

Sally eyes me, cagey. She crosses her arms in front of her T-shirted chest and tilts back in her chair, almost hitting the iPod-wearing teen in the chair behind her.

"Where do you live?" she asks, flipping the heel of one high-heeled strappy mule against the sole of her foot. Tap. Tap. Tap.

"Connecticut. Hartford. I'm an artist, just

130

visiting the Berkshires, you know, for the fall colors." I shrug, embellishing my cover story. "Can't make much money doing watercolors, you know? And my ex-husband . . ."

"What's your phone number? Write it down for me."

Ah. Now I'm going to have to think of a reason why I don't look in my purse. Although why should I necessarily have a pen? I'm not a reporter.

"I —" I begin.

"Look. Don't make a big deal out of this," Sally says. Her voice gets tough, dismissive. She clunks her chair back down onto all four legs, and plops her purse — a fake Coach, I can tell — on the table. "You ever hear of some mom in the suburbs hauled away to the slammer for selling purses? It's like Tupperware, ya know? Don't get hot over it. You want to sell purses?"

That phony Coach had better not contain a hidden camera. She'd better not be taking my picture.

Before I can decide on my answer, she yanks open the drawstring, and digs around inside, talking the whole time. "Listen. Who cares if those snazzy purse makers lose a little profit? We wouldn't be buying their overpriced stuff, anyway. It's not our money they're losing." Apparently not finding what she wants, she turns the bag on its side and shakes the contents out onto the table.

And voilà. There's no camera. She's just purse-pushing Sally, suburban entrepreneur, and I'm the only one undercover. I feel my shoulders relax, and glance at my own purse. Even if the battery runs out now, I've got the shots we need.

Sally plows through her belongings, and finally finds a slim black plastic cardholder. She extracts two business cards. They look like the one Regine gave me.

She then selects a pencil, and offers it to me, eyebrows raised. "You want to work for me? Here's the deal. I'm getting into this full-time. Frankly, it's a gold mine. And perfect timing for you. I'm dumping my supplier and going on my own. You don't need to know more than that. But if this all works out, there'll be plenty for everyone. So. Write your number on one card. Keep the other. So you have my number."

She nods as I follow her instructions. One card has a phone number on the back, local area code, written in marker. I tuck that in my pocket. On the other, I write the number for the safe phone line Franklin and I have set up for exactly these occasions. And now, my "name." Elsa, um. I consider using the last name Murrow, just for a little in-joke, then decide on Walters. Barbara won't know.

Sally's stuffing her possessions back into her bag. "Ever hear of a woman who said, sorry I don't need another purse? My new supplier . . ." she pauses, still smiling. "Well, I'll call you. Do what the message says. Soon you and I will be able to buy ourselves the real thing."

"It's in the bag," I say. Nervous Elsa pretends to stifle a giggle at her bad joke.

"You got it, girl," Sally replies, turning to go. "And you're gonna love it."

I watch the redhead wind her way through the rickety chairs and tables and out of the food court. I'm gonna love it? Flickers of suspicion are still flaring in my head, and I'm not sure how to extinguish them.

If Sally's the real thing, I'm in.

If she's not, I'm in trouble.

CHAPTER NINE

I haven't done this since high school. It was silly, as a teenager, to drive by Tommy Thornburg's house just to see if he was home. Or if any cars were in his driveway. Or maybe, to see if cheerleader goddess and most-likely-to-succeed-at-everything Nancy Rachel Hartline's convertible was in his driveway. To do it as a grownup is beyond explanation. Plus, driving barely five miles an hour past someone's house at ten o'clock at night is probably illegal. It's stalking, or reverse-speeding or something. I hope no Neighborhood Watch goon calls the cops.

I just couldn't stay away. But I can't bring myself to call him. Again, high school.

The front windows of Josh's house are dark. I can see one light, which I know is his study, still glowing out a side window of the first floor. I also know that's on a timer and doesn't mean he's home. The garage door is closed, so I know his Volvo might be inside. Or it might not be. And if he's not here, where is he?

I edge past number 6, driving toward the end of Bexter Drive. I'm still in my Elsa outfit and have a fleeting fantasy of knocking on Josh's door to see if he'll recognize me. He will, of course, and he'll laugh, and I'll laugh, and Penny will come running downstairs, and we'll all laugh. And then everything will be fine again.

Back to reality. Penny is with her mother. Two days ago, Josh stomped out of my apartment. I didn't try hard enough to stop him. And now I miss him. I don't need him, I insist to myself. I'm fine on my own. But that doesn't mean I can't miss him.

I yank my steering wheel toward Beacon Hill and home.

And when I get there, I see that Josh's car is parked in front of my house. I blink in confusion, then blink again, my brain trying to register this unpredictable occurrence. While I was in front of Josh's house, he was in front of mine.

I hope it's because he misses me, too. I hope he's not here to pick up his toothbrush.

My assigned parking space is in the back, in the lot behind my building, but I slide my Jeep in behind his car. My headlights illuminate his unmistakable shape in the front seat, his arms crossed over the steering wheel. He sits up as my lights hit him. Turns around. And opens his door.

We connect on the deserted street, hands searching, lips meeting, devouring each other, remembering. My arms wrap around his neck, his hands move down my back. It's not a toothbrush that he wants. We're ignoring the spotlighting streetlights, ignoring any nosy neighbors watching from their brownstone windows, ignoring the necessity of breathing.

"How did you know?" I finally tilt my head back, not letting go, not taking my eyes from him as I try to make sense of this. "When I would be home?"

"I would have waited. As long as it took," he whispers, eyes closed, and reaches up to touch my hair. He opens his eyes, smiling, and then his expression changes. He gently pushes me arm's length away, keeping his hands on my shoulders.

"My, my, Ms. McNally," he says. He looks me up and down. Then up again. "I fear I must inform you the summer of peace and love is long over. And I must say, I'm not sure how your fans will handle the reporter as hippie look."

"It's a long story," I say, tucking my arm

through his. I can feel the softness of his black sweater against my cheek as I curl closer to him. "How about if I tell you the whole thing — upstairs?"

But once we get inside, I can't ignore the flashing light on the message machine. Every muscle in my body longs for Josh. Every scintilla of my intellect understands that it won't matter if I wait until tomorrow. That if there are messages still waiting, unlistened to at this time of night, it can't possibly make a difference if they wait a few hours longer.

But as I told Mom when she caught me, nine years old, reading the last chapter of my Nancy Drew first: *I hafta know.* And now, thirty-seven years later, thirty-eight, shouldn't Josh understand that, too? I'm a reporter. Working on a big story.

"I'm so sorry, honey," I say. My arm is still linked through his as we stand in my entryway. I hold tighter as we both stare at the blinking light on the living room phone. Botox is winding her way through our legs, meowing a combination welcome and complaint. Josh is silent, ignoring both of us. I can feel his body stiffen.

"Why don't you open a bottle of wine for us?" I continue. "And I'll just see who it is." It might be news about Katie Harkins.

Franklin might have checked our outside line and might have news from Sally.

"It's just a message from me, sweetheart," Josh interrupts. I can see the beginnings of a frown on his face. "I called you. I left a message, wondering where you were. I realized that I can't remember the last time I didn't know where you were. So. It's me."

I can't stop myself. "Two seconds," I say, moving toward the phone. "Get the wine from the fridge and I'll meet you on the couch."

Josh is still standing where I left him as I turn to pick up the receiver and begin punching in the number to retrieve the messages. "Two seconds," I say again.

I feel Josh standing next to me. He does not have a bottle of wine.

The phone voice begins its techno-prompts in my ear. *"To enter your mailbox, press . . ."*

"I think we need to talk, Charlie," Josh says, at the same time. He puts his hands in the back pockets of his jeans. "Why is it that you're so compelled . . ."

"Please enter your code, followed by the pound sign . . ."

"It's just, well, this story we're working on, I'll tell you all about it. It's why I'm wearing this outfit, you know? And yesterday

138

the police came, they were investigating."
I'm talking to Josh and entering my code at
the same time.

"You have, two new messages and . . ."

"The police?" Josh says. "So you finally
did report that phone call?"

I interrupt the prompt, pushing more
numbers to retrieve my new messages. I
know I don't have any saved ones. "Well,
no," I say, "the police were here because . . ."

*"First new message, received today at 7:14
p.m."* There's a pause as the message loops
up from the digital recorder.

"That's me," Josh says. "As I told you."
He reaches over and hits the orange button
to activate the speaker phone.

"Hello, Charlie." Now we can both hear
Josh's tinny voice. It's quiet, subdued. "I
tried to call you at the station, but you're
not there, either." There's a pause, and we
hear Josh sigh. "Do you think we should
talk? I'll try you later."

"I told you," he says. "Now, can we please
sit down?"

*"Second new message, received today at
9:56 p.m."* The computer voice says. The
speaker phone is still on.

There's a beat. Then clicking noises. The
same ones I heard in that first phone call,
although Josh doesn't know that. Then

whoever it is hangs up. The silence echoes through the living room.

"Ah, wrong number," I say. I'm desperate to lighten the mood. Somehow this night is suddenly fragile and suddenly all the stakes seem high. Maybe if I ignore it, it'll go away. Right. That always works. "Oh, well, I guess that's the good news, right? Let's get that wine. And I'll fill you in on my latest adventures." I turn to Josh, my expression expectant and enthusiastic.

No answer.

"Josh?" I persist. "It's my job. You know? If a student called you, or if there were some emergency at Bexter, you'd have to be available, right? So it's the same."

Surprising me, Josh puts his arm around me, and shepherds me toward the couch. Botox bounces up beside us, and curls up on my lap. Maybe this will all work out.

Josh takes my hand, examining my fingers. "You know, Charlie," he says. "There's a pattern here. Isn't there?"

I don't answer, because I can't come up with a good one.

He sighs. "And the pattern is, when you have a choice, you choose your work."

"But I don't have a choice." I can hear the almost-whine in my own voice.

"It's all right," Josh says. "It's me who will

140

have to change."

"No, you don't," I interrupt. "We can —"

"We can't." Josh puts my hand back on my own knee, and gives it a lingering pat. "Was it just two days ago? I wrote a new address for you on that card? I thought our lives were coming together, and I was so eager to share, well, everything with you. I came to see you, decided I had been unfair the other night. That phone call was disturbing, Penny had been upset going to Victoria's . . ." He stops, and looks at the floor. "Whatever. So I thought, let's try again. Charlie's worth it. And then you chose your messages."

I'm staring at the floor, too. Afraid to hear what may come next. Dumb, dumb Charlie. Married to her job. Tears well in my eyes. And then I decide. No. Dammit.

I stand up, dumping Botox onto the couch. Whirl around and face Josh, who's looking at me, bewildered.

"I did not. Choose my messages. I did not." Anger, or disappointment, or loss, is selecting my words, not me. "You have to balance your daughter, your job, even Victoria and what's-his-name. Your students, now that Bexter's back in session. Your parents in Annapolis. I have to do the same thing with my life. We're trying to add each

141

other and trying to keep the balance. And . . . and . . . and —"

I feel my fists clenching. I bite my lip, fearing this might be goodbye. "Maybe it's just not easy. Maybe it takes some practice. Or maybe, it can't work. No matter how much you want it to. No matter how much you try."

Josh stands, his face inches from mine. "We're new at this, aren't we? Grown up and acting like spoiled teenagers. Wanting everything, maybe not wanting to work for it."

"I'm trying to work at it. It's just — old dog? New tricks?" I say. I reach up and touch his face, see his eyes close for a brief second. "And as for wanting . . ."

My heart is beating so fast, my chest is so tight, it's difficult for me to get the words out. *"Want"* is hardly enough to describe it. And then, I couldn't speak if I wanted to. Josh's kisses are soft and strong and full of tomorrow. And of right now.

"Shall we just take it slow?" he asks, his voice almost a whisper. "One day at a time? No plans? No predictions? See what happens?"

He pulls one end of the tiny ribbon bow that's keeping my peasanty blouse civilized. As gauzy fabric drops from both my shoul-

142

ders, I close my eyes, and feel his lips exploring my neck.

"Mmm," I murmur. "I think I can predict what's going to happen now, at least."

CHAPTER TEN

"What kind of animal?" I say to Franklin. We're in our office, desk chairs pulled up to our video monitor, watching my shaky pictures from the purse party. Video from a hidden camera is about ten per cent usable. Most of it turns out to be upside down, sideways, all swoops and blurs, or has someone's hand over it. Basically, a lot of it looks like someone's shooting out of focus movies on a storm-tossed ship. Screening raw video can make you seasick.

That's why I'm having a bit of a difficult morning. I'm still the tiniest bit hung over from the late-night champagne that my almost-fiancé and I shared to celebrate the beginning of part two of our relationship. I'm also the tiniest bit distracted by residual twinges and tingles from that same late night in places it's inappropriate to discuss with my colleagues at work.

So I'm trying to hide my potentially

embarrassing physical infirmities and focus on our story. And my mind keeps going back to the anonymous phone call. I finally told Franklin about it, including my worry about who might be on the other end. He agreed I don't need to run to the police.

"What do you mean, what kind of animal? That's what mob types call themselves, you know? They all have nicknames," Franklin answers, not taking his eyes off the screen. He's making a shot-sheet of everything that's usable, noting the time codes and a brief description so we can easily find it all later. "Billy the Animal, Steven the Rifleman. You've seen the court transcripts. Lattimer thinks the purse syndicate is terrorist-connected. Or mob. But that doesn't mean Billy the Animal called you. Whoever it was probably wasn't even referring to the purse story. I mean, how would anyone know about it? And the second call, the hang-up? Probably a wrong number, as you said. I suggest we just see. Are you comfortable with that?"

Franklin always seems to understand me, even when I pick up a conversation in the middle.

"Okay," I reply, still watching the video. So far we've seen great shots of the mounds of purses, women shopping, and lots of cash changing hands. And my close-ups on the money box worked perfectly. Sally is there from all angles: tight, medium and wide.

"And it's true, of course," I continue. " 'Billy the Animal' isn't that scary, if he's like, a hamster. Or, you know, Billy the Bunny." I burst out laughing, suddenly carried away by my own wit, then wincing with the noise level. I turn forty-seven and suddenly my body can't hack late hours and champagne? Advil. I need Advil.

Franklin hits the pause button, stopping the tape, and turns to look at me. Confused. "Charlotte. Do you need some Advil?" he asks.

"Did I say that out loud?" I reply. Now I'm the one who's confused.

"Nope, but you're, how shall I put this delicately? You're a little greenish this morning. And may I say you might be well-advised to get one of those refrigerated cold-packs for your eyes."

"Hey, Brenda. Hey, Flash. What's up in snoop-land? Getting any bad guys?" Maysie Green leans against the doorway to our office, her still naturally brown ponytail tucked into her Red Sox cap. Her maternity wardrobe consists of black clingy stretch leggings with one of her husband Matthew's shirts. Works fine for her weekday all-sports drive-time radio talk program. Sunday nights, she has to dress up a bit more for her TV show. Titled, much to her dismay, *Maysie Green, the Sports Machine.* "Catch any ballplayers in the act? I could use some of the video for this Sunday."

"Hey, Mays," I say. "How's the new kid?"

"Hey, Machine," Franklin says at the same time. "Welcome back from the road trip. This has got to be your last expedition before little number three arrives," he adds, pointing to her stomach.

He hates it when she calls him Flash. I'm not that hot on Brenda, either, since Ms. Starr is even older than I am. And only exists in the comics. But my bff Maysie has called me Brenda from the day we met, years ago, and I know she means it affectionately. She's ten years younger than I am, and she somehow manages to juggle career, husband and two-going-on-three children. She adores Josh, and insists we wait until after her new baby is born to get married. Right.

I really need to talk to her.

"Little Poppy or Theo is fine," Mays says, patting her five-month bump. "Matthew still wants another *M* name to match Max and Molly. I suggested Maris or Mantle to get him to back off. And nope, the Sox are off to Yankee Stadium. Can't miss that. So I'm headed out tomorrow for a triple header, then off to Tampa Bay. Anyway, I just came to see if anyone wants to grab Mexican food for a farewell lunch."

I almost fall off my chair. Franklin saves me.

"Our Charlotte is in a somewhat delicate condition, I fear, this morning." He smiles. "How about if I go fetch some tea from the caf? And leave you two a moment to catch up?"

"Thanks, Franko," I say. "I owe you."

"Yes, you do," he says. "Pop that video. We'll watch the rest when I get back."

I'm on the phone when Franklin arrives. I only got about halfway through giving Maysie the scoop on my Josh dilemma when the phone rang. And now my eyes are growing wider with each word I hear from the other end.

"What?" Franklin asks. He puts a paper cup of steaming tea on my desk, the tag on a string draped over the side. Constant Comment. Always a comedian.

I put down the phone and stand up. Moving Maysie and Franklin aside, I look down the hall toward the double-door entrance to our special-projects unit.

"That was the intern in Kevin's office," I say. The doors open. And I see the intern was right. "Look who's here. McGruff the Crime Dog."

Detective Christopher Yens, now in a sleek charcoal suit, tie loosened and carrying a black briefcase, advances confidently toward our office. Behind him, like a frantic little parade, a pencil-skirted Susannah pointing — at me — and struggling to keep up. And news director Kevin O'Bannon, navy double-breasted suit jacket flapping, talking intently into his cell phone.

Yens looks like he's on a mission. Kevin and Susannah are not happy to be conscripted into service.

"What the holy hell," I whisper to Franklin. Nothing like the cops arriving with your news director to snap your brain back from leftover lust.

"See ya when I get home, and can't wait to hear the rest about phase two," Maysie says, giving me a quick kiss on the cheek. She cocks her head at the hallway. "As for now, I know when I'm not wanted." She flutters a wave at Kevin as she heads away to safety.

The three non-amigos arrive at our door almost simultaneously.

"We —" Yens begins.

"He —" says Susannah.

"I —" says Kevin. He flips his phone closed, and stares at Yens. Defiant.

Yens shrugs, putting himself in charge by relinquishing the floor. He sets his briefcase on Franklin's desk, then crosses his arms, waiting with a look of infinite patience.

Kevin adjusts his jacket, smoothes his tie. Waits, just a bit longer than necessary, to begin.

"As I explained to Detective Yens, it's not part of our role as journalists to assist police in their investigations. And we certainly do not — ever — turn over any of our work product or notes to law enforcement." He turns to the detective, pointing an imperious finger. "You may have a copy of what goes on the air. Otherwise, get a subpoena. And we'll fight you every step of the way."

You go, Kevin, I offer in silent approval.

"And it was clearly out of line for you to visit Charlie and Franklin in their homes. I have detailed e-mails from each of them about that. And they'll stay in my files. And our lawyer's. However, in this particular case," Kevin continues, "we felt it not improper for all of us to talk, within certain boundaries, of course, about the matter of Katherine —" he stops.

"Harkins," Susannah puts in. She looks at

me and Franklin. "Isn't she the Prada — ?"

"P.I. Yes." Kevin finishes her sentence. "I decided we should talk here, up in your office, so as not to publicize our meeting to the newsroom. Now. Detective Yens. Charlie and Franklin will answer your questions. If they can. Briefly."

"Fine," Yens says. He snaps open his briefcase, and pulls out a manila folder.

I think I can see photographs inside. Which reminds me. I wonder if our videotape of the purse party is still rolling on our monitor screen. Franklin told me to eject the cassette when he went for tea. I hope I did. For oh so many reasons, including my future employment, that undercover video better not be visible. And I can't draw attention to it by turning around to check.

Moving carefully sideways, one step, then two, I plant myself in front of the television screen.

Franklin, apparently understanding instantly, sidles over next to me. Adding to the video barricade.

"But if you go too far with your questions, in any way, I have our lawyer on speed dial." Kevin flips open his cell phone with an I-dare-you flourish.

As the Kevin and the cop glare at each other, I reach over and wheel my office chair

151

toward me, and sit down, keeping myself in front of the screen. Franklin does the same with his chair. Talk about hidden video.

"Do you recognize this person?" Yens shows me a black-and-white, eight-by-ten photo, turns it to Franklin, then back to me. It's a corporate-looking portrait, a thirty-something woman. Severe. Serious. Dark hair, parted down the middle, pulled back somehow. Black jacket. Pearls. An executive. Or, it crosses my mind, an international spy. But this is clearly Katie Harkins. Who else would he be showing us?

I look at Franklin, who's shaking his head. No.

"Me, neither," I say. "She doesn't look familiar. Is it Katie?"

"How about this person?" Yens holds up another photo.

It looks like the same woman, but in this photo her hair is wildly untamed. Maybe with extensions. She's got raspberry glossy lips, a black T-shirt, a leather jacket. The same pearls. New York fashionista.

"Nope," Franklin says. He looks at me. "You?"

"Nope," I agree. "Is it Katie?"

"We know Katie Harkins was supposed to meet with you several days ago," Yens says, cutting me off. He shows us both photos again. Kevin and Susannah step into the room to get a look. "You're positive you haven't seen her? Looking like this? Or like this?"

"What are you getting at, Yens?" Kevin interrupts. "They told you they haven't seen her. I'm sure they told you she cancelled their appointment."

"She didn't cancel," Yens says.

"Of course she did," Kevin retorts. He looks at Franklin. "Isn't that what you told me?"

"Well, not really," Franklin says. "I said, *someone* called to cancel. I never spoke to her directly. All of our communications were by e-mail. I saved —"

"Stop," Kevin commands.

Franklin nods. He gets it. "Anyway, bottom line. She didn't call to cancel. Someone in her office did."

"That's what they said, at least," Yens mutters as he replaces the photos in the file folder. "Man? Woman? Who was on the phone?"

"Man." Franklin says. He tilts his head. "Almost certainly. Or a pretty deep-voiced woman."

"Have you found her?" I ask.

"Have you tried to reschedule?" Yens ignores me. "What happened?"

"Yes, several times," Franklin says. He flickers a questioning glance at Kevin, then continues. "I've left Charlie's cell-phone number and mine. But no return calls. I always get a voice mail, the same voice mail, saying she was out of the office for a few days and would be back Wednesday. But that was two days ago."

"Exactly. And in answer to your question, Ms. McNally, no. We haven't found her. We're told her home in D.C. is empty. Her car is not in the garage. Mail at the post office, unclaimed. According to our sources. Due to the nature of her job, of course, we know that's not necessarily alarming. But it is unusual. And that's why I'm following up. To see if you've heard from her. Or anyone in her office."

I totally get it now. No question about it. I should have thought of it when Yens paid me a visit, but I was so frazzled my brain didn't grasp it then.

"She works for you, doesn't she? She's an ex-FBI agent. Now a private investigator. Undercover, I bet."

I hear Franklin's intake of breath. Susannah looks at Kevin, quizzical, making a little what's-this-about expression. The news director holds up a hand, eyes narrowed, quieting her.

I point to the briefcase and the photos inside. "She works for you, as well as for the purse companies. Doesn't she? That's her agency photo, and then how she looks on the street. On the job. And let me ask you. Does she also work with Keresey?"

Will Yens say "Keresey who?" And I'm playing back my memories to see if I recognize the woman in the photos from the purse party. Now that I've seen the pictures, I can't wait to look at the video again. What if she was there? Would she have recognized me? It's so much simpler when people are who they say they are, and not someone — else.

"Keresey who?" It's Kevin. He's so concerned about what Franklin and I might say. He's the one who should keep his mouth shut.

"Yes, Keresey who?" Yens says. He crosses his arms in front of him, expression almost sardonic. Waiting.

I wonder if he really doesn't know her. Or if he's just trying to find out how much we know about the FBI's counterfeit operation. How many Kereseys can there be?

"Keresey Stone of the FBI," I say, then stop. I'm the reporter. Stay on the offense. "Do the state police have an undercover operation? Looking into counterfeit purses?

Is Katie Harkins undercover for you? Did she go missing on assignment?"

Yens looks amused.

"Good try, Charlie," he says, emphasizing that he's using my first name again. "We're done here. You'll call me if you hear anything."

"They will not," Kevin says. "They'll call me. Then we'll decide where to go from there. Susannah, will you show the detective the way to the front door?"

When Kevin turns around to watch the two depart, I whirl to the TV monitor behind me. The tape is still rolling, but the video is over and the screen is, thankfully, black. Who knows how long it's been that way. I punch the red stop button. Click the power switch to off. Franklin gives me a congratulatory nod. And by that time, I have a plan.

CHAPTER ELEVEN

"So what do you think, Kevin?" Now the parade is going the other direction. Franklin and I are accompanying Kevin back to his office. I think I can parlay Detective Yens's visit into an open door for us to get permission to change our purse story into a real investigation of the distribution system, showing the teeming black market kept thriving by greedy suppliers and fashion-addicted women.

I just have to lure Kevin into thinking it was his idea. Talking in bullet points so he can understand, I've told him about our visit to the FBI and Keresey's undercover work. I've told him about our potential access to the Delleton-Marachelle design studio in Atlanta. I've described the purse parties we could have access to. Of course, I left out the part about how I'd already been to one. Now I have to see if I can reel Kevin in.

"Do you think you could get into one of those parties? Maybe with a hidden camera?" Kevin asks. He opens the glass door to his office and gestures us in.

"Well, sure I do," I say, nodding oh-so-thoughtfully. "Don't you, Franklin?"

"Oh, yes, indeed," he replies. "We even have that new camera. In fact, I was fooling around with it and I . . ."

He pauses. I can almost hear his brain recalculating.

"I signed it out of the engineering department, just the other day," he picks up his sentence. "To make sure we know how to operate it properly. So, I'd say we're all systems go. If Charlie is comfortable."

"Oh, sure," I say again. "If it's all right with Kevin."

"You'd have to be in disguise," Kevin says, swiveling in his black leather I'm-an-executive chair. His desk is stacked with re-sumé DVDs. In front of him is a legal pad with a list of something I wish I could read. "You're so well known. How would you pull that off, Charlie?"

"Well, I think I could manage to look different enough. And, maybe, we could go out of the viewing area. Right, Franklin?"

Franklin nods. He's shifting, trying to get comfortable on the wooden arm of Kevin's ultramodern couch.

"And what are you efforting for this Atlanta shoot?" Kevin continues. "We'd have to pay for plane tickets, for an out-of-town photographer, hotel rooms. How will that be cost-effective? Can't you just do it by phone?"

"Oh, no way," I say. Hoping I'm right. "We're getting unprecedented access to the manufacturing and design process. Hoping for interviews with big shot, execs, designers. They'll explain how colossally detrimental the knockoffs are to legit businesses."

"We can't get to the bottom of it, of course," Franklin says. "Even the FBI admits, it's basically unstoppable. But the D-M people will show us evidence seized from the cargo ships that bring the stuff into the U.S. Huge containers crammed with fake bags. Customs nabs them, usually in L.A. But they know they barely make a dent. And we're getting exclusive stuff."

My turn at bat. "And also, of course, how the companies are taking law enforcement into their own hands. Forming their own in-house purse police. Tracking down the bad guys. Becoming kind of fashion vigilantes."

"Fashion vigilantes," Kevin repeats. "I like it."

"Problem is," I say. Going for the kill. "Susannah says she wants just the feature. I wonder if she might not be happy with the bigger story."

"I'm the news director," Kevin says. "She doesn't need to know everything we do."

I'm trying to keep a straight face. And I can't possibly risk a peek at Franklin, who I'm sure is amused by Kevin's insistence he's in charge. But I've never been quite comfortable with hiding what we're doing from management. If Kevin now gives us the go-ahead, he'll never know we had already gone ahead without him.

"When a true journalist gets turned on to a big story, it's our job to do it right," Kevin says. From on high. "Not doing our job if we turn our backs on it. It may be tough, but you know the old saying. When the going gets tough —" He looks at me, as if to make sure I know how to finish the line.

And I know he expects me to say "the tough get going."

But I don't.

"The tough go shopping," I say.

"Well done, Charlotte," Franklin says. "At least now we're not faking it."

"Yup," I say. "Telling the truth is always my first choice. It just doesn't always work

160

when you're an investigative reporter."

I throw my briefcase and purse into the backseat of Franklin's immaculate silver Passat. Both car doors slam, and Franklin maneuvers us out through the overcrowded obstacle course of news trucks and microwave vans in Channel 3's cramped basement parking lot.

"What does Keresey want anyway? Why do you think she's asking to meet us out of her office?"

"Why are you asking me?" Franklin holds up the gizmo to open the garage door, pointing, then clicking. He eases the Passat up the ramp and into the sunlight. "The message was on your phone."

"Just brainstorming," I reply. "We can ask her about the raids, at least."

"Yeah, good idea. I couldn't find any mention of any enforcement actions that had resulted in agents being killed. Nothing. There were some Justice Department news releases about seizures of counterfeit goods. Lattimer's successful bust in Atlanta. But nothing in warehouses."

As we pull out into traffic and head toward our destination, I buzz down my window, hoping to let in the autumn day. Instead, I hear car horns blaring, irate drivers yelling at kamikaze bike messengers, crosswalk-ignoring pedestrians swearing as they claim the whole of Cambridge Street as their personal domain.

"I suppose they only put out press releases when something goes right. If an agent were killed in the line of duty, but the mission failed, maybe they'd just keep it quiet."

"Maybe. And of course 'Operation Knockoff' . . ." he looks at me, raising his eyebrows to scorn the pretentious name ". . . is still a work in progress. So maybe all of it's still hush-hush."

"There she is," I say, pointing to a familiar shape. "See? Keresey's on the sidewalk. Over there. Right under the entrance to the Charles Street T Station. You don't think she's expecting us to get on the train, do you? You have tokens?"

Franklin taps his car horn and Keresey looks up. Recognizing us, she points us to the Longfellow Bridge, the one everyone calls the "salt and pepper" bridge because of the huge shaker-shaped pedestals that line the edges.

I wave at her, signaling we understand. Genius Franklin even finds a legal — legal for thirty minutes at least — parking place in front of Mass General Hospital. We hurry to catch up with Keresey, who's leaning back against the rusting wrought iron sidewalk railing and staring out over the street to the river beyond. She's dressed in blue jeans tucked into high-heeled black boots and a dark chocolate leather jacket. Flat messenger bag over one shoulder. Sunglasses, baseball cap, blond ponytail. No necklace of ID tags.

The wind kicks up, the Boston promise of the cold to come. I'm glad I wore a leather jacket of my own over my black turtleneck sweater dress, and happy for my flat boots as we trot along the sidewalk. A fleet of J-boats glide, sails stiff, across the choppy water, and a few sculls power their way back up the river toward MIT. Beside us, a parade of cars and bicycles cross the wide expanse.

"You undercover?" I ask, as we arrive. "Headed to a purse party? Or sneaking out of the office to the Red Sox game?"

I'm trying to be casual, but I can already feel she's all business.

"Hey, guys," she says. Her smile is tense. "Walk with me, okay?"

The three of us turn toward Cambridge, the sidewalk just wide enough. Keresey's in the middle. Across the way, a Red Line train, passengers in each window, hurtles by, headed into the tunnels of the Boston-side subways.

"I know it's not SOP. Meeting you like this," Keresey begins. "But standard operating procedure means I have to notify the PIO, and the SAC, if I want to talk with you."

I wait, pulling my jacket more closely around me as the wind picks up over the water. Franklin stuffs his hands into the pockets of his maroon suede jacket. He's silent, too. We know it's best to just let her talk.

"I don't want to put you in an awkward position. Let's put it this way. I didn't want to put any of us in an awkward position. But, Charlie, I saw your eyes light up when the SAC was discussing our undercover operations. And don't even begin to try to convince me you two don't have a plan to do some U-C investigating. Attend some purse parties on your own. I've known you both long enough."

I halfway open my mouth to reply, then think better of it.

Keresey holds up a hand, then turns to me with a rueful smile. "Hey. I don't want to know. That's the awkward part. If I know, I'll have to order you to stop. I'd also be obligated to ask you if your expeditions are already underway. So I won't ask. You don't tell."

She stops, mid-river, and points to an alcove where a concrete bench carved into the side of the bridge provides room enough for us to sit down. As we sit, she takes the strap of the messenger bag from her shoulder and, slowly, zips the pouch open.

Franklin flickers a questioning glance at me. *What?*

I reply with the briefest shrug. *No idea.*

Keresey is pulling out a brown legal-sized envelope. She unwraps a red string from around the two paper discs on the flap, then reaches in and extracts an eight-by-ten photograph. And another. They flutter, caught briefly in a puff of wind. She juggles the envelope and the photos to keep it all from blowing away.

I crane my neck to see who's in the pictures, but she's holding them face-to-face. I can tell Franklin is checking them out from his side, too, but he signals with a slight shake of his head. *Nothing.* Nothing to do but wait.

Keresey puts the envelope back into the bag, and puts it down on the sidewalk, taking a moment to balance it so it's standing upright. Apparently she doesn't want to spill what's still inside. Apparently she's trying to drive me crazy with suspense.

Finally she holds up the two pictures.

Shows them to Franklin, then turns to show them to me.

Keresey, with her back to Franklin, doesn't see him put a hand to his mouth. I understand his startled gesture. We saw these same photos earlier this morning. The international spy. And the raspberry-glossed fashionista.

I see Franklin's eyes widen as he watches me examine the photos. He bites his lower lip. We have no way of communicating. No way to collaborate. No way to plan our response. Do we reveal the state police are asking us the same questions?

"Charlie?" Keresey prompts. "I'm betting you've attended a purse party or two. You don't have to tell me any more. All I want to know is whether either of you have seen this woman at any of the parties? And if you have, did you get video of her? So, Charlie, you first."

Which means I'm the one who has to make the strategy decision. Right now. Three long-legged girls jog by us, wearing crimson Harvard T-shirts and tight black shorts. We have to pull our legs in to let them by.

In that second, I decide. I'll tell her the truth.

But not the whole truth.

"No, I never saw this woman at a party," I say, shaking my head as I point to the pictures. Which is true. I didn't see her at the party. Or on our tape. Or anywhere in real life. Keresey didn't ask if I'd seen her *photograph.*

"Franklin?"

"Nope." His dark skin goes a little gray, which only I would notice. Franklin, son of a Mississippi minister, still has a tough time lying.

"Who is she?" I ask. I do want to know, but I also want to let Franklin recover. I hope Keresey doesn't push us here, because we're headed toward some murky journalism waters. As Kevin explained to Detective Yens, sharing our raw information with law enforcement is totally taboo. We do research, we examine documents, we get the scoop. And we keep it to ourselves until we decide how much of it goes on the air. What's kept off the air stays off-limits.

Plus, if the FBI doesn't know what the state cops are doing, maybe there's a good reason. I'm not going to be the doofus who compromises some complicated investigation.

Keresey tamps the photos on her knees, lining them up, then slips them back into her bag.

"It was a long shot. Look," she says. "I'm not saying you guys are going undercover. But if you do — keep an eye out for her, okay? Just let me know, back channel, if and when you see her. And where. Can you do that for me? I promise, I'll make it worth your while."

A little journalism bargaining is fine with me, but I'm still curious.

"Keresey, who is she?" I ask, ignoring her proposition. "And forgive me, but does Lattimer know you're here?"

Keresey stands, and turns back toward the Boston side of the bridge. She gestures with a hand, *let's walk.* "I've only talked with her via e-mail. She's a former agent, Lattimer says. Years ago. Ten. Maybe more. Lives in D.C. now. Knows Lattimer."

"And what does she do these days?" Like I don't already know.

"Out on her own, Lattimer says. Private investigations. Lots of retired agents go that route. No money in working for Uncle Sam, as we all know. Guess she figured she paid her patriotic dues. Anyway, apparently she's working with some big purse companies. Tracking down counterfeits. Her name is Katherine Harkins. Katie Harkins. Lattimer calls her the Prada P.I., though he says she works for several companies. Fendi.

168

Delleton-Marachelle. Ever hear of her?"

I calculate, hesitating before I answer. I'm exceptionally fond of Keresey. But it's tough to have friends when you're a reporter. I need to balance our relationship with our responsibilities. The almost-truth will work here. "I think I've seen her mentioned in newspaper articles, yes," I say.

"Anyway, she's been feeding us info on some in-house investigations, leads they've picked up," Keresey says. "Many companies now are trying to track counterfeiters on their own. They're looking for manufacturers. Suppliers. Distribution chains. Even little fish. But they have no police powers. They rely on law enforcement to take them down."

"And so?" Franklin asks. "This Katie Harkins? What about her?"

"And so," Keresey says, "we haven't heard from her in a few days. And that's unusual."

We divide up to walk down the final steps off the bridge, arriving in a grassy mini-park at the end of Charles Street.

"Dammit," Franklin interrupts. He points a finger ahead of him. "Look."

We both follow his instructions. And we a see a bright orange piece of paper on our windshield. We've gotten a parking ticket.

"I'll be right back," Franklin says.

He strides toward the car, holding up his arm, and pointing to his watch. "I'm positive we had five more minutes on the meter," he announces over his shoulder. "City Hall, here I come."

"Franklin never gets a ticket," I explain. "He's very organized."

Keresey smiles. "How well I know. Wish I could fix it for him, but we don't have any control or connection with the Boston cops. Or the staties, for that matter. We're federal jurisdiction only."

Aha. So the FBI may not know what the state cops are doing. Which means it may have been a good thing I kept quiet about Detective Yens and his set of photographs. But why do they have the same photos? Certainly can't ask Keresey. Time to change the subject.

"How are you, anyway?" I ask, touching Keresey on the arm. "I don't see you enough, and Maysie's always asking for you. You liking your assignment? You having any fun?"

"Well, you know, I'm just a middle-aged married lady," Keresey says.

I step back, hands on hips. "Keresey Stone, you're holding out on me. Last time we talked you were bemoaning your 35-year-old fate. 'No one wants to date a sharpshooting, drug-hating, law-abiding federal agent,' was, I think, along the lines of your complaint. And now you're telling me you're married?"

"Yup," Keresey says. Then she smiles. Twinkling. "I gave up on the whole man thing."

This is surprising. "You — ?"

"Oh, not that," says. "Not that there's —"

"Anything wrong with that," I finish.

"Right. But I realized I couldn't find the perfect man because I had already found him." She opens her jacket and flashes the black-and-silver FBI badge pinned to the sleek satin lining inside. "I realized I was already married. To Uncle Sam."

Single. *Been there.* Married to her job. *Done that.* Do I tell her how she may feel in ten years? Do I warn her?

Every time Mom tried to convince me to "forget about that silly local television" and "come home to Chicago" where I could be "truly happy," I politely went to her dinner parties. And then came home. Did what I thought was right for me. When Maysie urged me to "be flexible" and "open-minded" with a parade of single but impossible judges and CEOs, I politely went on the dates. And then came home. Did what I thought was right for me.

171

But now, having settled all these years into single, my heart is having a bit of a struggle adjusting to the possibility of "my life" becoming "our life." Making room for Josh. And Penny. And it could be I'm meant to be single. Maybe that's what's right for me.

To each her own. Slinging one arm over Keresey's shoulders, I give my pal a quick hug. "Congrats, Mrs. Sam. At least you won't have to write thank-you notes."

CHAPTER TWELVE

"Speaking of tickets," Franklin says. He stabs his orange violation notice to his bulletin board with a pushpin. "The good news is, the Delleton-Marachelle visit came through. Done deal. Got the message on my voice mail when we got back from Keresey. I already called the travel agent to check out schedules and plane tickets."

"For when?"

"Tomorrow, if we can get there. Or the day after. Apparently the D-M marketing director." He consults a pad on his desk, and holds it up to show me the name. "Someone named Urszula Mazny-Latos? She's called Zuzu. Is jet-setting back to Paris first thing Monday. So it's got to be a weekend deal. Saturday or Sunday. Maybe both, if tomorrow works out. I'll work on getting us a crew from the Atlanta affiliate. If this Zuzu will let us bring a camera."

This is great news. We're getting unprecedented inside access, and the potential for fascinating video. I should be thrilled. Instead, I'm seeing a romantic makeup weekend with Josh slip-sliding away. And at a deal-breakingly terrible time.

"No way to do it Monday?" I ask. I twist one of my legs around the other. "You sure?"

Franklin looks at me quizzically, then snorts. "What happened to Miss 'there are no weekends in TV news'? How many times have I heard you pronounce that j-school credo to your eager little interns? And now, suddenly Saturday exists?"

He's right. For the last twenty years, almost nothing has come before my job. Dad's funeral, of course. I struggle to come up with another example. And fail. Now I'm trying to change the date of an important interview to protect an important dinner date. Am I losing my edge? Or gaining something else?

"Don't 'oh, ho' me, Franklin B. Parrish. Stephen is out of town anyway, right? On one of his accountant things? So you don't care. But my future is probably at stake here."

"Well, it certainly is if you don't get on the plane to Atlanta G-A." Franklin gives me an evil smile. "Unless you can explain

174

to Kevin and Susannah why Brenda Starr has suddenly turned slacker."

I sigh, and check the wall clock. Josh and I have dinner plans for tonight. Penny's favorite Chinese carry-out at his house. Over egg rolls and dim sum, I'll soon be forced to explain how our weekend just crashed and burned.

Crashed and burned. Not the best words to use before getting on an airplane.

A thought skitters through my head. A good one.

"Charlotte?" Franklin asks. "Yoo hoo, reporter girl. I've been talking for the past two minutes about the plane schedules the travel agent just e-mailed. Did you hear anything at all?"

"You know what I was thinking?" I ignore his sarcasm. "Let's look at the undercover video again. You have the tape handy?"

Franklin pulls out a green plastic bin marked "Purse" from under his desk. Inside is a series of yellow tape cassettes, each carefully labeled in Franklin's precise handwriting. He selects the one marked "UC-1. G Barrington. Exteriors and ints. Sally," and hands it to me.

"Here. Pop it into the viewer," he says. "But why?"

"Go with me here," I say, sliding the cassette into the opening. I push Play and the black screen dissolves into those shaky pictures.

"Let's look again, in another way," I say, peering closely at the screen. "I'm wondering. What if just-call-me-Sally is actually the Prada P.I.? Let's say, she's infiltrated the Designer Doubles organization. Talk about counterfeit. You plop a wig of coppery curls on someone, you know? Change the makeup? We know my disguise worked for me. Those waitresses at the restaurant didn't recognize me. And if Sally is actually Katie, she might not have recognized me, either. Katie's not even from around here, remember? And I did wonder, in that mall, whether we were both pretending to be someone else."

"Only you saw Sally in person," Franklin says. "I probably won't be much help. But, hey, it could happen. Brilliant idea, anyway."

I scroll the video into fast forward, searching for the first time I got Sally on camera.

"Wish we had those photos," I murmur. "It would make this easier."

"Want to call the cops and ask for copies? Or call Keresey? I'm sure they'd be more than thrilled to help us." Franklin wheels his chair up to the monitor, then takes off his glasses, cleaning them with his special wipe. "You know, that was quite the morning we had, wasn't it? You, me, Yens, Keresey. And every one of us, at some point, was lying."

Nothing like the smell of fried food. The pungent mix of salt, oil and forbidden carbs draws me, irresistibly, through the back screen door and into Josh's kitchen. A brown paper bag, the top rolled down and stapled closed, waits tantalizingly on the island in the middle of the room. Grease stains already darken the bottom. Another brown bag, smaller, has already been ripped open. Beside it someone dumped a pile of chopsticks covered in paper sleeves, shiny plastic packets of duck sauce and hot yellow mustard, and a plastic-wrapped selection of multicolored rice puffs. Next to that, a crinkled pile of cellophane suggests a certain nine-year-old has no willpower. And proves her father has been out of the room.

"What does 'Confucius say' mean?" Penny is studying a strip of white paper, crumbles of fortune cookie still clinging to her mouth.

"It means your father is going to flip when he sees you've already eaten all the fortune cookies, my little unfortunate cookie," I say, giving the top of her head a quick kiss.

"Not all of them." Penny, the picture of

innocence, pulls out one cookie from the flapped pocket of her cargo pants, then another. They're crumpled and battered in their plastic pouches. Used cookies.

"I saved one for you, Charlie Mac. And one for Daddy." She examines the brown bag, now literally oozing kung pao sauce. "Mom never lets us have Chinese food. She says it has monster glutamate."

She starts unwrapping chopsticks, breaking each set apart with a twist and a crack. "I'll help," she says, putting the two "saved" cookies on the counter.

Maybe mine will say "you are going on a long journey." That would at least provide a much-needed segue to the unfortunate conversation I'm soon going to have. I'd already gone home to pack my suitcase for Atlanta and it's waiting now in my trunk. My plan is to leave my Jeep in Josh's garage until I get home. Turns out, our plane leaves first thing in the morning. Josh doesn't know any of this. Yet. And I want to savor tonight as long as I can.

"Where's your dad?" I ask.

"Right here, of course." A voice comes down the hall, followed by my darling Josh. He looks just out of the shower, hair still damply tousled. And he's particularly fetching in his oldest Levi's, ripped at the knees, and a stretched-out V-neck sweater, gray T-shirt underneath. It's all I can do to keep from running my hands up under that sweater. I've always thought he looks just like my teen pin-up heartthrob from *To Kill a Mockingbird,* Atticus Finch. At least how Gregory Peck looked as Atticus in the movie.

"Hey, sweetheart," I say. I fiddle with some paper napkins to give my hands something more socially acceptable to do.

"Hey, Daddo." Penny looks up from her chopsticks project. A pile of shredded chopstick sleeves now litters the counter. "I'm helping."

"I see that, Pen. Great job. Hey, sweetheart." Josh smells of citrus and toothpaste as he winds an arm around my waist. He gently kisses my ear. "Weekend plans," he whispers. "Listen to this."

Josh keeps his arm around me, but focuses on Penny. His voice changes to the parental tone designed to convey information to me without letting Penny know his true meaning. "So tell me again — what time is Emma's mom coming to pick you up for the slumber party?"

"Oh, Daddo, you know it's seven, right?" Penny says. She's using her long-suffering-child tone. "And then I get to stay all night at Emma and Kristin's. Then Mom will pick me up tomorrow. Don't you remember anything?"

"Nope," Josh says. He reaches over and taps her on the head with a duck sauce packet. "That's why I have you."

I see what's going on. And any other night, I would be doing a quick personal inventory — slinky-enough underwear, sleek-enough legs, toothbrush available — in preparation for the deliciously private and child-free romance-novel evening Josh clearly has in mind. This night, though, I fear his plot is going to be thwarted.

My stomach twists with what's ahead. And I don't mean the monster glutamate.

I have to tell him soon. I've stalled through the spring rolls and dim sum. I've stalled through the reheated General Gau's chicken. Penny's upstairs doing the last of her slumber party packing and Josh and I are trying to figure out what's in a dish the Shing Yee Palace carry-out menu calls "Two Delights in the Nest."

"I couldn't resist," Josh says, picking through the exotic concoction with one chopstick. "I could only think of you as a 'delight in the nest.' And once I had that mental picture, well, it just seemed too perfect."

"You're in a goofy mood, Professor Gelston," I say. "I remind you of Chinese food?"

"Well, it's delicious. And unpredictable. And always wonderful." Josh points to me with his chopstick. "And I love it. So why not?"

The three white pillar candles on the dining room table flicker and drip into their chunky glass holders. I had snipped some bronze and crimson leaves from the backyard maple, and arranged them as a centerpiece among the candles. It's just the two of us, Josh at the end of the table, me beside him, both with a view of the first fire of the season — unnecessary but hypnotic — crackling softly in the living room. We've uncorked a special sauvignon blanc. Our favorite Ella CD plays in the background. We're a glossy ad for middle-aged lust. Exploring the second time around. And as soon as Penny leaves, I've got to stop the music.

"So listen," Josh interrupts my doomsday thoughts. "What are you doing tomorrow night?"

I hold my chopsticks in midair. A noodle dangles, then slithers back to my plate. "Tomorrow . . . ?"

"Yup. If you're not busy —" He pauses, smiling mysteriously, letting this preposterous idea hang briefly between us. "If you're not otherwise occupied, I have a little treat in store."

My chopsticks haven't moved. Tomorrow night at this time I'll be in Atlanta. There's no way out of that. Even under normal circumstances, that was going to be complicated enough to explain. Now some unknown "treat," which my frazzled brain is unable to fathom, is about to be dropped like a grenade into my life. Our lives.

"Treat?"

"The Royal Shakespeare Company. One performance only. And you know it was instantly sold out." Josh is looking so pleased with himself, it brings tears to my eyes.

This is unstoppable. Maybe I could faint. Maybe I could throw up. Which actually doesn't seem too unlikely.

"So anyway," Josh continues, apparently unaware of my increasing distress. "Westy Peabody? Big shot on the Bexter board. Had two tickets and couldn't use them. And now they're ours. Tomorrow, the Opera House, *The Comedy of Errors*. And I made dinner reservations at Grill 23. Your favorite."

Josh points a chopstick at me. "What do

you think of that, my little delight in the nest?"

I think I have to kill myself. *The Comedy of Errors*. Thanks, universe. Irony is always welcome.

The Chinese food, remnants still on the table, has congealed into a toxic waste site. Josh has pushed his chair back from the table. He's still sitting next to me, but he's positioned himself as far away as possible.

"But I couldn't know." I'm pleading with him to understand my hopeless case. "About the tickets. I mean, it's wonderful. And you're wonderful. I'm devastated. But I have no choice."

"There's always a choice," Josh says. "I'm not sure how often I've said that to you. I'm not sure how often we've had exactly this same conversation. You do have a choice. And you always choose work."

I put my elbows on the table, and drop my forehead into my hands. How can I convince him? I look up at Josh through my fingers.

"I know we've had the conversation. I know sometimes I have to work. But in my heart, I choose you. You know I do. And Penny. But this is the only time Franklin and I can get into the . . ."

Josh is shaking his head quickly and decisively. Dismissing.

"Charlie, maybe it's not even you. Maybe I'm just not ready for this. Maybe the whole Victoria thing is still too raw. I never saw it coming, how she was pulling away. I worked, she worked. We had our jobs. And we had Penny. I thought everything was fine. And suddenly, it wasn't."

Maybe there's hope here. "Maybe it's that I've been on my own for so long," I say. "I'm not used to making decisions that include, you know, other people."

Josh backs his chair away from the table, stopping me. "You know what, Charlie? This is making you upset and defensive. I feel like I'm forcing you to explain who you are. And you shouldn't have to do that. But I can't let my life be controlled by your job. The other day, we decided to take it more slowly."

He stands, waving his hand over the wine, the flowers, the candles. "Maybe we should have taken it even more slowly. Much more. Maybe we should take a break."

His eyes narrow behind his tortoiseshell glasses. He puts both hands on the back of his chair, supporting himself. A thatch of charcoal-and-silver hair falls onto his forehead. He takes a deep breath. "You go to

Atlanta. And then we'll see."

We'll see what? See if we still love each other? See if we still want to be together? Are we supposed to know that yet? I swallow my fear and struggle to keep from asking the questions out loud, even though I'm aching for answers.

Suddenly, the aching flares into anger. Why does he get to make the decisions?

"We'll see?" I can't keep the sarcasm from my voice. I'm not this angry, but I'm hurt. And sorry. And trapped. And I know I'm saying the wrong things. "You mean, *you'll* see. Whether what, it's worth it? Whether maybe you'd like to date other people? See if you can find someone who'll be available every minute?"

Say no, I plead silently. *Tell me you love me, and I'm worth it, and we'll work it out.*

Josh looks up at me. "Is that what you'd like to do?"

No. Of course not. But of course that's not what comes out of my mouth. "Is that what you'd like to do?"

"Daddy?"

Penny, lavender suitcase in one hand and a droopy-eared stuffed rabbit in the other, is peering through the banisters of the front hall stairway. She takes the last two steps down, deliberately, one step at a time,

185

balancing her possessions. At the bottom of the stairs, she stops. Staring at us.

"Daddy?" she says again. And then she turns, drops her bunny and her suitcase, and runs all the way upstairs.

"I'll — she's — I wonder how much she heard, or if —" Josh begins. He starts toward the stairs.

"No. Let me. I'll be right back." I race after Penny, not waiting for his answer, taking the steps two at a time. This is my fault.

Penny's sitting, back to the wall, on the window seat on the landing. Her feet are up on the navy-striped cushions, her pink sweatshirt stretched out to cover both knees.

"Penny?"

She's silent, looking away from me.

I sit down beside her, slip off my heels and pull my feet up the same way. "Remember when Emma and Kristin went to the movies that time? Without you?" I twist my head around to check her expression. She's staring, determinedly, straight in front of her.

"Their mom said only they could go." She says to the hallway. "So what?"

"So remember how angry you were? We were in the kitchen and you told me you hated their guts?"

Penny looks at me sideways, just a flicker.

186

"Yeah. It was unfair. My dad let them both come with me when I went to see *Princess Diaries*. It was mean."

I nod. "And you told me they were 'gross,' and you never wanted to see them again."

"Uh-huh."

"And tonight, where are you going for your slumber party?"

Penny does a full-body sag. "Emma and Kristin's."

I pause, letting this sink in.

"So your dad and I . . ." I take a hesitant step into an emotional minefield. Realizing I'm explaining the situation to myself as much as I am to her. "Just tonight, we're feeling a little like you did that time about Emma and Kristin. Sometimes people argue. And they have angry feelings. But that doesn't mean they don't feel different a little later. And they say they're sorry. And your dad and I — love each other."

I check for a reaction to what I hope is not overstepping. Am I going to make this worse?

Penny just nods. "Dad told me that."

"Okay," I reply. *He did?* I'm aching to hear more. When? Where? Why? But this time is for Penny. She's scared and needs a friend.

Penny lifts the sweatshirt from her knees and turns toward me. Her feet, dangling in clunky thick-soled sneakers, still don't reach the floor. She plucks at the pockets of her cargo pants. "Mom and Dad told me they loved each other, too," she says. "I remember perfectly. But they got a divorce."

I nod. Reality is reality. "Yes," I say. "It happens."

We sit quietly for a moment, then Penny thuds one rubber heel, then the other, against the base of the window seat. Punctuating our thoughts.

The thumping sound stops and Penny turns her head up to me. She tucks a lock of brown hair behind one ear, revealing a tiny pearl earring I hadn't noticed before. Cargo pants, sneakers and pearls. Adorable.

"Charlie Mac?" she says. She locks her eyes with mine. "When is it real? How do you know when a fight is forever?"

I bend down to touch my forehead to hers and tell her the truth. "I wish I knew, kiddo," I say. "But don't worry —"

"You have to trust those you love," Josh says, finishing my sentence.

We both turn to look at him. He's two steps down on the stairway. Holding the banister. Who knows how long he's been listening to us.

"Your dad is right," I say. I'm looking at Penny. But I'm talking to Josh. "Life is complicated, sometimes. You know? But love makes it worthwhile."

CHAPTER THIRTEEN

"Why do we have to get here so early? It's still yesterday, as far as I'm concerned. Six in the morning? Our plane isn't till eight," I say, wheeling my new black canvas suitcase down the sidewalk and through the doors to Terminal B. Grumbling. They still haven't found my old one. "I wish I didn't have to let them take another of my suitcases. At least till they give me back the one they swiped. Lost."

"Charlotte, nix on the complaining," Franklin replies, following me inside. "I told you to bring a carry-on instead. Besides, the TSA rules say get to the airport early. What if there are lines? What if there's some security backup? Better to be safe."

"Coffee," I say. "That's the only thing that'll make this work."

We drag our luggage through the semideserted airport terminal, stopping briefly at the multiple screens of the destination monitors, confirming our flight to Atlanta is on time. We hand over our bags to the way-too-perky agent at the ticket counter. "Ninety minutes till takeoff," I say, pocketing my claim check. "Great. Maybe we should catch a movie."

"Let's just get ourselves through security," Franklin says. He gestures as we approach the checkpoint. "See? No lines. No waiting. We'll get to the gate, then we'll get lattes. You can read. You can relax. You know you're cranky because you hate to fly. Why don't you just take a Valium like everyone else does?"

"You don't take them," I retort as we send our stuff through security. "Plus, if the plane crashes, I don't want to be too doped up to get us out alive."

Down the long corridor, we see Gate 32 is deserted. Apparently it's even too early for the agents to be at their desks. A motorized golf cart, piloted by a woman in a navy uniform, beeps its way past us, empty. The waiting area looks more like a hotel. Two college-aged bodies, arms wrapped around each other, sleep head against head in a corner by the window, bulging backpacks as footstools under their feet. Three sleeping soldiers, in full camouflage except for their Red Sox caps, drape themselves stolidly across two seats each.

"And no waiting for caffeine." Franklin gestures toward Dunkin' Donuts, then points me to a row of empty chairs. "Stake out those seats. You take my suitcase, and I'll go get newspapers and coffee."

"Sounds good to me," I say. As Franklin heads off, I think about the cell phone that's inside my purse. And whether it's too early to call Josh and say goodbye again. He'd been asleep, peaceful, when the cab picked me up. We'd stayed up too late. Analyzed too much. Hedged the "dating other people" issue. Decided to talk when I get home. Decided not to do anything drastic. Unless you count what happened between two and three in the morning. Which did not include talking or sleeping.

I'm hoping to catch a quick recovery nap on the plane. Or maybe I could sleep a bit now. While I'm waiting for Franklin.

I close my eyes, just for a moment, I promise myself. Then I feel a shadow in front of me. Blinking, with a start, I sit up straight. Something's wrong. I can tell by Franklin's face.

He's standing in front of me, wordlessly holding out a newspaper. I can see from the size and typeface that it's not either of the Boston papers.

"Franko? What?" I take the paper from him. And follow his finger to an article on the front page. Damn. I give the paper back.

"Need my glasses," I say. I burrow through my tote bag. There should be three cases of reading glasses in here. I can't find even one.

"Just tell me what's in the paper," I say, still rummaging. "What paper is it, anyway? What's it say?"

I freeze, midsearch. A tragic thought has occurred to me. I look up, both hands still in my bag. "Do not tell me someone's done a story about counterfeit bags. I mean, do not tell me that."

"Nope." Franklin sits in the chair beside me and folds the newspaper in half with a crinkling snap. "The *Barrington Eagle-Tribune*. I found it in Dunkin' Donuts. Story on page 1. Headline. House fire destroys vacant house, threatens neighbors."

"Barrington?"

"Firefighters responded to 59 Glendower Street in Great Barrington late Friday afternoon after residents reported seeing smoke from a basement window," Franklin reads out loud. "By the time all units arrived at the address, the house, which according to a posted yard sign is for sale, was fully engulfed. Firefighters blame the unseasonably gusty wind conditions for causing the flames to spread to nearby homes. Some sustained what firefighters termed 'major' damage. 'It went up like a bonfire,' said a neighbor who refused to give his name. 'The place was empty. Renters just moved out.'

"Officials said the adjacent home at 57 Glendower was also uninhabited at the time of the fire, although neighbors told this reporter it was recently rented. Neighbors report a large gathering at the home the day before. Police will not comment on whether that is relevant to their investigation. Much of the contents of that house were destroyed, although investigators also refused to discuss the extent of the damages or loss. The tenant was not immediately available."

I flip open my glasses and grab the paper for myself. I read it, scanning.

"Holy —"

"Shit," Franklin finishes. "Just say it for once. It's the house next to the party house? Right?"

"Well, yeah, from reading this, sure. Seems to be." I put my glasses on top of my head, and squint at the annoyingly unrevealing black-and-white photo beside the story. "Can't really tell, but the address is right. So the 'tenant' of 57 has got to be just-call-me-Sally, don't you think? And as for the fire, and the 'contents' of that house being destroyed. You think, coincidence?"

"Well, burning down a house to send a message about selling fake purses is somewhat heavy-handed," Franklin says. "But I suppose if you could make a warning appear to be collateral damage in a separate house fire, that might be pretty effective."

"A warning — meaning someone could have been sending a message to just-call-me-Sally. Remember she told me she was — how did she put it — branching out on her own?"

"Of course."

"And maybe someone's making it clear that's a bad idea. Which is more than disturbing. The key now would be to find her. Make sure she's okay. Although I suppose the police are already looking. And it's not like she wouldn't already know her house caught fire."

"True."

"So now that's maybe two people missing. Sally. And Katie Harkins. And as far as we can tell, from looking at the video at least, that is actually two people. Not one." I take a sip of latte. "Maybe the D-M execs will be able to tell us something about Katie. Who knows."

We're both silent for a moment. Calculating.

"Think it's conspiracy, kidnapping, arson, extortion and grand larceny counterfeiting? Or a coincidence?" I ask. "Or maybe, some of each?"

"Who knows," Franklin says.

I have a fleeting glimmer of fear about my little apartment. Botox, on her own. Tolerating Amy the cat sitter, trusting I'll come home. How frightened my sweet kitty would be if some bad guy broke into our apartment. Set it on fire.

Josh and Penny. A potential reality descends with an ugly thud. Are they vulnerable? Could — whoever it is — find out who they are? Do they already know?

News is what happens to someone else. But now my world includes someone else. Josh. And Penny. And that's a different story.

I think of little Penny, sitting on the stairs, worrying. Anxious. Josh, silently arriving to reassure her. To reassure us.

Am I putting people I love in danger? People who love me?

I shake my head to erase the thought, as if there's some evil kaleidoscope in my head making creepy designs. I watch too much television. I'm nervous because of my imminent plane flight. Nothing is going to

196

happen.

The flight attendants look like Kabuki dancers, lined up in the aisle of our 737, making synchronized pointing gestures as if we couldn't find the two forward and one rear exits for ourselves. They pretend the oxygen masks are falling from the overhead compartments. I'm pretending I'm not terrified. Franklin is pretending he doesn't know I'm pretending.

"Three annoying things," I say, adjusting my seat belt again. "One. It's the crack of dawn on a Saturday and we're on a plane so no way we can call the Great Barrington PD to get more info about the fire. Two, no way I can call Sally at that number she gave me."

Franklin has one earbud in, clicking through the flight's selection of music. He's listening to me through the other ear. "And number three?"

I bonk my head against my fully upright seat back, and stare at the nubby blue-on-blue upholstery of the fully upright and knee-threateningly close seat back in front of me. "Yeah. Number three is a doozy. We're doomed on so many levels. Think about our undercover video."

Franklin takes out the earbud and slowly

winds the headphone cord around one hand. And then unwinds it.

There's a squawk from the public address system. Which makes my heart leap before I can stop it. The plane hasn't even moved yet and I'm already awaiting the announcement of approaching disaster.

"Flight attendants, prepare for cross-check," a voice demands. The blue uniforms stride down the aisle, seeking out delinquent seat backs and tray tables. I kick my tote bag farther under the seat in front of me.

"The police. Kevin. Arson. Evidence." Franklin's voice is hushed.

"You got it, bro," I say. "A doozy. Kevin gave us the okay to go undercover. But that happened *after* the fire. So as far as he's concerned, we would not have video of the party house. Remember, I shot pictures of the houses on both sides, too, just to get some context. So we have exteriors, and interiors, of places where there may have been arson. And yet, if I say I was there, so much for our undercover operation. And so much for our story. And, potentially, so much for our jobs. Since as far as permission from management to shoot undercover goes, we didn't have it."

Our plane creeps backward and I can see the jump-suited tarmac crew waving those orange flashlight signals to make sure the pilot knows where he's supposed to go. Preflight jitters are not the only thing that's making me nervous.

"Wait, Charlotte," Franklin says. "Don't freak."

"Too late," I reply.

"Listen. I agree that in the worst possible scenario, we're in a bit of a bind. But let's think about a best-case scenario."

"Best-case scenario in a situation where one house burned to the ground, another is ruined, and one person is missing? And where we lied to our news director?"

"House fires happen all the time, Charlotte. You know that. In addition, the house at 59 was vacant. I saw the video. Decrepit. Maybe some slimeball absentee landlord decided to torch it and get the insurance money. Maybe something happened with the gas. Maybe someone was burning leaves and a spark hit the house. You're making it a melodrama. And it probably isn't."

My hands clutch the armrests as the plane lifts with a roar from solid ground into the mystical land of aerodynamics. I watch the wings to make sure the flaps are operating properly, in case someone in the cockpit forgets. I listen for the landing gear to retract. I wonder how I wound up in such a complicated journalism situation. Again. I was just trying to get a great story.

"Here's a plan," I say. "Nothing we can do now. We go to Atlanta. See what we can find. We'll be back at the station Monday morning. Avoid Kevin. We can both drive to Great Barrington and scout. Talk to neighbors. And the police. We can pretend we're just working on the fire story. See if we can gauge whether it's an accident. See if Sally shows up. And see if buying a counterfeit purse has made me a possible witness in an arson case."

Franklin tucks a pillow behind his head, then turns to look at me. "Nice going, Charlotte. Talk about accessory to a crime."

CHAPTER FOURTEEN

"Let me show you what we call 'the magic closet.' " Urszula Mazny-Latos, marketing director of Delleton-Marachelle, is impossibly chic in precariously high burgundy lizard pumps, an impeccably tailored black suit, and a recognizably Hermes scarf around her neck. Tied in a way that, somehow, only someone who's studied scarf-styling in Paris can carry off. She's leading us down the lushly carpeted corridor of the D-M design headquarters, past closed doors marked Art, Graphics, Fabric.

Our taxi had dropped Franklin and me at what turned out to be a startlingly authentic copy of pre-Civil War Tara, opulent and luxurious. White Corinthian columns fronted the vast stone portico, the red-brick edifice stretching on either side, massive banks of rhododendrons surrounding what looks like a renovated mansion.

Up the wide front stairway and through a

lofty set of double doors. Inside, a guard in a sleek charcoal jacket, that iconic D-M logo of intertwined initials on a front pocket, greeted us from behind a spacious glass-topped rococo desk, all swirls and carved curlicues. He'd waved us to a white-on-white striped settee along a dark mahogany-paneled wall.

"Miz Mazny-Latos is expecting you," he'd said, as graciously as if we were arriving for afternoon tea with Scarlett and Melanie. "May I get y'all anything?"

No sign-in, no security check, no asking for IDs.

For a city girl, I'm now feeling pretty country mouse in what I'd thought would be an appropriate "yes, I'm a reporter but I'm still fashionable" look, a black knit dress with a curvy black jacket. Pearls. No scarf. I suddenly feel short in my mid-heels.

She's already instructed us: "Just call me Zuzu." On anyone else, Zuzu would sound like someone's poodle. On her, Zuzu is so cosmopolitan it makes "Charlie" sound like a klutzy fourth-grader.

Zuzu selects a key from a crowded, jangling key ring. I notice it, too, has the D-M logo stamped on a pale green circle of leather. She puts it in the lock, and with a flourish, waves us into fantasy land.

I can't even take a step as my brain struggles to assimilate acquisitional overload. I'm hoping my country mouse jaw isn't dropping. On long white-lacquered shelves, floor to ceiling, is every Delleton-Marachelle purse I've ever seen in their Madison Avenue atelier, posh department store catalogs, the pages of *Women's Wear Daily*. It's a purse museum.

We walk past dozens of them. Hundreds. Each in clear plastic, each nested in white tissue paper, coddled as if they were irreplaceable jewels or antiquities. There are rows of black with glints of brass and gold trim, then a section of beiges and cream, camels and chocolate, a row of white. And then, a rainbow. Red, lilac, yellow. A vibrant orange. Braiding, piping, tassels and fringe. The place smells of leather. And money.

Thou shalt not covet? Not a chance.

"Wow," Franklin says. Luckily one of us is not speechless.

Zuzu steps across the deep pile of the champagne-colored carpeting, taking center stage, surveying her domain. "This is where we keep all of our prototypes, as well as the first off the production line for each design."

Based on her accent, I wonder if she's Polish, or Russian. Austrian, maybe.

"I brought you here, first," Zuzu continues, "to illustrate we feel our products are precious. Treasures. To show how —" she pauses as if searching for a word. "Despicable. Despicable it is that these people steal our designs, have someone in Asia duplicate them with inferior fabric and construction, and then sell them. You got the example I sent, yes? As if they are authentic."

She reaches to a shelf beside her and unwraps a red leather tote bag, tenderly as if it was a living thing. "Our chief designers, Luca Chartiers and Sylvie Marachelle, designed this Diana bag." She holds it up to us, tilting it so we see every angle. It's a shiny deep claret rectangle, two midlength straps linked with circles of gold. The D-M initials, infinitesimally small, encircle a golden clasp. A tiny key on a slender leather braid dangles from one corner.

"The princess carried it. And Caroline of Monaco. And of course Mrs. Schlossberg. It was not even in stores."

"Not in stores?" I ask. That's not your typical sales model. "So how do you . . ."

"It is a question of . . ." She tilts her head. "Reputation. Creating desire for the most desirable. A fantasy purchase. Every woman wants something that is perhaps just out of her reach. So they would contact us. Inquire about the Diana. And then we would tell them how they could carry the same bag as a princess."

"For five thousand dollars," Franklin says.

"Ten." Zuzu smiles. "That is part of the fantasy." She puts the bag, carefully, back in its wrappings. She pats it into place with a maternal smile. "And every one of these is as much a treasure. Some you have never seen, the ones we're premiering in our spring line. We expect it will be an international triumph."

She looks at me, conspiratorially. "Would you like an advance look?"

Oh, no, I don't say. We're working. I'll just buy mine later at Bergdorf's.

"Of course," I reply.

"Wouldn't miss it," Franklin puts in.

Zuzu unlocks a door which covers one row of shelves. She pulls out a chocolate leather pouch, so buttery soft it barely keeps its shape. She holds it out toward me, keeping far enough away so it's clear I'm not supposed to touch it. A braided drawstring, tipped with three tiny gold balls on each end, is woven through the leather. Across the top, a horseshoe-shaped gold medallion holds down a thick strap.

"The Angelina," she pronounces.

She might as well be saying "The Mona Lisa." "The David." "The Hope Diamond."

"This is the only one in existence. The production will begin in two months. By showing you this, you know I must trust you."

Her face hardens as she gestures us toward the door. "Come with me now to our principal design room. I will show you how they cheat and steal and lie and take our designs for their own. Why we must find out who is behind this. Why we must stop them."

It takes us three locks and a keypad code to enter the design room. This closed-access hideaway, at the dead end of a long hall, is as much about security as style.

"It is — pornography," Zuzu says as she walks to a bank of glossy white cabinets and closets, arranged floor to ceiling along one wall of the design room. The noontime sunshine blasts through a skylight, pouring natural light across the three tilt-topped drafting tables set up underneath. No one is at work now, but I see silver-framed photos on the three elegant wooden desks spaced for privacy along the walls. A conference table.

Opening a tall cabinet, Zuzu extracts what I now recognize as a Diana bag. She holds it up, using only two fingers of each hand.

"Diana?" I say.

"Disgusting. It is trash," she replies. She

yanks open the flap and shows us the inside of the purse. "Look at this lining. It is not the quilted silk of a true Diana. This is cheap nylon. Feel for yourself."

I take the bag, showing it to Franklin at the same time. "How else, Zuzu, can you tell this is not real?" I pause, not wanting to offend her. Or sound like a clod. "To the untrained eye, of course, this is a very good copy."

Franklin takes the faux Diana, examining the straps, the zippers, the hardware. "One of the key elements of our story, we hope," he says, "is not only to educate buyers on how to discern whether a product is authentic, but also to let them know how destructive it is to your business. And to see if we can discover where the knockoffs are coming from. And stop them."

A buzzer sounds from a telephone on one of the desks and a crackly voice comes over the intercom. "The cameraman is here, Miz Mazny-Latos."

Zuzu pushes a button. "Conference room six, William." She turns to us and retrieves the purse from Franklin. "I will agree to describe for you, in this interview, just two or three 'tells,' the security devices we have used in the Diana bag. Just to let customers know when they are buying a fraud like this one.

"Of course there are many more tells." She gestures to a row of red notebooks on the wall. "They are catalogued in these notebooks. But I will not reveal them all."

"Of course," I reply. "Then the security tells would cease to be effective. And I do want to ask you about that in the interview. Perfect. I'll also want to ask about your own security police. Do you have them?"

"They are not police," Zuzu interrupts. Imperious. "We simply have consultants. Who we hire to monitor the sales and distribution of knockoff products."

"Of course," I say again. "And we have been in contact, as you know, with Katherine Harkins?" I pause, waiting to see if Katie is off-limits somehow. I'm haunted by where she is. Wondering what happened to her. Maybe nothing. Maybe nothing good. I keep the follow-up question unspecific. "Have the authorities contacted you? Asking if you've seen her recently?"

"Or have you seen her recently?" Franklin puts in. Ultra-casual. "Has she come to Atlanta in the past few days?"

There's a knock on the door frame. "Miz Mazny-Latos?" William says, opening the door. "Here's the cameraman from Channel 12."

And he's a knockout, my brain replies, before I can stop it. Levi's, plaid flannel shirt, work boots. I can't decide to check whether my bangs are straight or whether to check my teeth for lipstick.

He puts his camera and a dark green light kit down on the floor. Dusts his palms.

"Hello, Charlie." The barest hint of a drawl. "I'm Brian Jordan." He walks toward us and holds out a hand to Franklin.

Franklin loves when this happens. Says it proves I'm not a hotshot. Which I've never said I was.

Franklin shakes Brian's hand, then gestures with his head. "That's Charlie," he explains. "I call her Charlotte. Makes things a lot simpler. I'm her producer, Franklin."

Brian holds out a hand to Zuzu. "Sorry, Charlie," he says. His smile is killer.

Zuzu keeps her arms folded around her detested bag for a fraction of a second, then shakes Brian's hand.

"I am Urszula Mazny-Latos," she says. Giving him the full-name treatment. "Marketing director at Delleton-Marachelle. That — is Charlie."

Comedy of errors, I think. Then a wave of sadness washes over me. Why? And then I remember. Pulling myself back to the present, I walk toward Brian, offering a welcoming hand.

"Happens all the time," I say. "And thanks for coming. We'll do the interview in a moment, but first we need to get some shots of these purses. The fakes."

I turn to Zuzu. "Correct?"

Zuzu nods. "The counterfeits, I will be delighted to show you. There are more in the cabinet, evidence seized in Customs raids. Now in our possession. Each one worth — pennies. Like the one I sent you. And sold for sometimes hundreds of dollars."

She deposits bag after bag on the gleaming conference table, gingerly, as if she were reluctant to touch them. Faux Dianas in all colors, tiny clutches and chunky hardware-laden shoulder bags. Even a fringed suede, exactly like the one I purchased at the party. Zuzu's every move transmits her anger and repugnance.

"At least this trash never hit the markets," she says. "I show them to you as proof we are serious. And on the trail."

I flip through my notebook, checking my notes for questions I may have missed. Or answers Zuzu gave that may not be quite right for television. Too long. Too many pauses. Too technical. Too vague. Actually, just about every answer she's given. I'm on the verge of freaking. Zuzu, so poised and well-spoken all morning, turned wooden and inarticulate on camera. Perhaps she was worried about her accent, but whatever, she was a deer in the Klieg lights. I just needed to elicit one usable sound bite. But even though I've used almost every interview trick in my repertoire, I'm not sure I have it.

"Hang on one second." I signal Brian with a quick finger-across-my-throat cut sign.

He punches the blue button on the camera, putting his Sony on pause, then clicks a lever, adjusting his tripod.

"Don't move yet for the wide shot, thanks. I'm just thinking if there's anything else." I look at Franklin, knowing Zuzu can't see the panicked look on my face. Knowing Franklin will give it a try.

Franklin, sitting on the other side of the oval conference table and out of camera range, gets the message. "I have a question," he says.

Zuzu turns to look at him. "Yes?"

"Just pretend you're talking to Charlotte when you answer, all right? I know it seems unnatural, but it's so the camera angle is correct. I'm just wondering — there wasn't any security when we came in. No sign-in. No inspections. In a place where your trade secrets are so critical, how concerned are you there may be a breach?"

"Well, that's what you noticed when you arrived at the front door," Zuzu says to Franklin.

"Zuzu?" I gently prompt her. "Remember to look at me when you answer?" I give Brian the one-finger sign to roll tape.

He nods. "Rolling."

"So?"

"As I said, that's when you arrived," Zuzu begins again. "But you may not have noticed our surveillance cameras. And when you leave, when anyone leaves, it's a different story. Everyone uses the back door. Everyone signs out. Rejected designs are shredded. Personal bags are searched. Employees. Visitors. It is all the same."

She looks at her watch, signaling time is up. I look at mine, knowing I'm doomed.

"Time for wide shots?" Brian says. He means: time to cut your losses? He knows a bad interview when he hears one.

"We need to get some pictures of the two of us talking, a wider angle than during the interview," I explain to Zuzu. I'm keeping my voice casual, to convey we're finished with that segment. "Also, you said you're taking us back to the studio, as soon as the designers arrive. Would it be possible for Brian to get some video in there, as well?"

"Impossible." Zuzu ends that discussion with one word.

Brian begins to unclick his camera from the tripod. I hear Zuzu take a deep breath, then let it out.

Bingo. After years of doing interviews, I know what this means. She thinks she's off the hook. Sometimes even the most stilted and terrified subject will relax when they think the camera is off. Maybe this last-ditch tactic will work.

"Zuzu, are you perhaps making too much of this?" I say, my voice still casual. "Forgive me, but just devil's advocate, isn't it simply capitalism?"

Her eyes flare. Her back stiffens. Her posture changes. She glares at me.

I give Brian a quick nod and make the one-finger signal again, holding my hand below her eye level. Roll tape.

"Would it be acceptable to put someone else's signature on a Picasso?" she asks. Her voice is bitter, accusatory. "Put your own name on *Gone with the Wind*? And then try to sell them as real?

"It would be laughable," she says, punctu-

213

ating her disdain with two French-manicured hands. "Absurd. And yet, these people brazenly, blatantly, steal our designs. Our trade secrets. They copy them. And offer them for sale. And what do customers do? Without a thought, except for their personal greed? Knowing they are paying for fakes? And sometimes even proud of it? They participate in crime. They are stealing our profits, just as if they came into our building and took the money from our safe. It is greed. It is fraud. It is scandal."

She pauses, and looks down at her hands. As if she's almost surprised by her tirade.

I raise my eyebrows at Brian: "got it?" He closes his eyes briefly in salute, then signals back with the quickest of nods. "Got it."

As Franklin helps Zuzu unclip the tiny microphone from her lapel, I'm calculating. Ten thousand dollars for one purse. Ten thousand dollars times who knows how many glamour-hungry fashionistas. And that math, I can do.

So where is Zuzu in this equation? How far would someone go to protect a multimillion-dollar business?

Maybe Zuzu's hired "consultants" do more than "monitor" the distribution of knockoffs. Maybe they also try to stop them. Maybe that fire in Great Barrington originated here in Atlanta.

Maybe who you call a "bad guy" depends on what you think is good.

CHAPTER FIFTEEN

"Think what we could find out if we just had the nerve," I say. I look, longingly, at the row of identical red leather notebooks lined up on the shelves behind us. Franklin and I are back in the principal design room, parked at the Louis XIV style conference table, each with a crystal glass of iced San Pellegrino on a silver coaster. Zuzu's left us, just for a moment, she emphasized, saying she'd soon return with D-M's artistic directors.

"I'm lusting after the design secrets in those books," I continue. "Every 'tell' is there. All we'd have to do is grab one each, get some shots with our cell phones, and have more inside scoop than anyone could even imagine."

"Good idea," Franklin says. "We could maybe write a book about them, from our deluxe accommodations inside the Atlanta Federal Pen. That would be what? Larceny of trade secrets? Theft of intellectual property? Unauthorized dissemination of proprietary —"

"I'm just saying," I interrupt. "It's not like I'm planning to do it. Although we sure do need some more video. Maybe we should just snap some quick cell phone shots in here."

"Charlotte," Franklin begins.

I recognize the tone. Franklin can be such a Boy Scout. "Kidding," I say. "But this is such a gold mine."

I get up and stroll through the room, trying to soak up atmosphere that might help me write a more compelling story. On one of the desks, I see an array of photographs. Silver frames, smiling faces. A tall, elegant man in black tie, holding some sort of award, his other arm across the shoulders of a much shorter, but equally elegant, middle-aged woman. Brother and sister? Married? Another photo. The woman with someone who might be her sister.

Then there's the same man, in khakis and a sweater, in a garden somewhere, this time with a much younger woman, her face partly in shadow. Father and daughter? I suddenly feel old. And old-fashioned. Maybe lovers? I do a double take. The girl looks awfully familiar. I shake my head, dismissing the thought. The next photo has same man, again with one arm around the short woman, and the other around Zuzu.

"Look over here," I say to Franklin. I'm still holding the last photograph but I can't help thinking about another one. "Remember I told you about that girl in the airport?"

There's a tap on the door, then it instantly opens. Zuzu enters first. A man and a woman behind her. I'm caught, photo in hand. And I'm looking at all three people in the picture. Petite chic woman, elegant black tie man and Zuzu.

"Sylvie Marachelle, one of our chief designers," Zuzu says, raising one eyebrow as I put the photo back in place. "And the other, Luca Chartiers." *Shar-tee-ay.* "Luca also creates the special elements we use to insure our bags are authentic."

We all shake hands, saying hello. Sylvie's "good afternoon" is smoky-soft, unmistakably French, her handshake quick and perfunctory. Luca actually says *"Bonjour"* before switching to almost accent-free English.

"I hope you enjoyed my little collection," he says. He points to the black tie photograph. "Sylvie and I are especially proud of our Coty 'Designer of the Year' Award."

"I'm so sorry about the photograph," I

begin. "I was just curious, and . . ."

"Not at all." Luca waves away my apology.

Zuzu shoots him a look, then moves to center stage, checking her watch.

"Sylvie and Luca have agreed to show you the prototype room," she says. She scans the room as if there's something she's missed. She looks pointedly at me, then Franklin. "You have no cameras, of course? Anywhere? And please do not use your cell phones."

"Well, of course," I say. "Of course not. My cell is off." Whoa. I wish I could look at Franklin. Were people listening to us?

"We understand. Of course," Franklin says at the same time.

"Then please follow me," Zuzu replies. She shows us down a long hall, framed poster-sized photographs of D-M's legendary purses, bags and wallets and scarves hanging pin-spotted under recessed lights along the way.

Franklin and Sylvie Marachelle walk side by side in front of me. She's a middle-aged pixie, diminutive, her silver-blond hair so casually chopped off it must have cost a fortune. Her tiny waist is emphasized by a wide leather belt and flowing calf-length suede skirt. Even in high-heeled boots, she

219

barely reaches Franklin's shoulders. I can see Franklin pointing to the photos on the walls, asking questions. Sylvie answers him briefly.

Luca Chartiers falls in step beside me. He's maybe fifty. Effortlessly fashionable in a French-cuff gray-on-gray silk shirt, intricately tailored navy blazer and an almost-white tie. Pushing it in Atlanta, perfect for Paris. Hair is a bit too long, nose a bit too long, a bit too tall. It's difficult to ignore that somehow it all works. Very nicely.

"Forgive Sylvie, she is somewhat pre-occupied." He bends down to explain, touching my back as if guiding me down the hall. "We are consumed with the debut of our newest confection. Did Zuzu show you?"

"The Angelina," I say. I can still feel his hand on my back, although it's no longer there. "Yes. Did you design it?"

"Sylvie and I, yes," he replies. "She is a descendant of the original Marachelle family, did you know? She and her sister? It was their grandfather's company, then their father's. Before it was purchased by the cartel that owns it now."

"Ah." He interrupts himself, briefly touching my back again, I suppose to indicate

we've arrived. He points to a door. "Prototypes."

We all stop at the end of the corridor. A
brass plate on the otherwise unmarked door
in front of us commands Authorized Entry
Only.

As we enter the room, I realize that I
would kill for a camera. It looks like the
secret hideout of the mad architect and sewing society. Euro hip-hop music, insistent
and throbbing, thuds from a docked iPod,
the lyrics incomprehensible. Desks and long
tables, some with sewing machines, are set
in a double line across the wooden floor.
Maybe half a dozen people in black lab
coats are at work, some sewing, some drap-
ing fabric onto the muslin-covered shoulders of human-shaped mannequins. Everyone is talking to someone else. Not one
looks up at us as we enter their domain.
They probably can't hear over the din.

Sylvie holds her hands high over her head,
clapping twice to get the workers' attention,
jangling her armful of gold bangle bracelets.
"I will explain to them," she says to us, then
crosses the room toward the group.

The studio is a chaos of color and texture,
every wall transformed into a floor-to-
ceiling bulletin board. Along one side,
rainbow displays of fabric swatches, squares

of frayed-edge satin canvas, vinyl, corduroy, with clear plastic push pins securing each one in place. Straps of all sizes — braided piping, multicolored leather, silver and gold chains, clear plastic and strips of suede hang from metal rings. Along another wall, a row of blueprints. Even this far away, I can tell they're not of buildings. They're sketches — front, side and back views — of purses.

Zuzu draws us closer to her, as a purple-haired woman across the room turns down the hip-hop volume from eardrum-assault level to mere nightclub drumbeat.

"This is our beta-testing stage," Zuzu explains, now that we can hear. "Each of these *faiseurs* takes the blueprint designs drawn by Sylvie, and by hand, creates a prototype of the actual bag."

"Fie-soors?" I say. *Merde.* My once not-terrible French is instantly *disparu.*

"*Faiseur* is French for miracle-worker," Luca explains with a smile. "Sylvie's grand-father, Jean-Paul Marachelle, started the tradition when his atelier was still on the Rue de Sevres in Paris. When the first *faiseur,* in the thirties, managed to create what he called a miracle bag — *pochette mirac-uleux* — from his first hand-drawn design. And it's simply never changed."

He gestures to the group. "These are all

fine arts and fashion students, some from colleges here in the U.S. and some from France, students who learn their craft by creating our current *pochette miraculeuses.*"

I'm intrigued, and not just because Luca is so charmingly continental. And attentive. And seems to be looking at me the same way I'm sure I was looking at the Angelina bag. As if I were the only one in the room.

"Forgive me," I say. This room looks like a security breach waiting to happen. "All of these people, and they all look so young, are the front lines of your design team? Couldn't any one of them be a conduit for information? Passing your design secrets to anyone willing to pay them enough?"

Luca shrugs. "Perhaps," he says, "but —"

"Never," Zuzu interrupts. "You see, Charlie. The *faiseurs* simply create, shall we say — options. We choose the final version, and it is only then we insert the special elements Luca has created to insure the bag is authentic. None of the *faiseurs* see it until it is made public. And even they do not know which 'tells' are selected."

"And it's clear why the Delleton-Marachelle line is so expensive," Franklin says. "The building. The staff. The materials. The production."

"It is the same with every true designer,"

Zuzu replies. "We are not just profit. We are art. We are fashion."

"We are in trouble," Luca says. He's looking at his beeper. Then he looks toward the doorway. "Nell."

My phone is trilling the text message signal. This, after the photograph debacle, is at least the second embarrassment of the day, since I had assured Zuzu my cell was off. Fortunately, Zuzu, Luca and Sylvie are completely focused on the woman who just arrived. I turn my hearing to parabolic, unable to switch off my compulsion to eavesdrop. *I hafta know.* I manage to pick up some snippets of French. And maybe the word — Angelina?

They're engrossed, listening intently to the woman at the door. She's pointing to a clipboard, whispering. Carrying the conversation. She's as self-assured as a ballerina, white silk shirt and black patent stilettos, sleek and severe as an arrow. Except for Sylvie and William the guard, everyone in the building could do double duty as magazine covers.

I glance down at my purse, longing to zip it open. A text message. Could be Josh. Could be Katie Harkins. Could be the Great Barrington Fire Department returning the call we made in the taxi from the airport. I'm deeply tempted to sneak a peek while the quartet of fashionistas is huddled in their doorway conference.

"Take out that phone and they'll throw us out of here," Franklin murmurs.

I nod, reluctantly acquiescing. I keep my voice low. "We've just got to follow up on that Great Barrington fire. We're getting some good info here, but Just-call-me-Sally is our only link to the distribution and supply system of the fake purses."

"And also the number on that business card she gave you, remember?" Franklin guardedly points to the group at the door. "What do you suppose is going on? Look at the worried expressions on all those beautiful faces."

I see Luca pull a BlackBerry from his jacket pocket. Still frowning, he uses both thumbs at light speed, texting. Sylvie, with a nod, strides away down the hall. Zuzu, her face solemn, brings the newcomer toward us.

"This is Nell Follatrera," she introduces us, and continues as we all shake hands. "Director of our legal department. I'm afraid we'll have to cut our conference short."

"We've had word from the authorities,"

Nell says. Her voice is strong and confident, with a tinge of the south. Her tone is confidential. "As I'm sure you've been told, the FBI has not been terribly successful at finding the distribution warehouses holding the copies of our products. We've just had word another raid has failed. They found nothing."

"Failed?" I ask. "Where was the raid?" I drag open the top of my tote bag. I need a notebook and pencil. I hope nothing's happened to Keresey. Or Lattimer. Wonder if they were in on it.

"Please," she holds up a hand. "We have no comment for the record. You'll need to call FBI officials for a statement."

"But it's Saturday, and their Public Affairs office isn't staffed," I protest. "So let me just ask you, was anyone hurt? Where was the raid?"

"What did they find?" Franklin puts in. "Was there an undercover element?"

Another idea. "Did it have anything to do with your new Angelina bag?"

"All good questions, and all questions I suggest you put to the authorities," the lawyer answers. "Now, if you'll excuse me." She bends to whisper something in Zuzu's ear, then strides out of the room.

"So I am fearing, now, we'll have take you

226

out through security," Zuzu says. "We have to . . . solve a problem. I am so sorry."

I know there's an emergency. I know these people are ready to bolt. And it appears, with good reason. But I can't let this fall apart. I have to protect our story. Ask every question I can.

"Zuzu," I interrupt. Might as well ask while I have the chance. "Did you know Katherine Harkins personally? I know she set up this interview for us."

Zuzu looks confused. "Katherine . . . ?"

Franklin frowns. "Charlotte, I tried to tell you in Kevin's office. Katie didn't set this up for us. I did."

My turn to frown. Okay, then. "I'm sorry, Zuzu. I should have asked you. Did your lawyer say anything about a fire in western Massachusetts?"

Now Zuzu looks doubly confused. She shakes her head, and turns to Luca, who's tucking his BlackBerry back into a pocket. "Do you know a Katherine — ?"

"No," Luca replies. "But I will be delighted to escort our visitors to the door."

This is probably a colossal mistake.

Luca, smiling as if we've known each other for years, is pouring what I learned from the menu is an expensive burgundy into my

227

crystal globe of a glass. The atmosphere at La Caleche is flickering candles, caressing music. And one confused reporter. Luca had invited both of us to dinner, of course. Franklin had begged off to call Stephen and order room service.

But I couldn't resist. I'm certainly allowed to have a business dinner with a man. Josh was the one who floated the possibility of us taking some nondrastic time off. That's not what this is, of course. But no one had lunch today. And I'm curious. About a lot of things.

Luca's gray silk shirt shimmers almost silver in the candlelight. Matching his eyes, I can't help but notice. I also couldn't help but notice he's not wearing a wedding ring. He'd pulled out my chair, ordered the wine, ordered our appetizers, suggested sharing the rack of lamb. Waved off the waiter's offer to pour more wine so he could do it himself. He's the un-Josh. And at this moment, he's making me feel like a very pampered, very coddled, un-Charlie. Or at least, a different Charlie.

"Did you hear any more about the raid?" I drag the real Charlie back to the table, risking a sip of wine. I'm strictly sticking to the purse business. If I can extract some info for our story, no one could raise an eyebrow at this dinner expedition. The text message turned out to be Kevin, making sure we were getting the goods. So I'm getting them. I remember the word I think I heard the lawyer say. "Is it the Angelina bag they were concerned with?"

Luca shakes his head, lifting both hands as he pretends to fend off more questions. "You must always be the reporter, I suppose. But our lawyer must always be the lawyer. And she insists, and I know you'll understand, I am prohibited from saying anything."

I shrug, as if defeated. But I'm still concerned about Keresey. Wondering if she took part in the raid. Wondering if something went wrong.

"It's just," I say, "I have a friend who may be working undercover with the federal government. A woman. Do you know if anyone was hurt in the raid?"

"I'm so sorry," he begins.

I feel my face flush, then go cold.

"No, no," he says. "I was going to say — I'm sorry, but I don't have any details. And again, I must insist. May we . . . talk about something else? Your life, perhaps?"

No way. "How about your life? How did you get into the purse business?" Friendly and professional. Maybe I can get him to

229

open up this way. Find out something later.

"It was Sylvie and her father who brought me in. Now her father's gone, she and I are chief designers. We met in school, and after we were married, of course, it all just evolved."

Luckily I wasn't in midsip, or expensive Côte de Beaune would have splatted across the pristine white tablecloth. I can't resist looking at his left-hand ring finger again. And this time, he notices. I'm caught.

He holds up his hand, waggling his slim fingers as if making it easier for me to see. His eyes twinkle. Or maybe it's the candle-light. "We are no longer married, of course," he explains. "And she never changed her name from Marachelle. But we worked together for so long our careers were more inextricably intertwined than our personal lives. We parted. So many years ago. But professionally, we stayed together."

A white-coated waiter arrives, fussing with our lamb, using silver utensils to serve haricots verts with slivers of almonds, and minuscule purple potatoes. As the waiter leaves, Luca relates the history of the once-struggling Delleton-Marachelle, how it relocated to the United States after the death of Monsieur Delleton, the arrival of Zuzu three years ago, and then the sale to

ITC Conglomerate. How back in the '90s someone managed to give Meryl Streep a prototype bag. When the movie star was photographed with it, the demand for the "Meryl" launched the tiny company into the fashion stratosphere. How he and Sylvie were suddenly in vogue. And in *Vogue.*

I lean forward, elbows on the table, fascinated. Then I remember the elbows on the table thing. You'd think I'd never shared a rack of lamb with a charming and successful French fashion designer. I guess I haven't. Luckily Luca's eyes are focused far away as he tells his story, maybe remembering.

His accent makes his still-careful English intriguingly continental. Our dinners disappear. Time disappears.

"Did you have children?" I ask. I remember the photo I picked up, the one of him in the sweater. With the beautiful young girl. Maybe there's an obvious explanation.

The waiter arrives, offering the check in a cordovan leather flap. I reach for it, but Luca stops me.

"Someone as lovely as you," he says, narrowing those eyes at me. Engaging, almost mocking. "I noticed your left hand, too. Are you, like Sylvie, married to your work?" He hands the leather flap back to the waiter. I half notice he's paid in cash. "Or are you — forgive me — involved?"

I look away, at my wineglass. At my plate. At the candles. Anywhere to avoid stepping into that quicksand of a question. I knew this was a mistake.

"Yes," I say, struggling to keep my tone casual. I can handle this. "And no. It's complicated." I put my linen napkin on the table, international signal for "we're done." And I don't just mean dinner.

Luca looks at me. Amused? Assessing. "I'll show you to your door," he says.

"Oh. No. I'm fine." I stand up. Why didn't I just order room service?

"I insist," he says.

I hold out my hand. The one without the key. Behind me, the door says room 965. There are two of us in the hall. And only one of us is going inside.

"Thank you so much, Luca," I say, shaking his hand goodbye. I can hear the nerves in my voice, hear my long-departed midwestern twang somehow remerging. My words sound first-date stilted. And somehow the more I fight the onslaught of inarticulateness, the worse it gets. "It was fascinating. And so interesting. And I hope we will meet again."

232

Ah. Possibly the wrong thing to say. I turn my body toward the door, brandishing the key, attempting to telegraph *I'm going in now. Alone.*

But Luca has not let go of my hand. "A little surprise?" he says.

I turn back to look at him, trying to gauge what's he's planning. We're in the middle of a hotel corridor, a public place. Deserted, yes, at eleven at night, but public enough, where anyone could open a door at any second. So the surprise can't be that surprising.

"A little anticipation?" he continues. His voice is not quite a whisper, but muted, personal. Meant only for me. Someone five steps away could not hear him.

His eyes, the gray now turned steely and intent on mine, are putting me a little off balance. I take back my hand, as politely as I can. I keep my voice down, too. "Anticipation?"

Luca reaches into his jacket pocket and draws out a small box, the signature lavender and gray of Delleton-Marachelle, tied with a lavender silk ribbon. "Don't open it until you get to the airport," he says. "A little anticipation always will make the journey's end sweeter."

I only had a glass and a half of wine. But

this isn't making sense. Still, no matter.

"Luca, that's terribly thoughtful," I say. I drop my voice even lower, suddenly concerned someone will hear us. Come out and see us. Even though there's nothing clandestine to see. "But as a reporter, I can't accept anything of value from someone involved in a story. Even dinner was, perhaps, pushing it. And now I should say good night."

"It is just a small token," he says. With a quick gesture, he tucks the tiny box into my tote bag. "A thank-you from all of us, for your efforts."

For a moment, we look at each other. The hall is silent, still. A softly lighted corridor of closed doors and the secrets behind them.

I feel Luca make a decision, and in that instant, he leans over and kisses me on the cheek. Softly. Fleetingly.

"*Au revoir,* reporter," he whispers.

Before I can respond, or recover, he's gone.

The glowing green numbers on the hotel nightstand clock now read 3:30 a.m. I've seen them say 1:34 a.m. and I've seen them say 2:31 a.m. And I know I must have slept at least some of the time in between. The green glow also illuminates the lavender-

and-gray D-M box, the sleek lavender satin ribbon still pristinely tied in its bow. I've seen the box every time I check the clock. I shook it once, with no resulting clues as to what's inside. But I haven't opened it.

Yet it's not only Luca I'm thinking about. It's Josh. Maybe life's sweetest moments only come after a little tension. A little suspense. And nothing that's worthwhile is easy. Every investigative reporter knows that.

Punching my unfamiliar pillow into submission, I wish I could do the same to my buzzing brain. Maybe what Josh and I are doing is moving into new territory. Maybe that takes some patience. Maybe that's how you know it's the real thing. If you're willing to wait for it.

CHAPTER SIXTEEN

I dive for my cell phone. It's in my purse, somewhere. I turned it off to save the batteries last night, and forgot to turn it on before we left the hotel. Kevin probably called. Again.

We're crammed into the back of a ramshackle taxicab, trapped in out-of-control highway traffic, twisting and turning our way to the Atlanta airport. The car smells like some maniac's idea of strawberries. There must not be one functioning spring left in the low-rider backseat. Whatever music is blasting from the radio surrounds us like a swarm of demented bees, the buzz punctuated by the driver's unintelligible and probably untranslatable challenges to the cars he insists on passing. Franklin, his face headed for green, clutches his briefcase as we weave across two lanes of cars, then back again, on the NASCAR-wannabe free-for-all that's Georgia's I-85.

"Don't you get carsick? Checking your messages in the backseat?" Franklin manages to say.

"Nope. Reading, texting, using my laptop in a car? No problem. I spent my childhood reading *Mad Magazine* lying across the way-back of our station wagon," I reply, punching buttons on my cell. "Mother was in despair, but turns out, it was all practice."

"We're flying home through Baltimore again, I told you, right?" Franklin says. "I hope you make it all the way home this time. With your suitcase."

"Yeah, I'm living dangerously, though. Checking it. You should, too." I say. "It too much of a pain to lug it through security. Besides, how many suitcases can the airlines lose?"

"Well, the latest Department of Transportation statistics show it's about —"

As the phone powers up, I whap Franklin in the arm before he can reel off his stats again. "Rhetorical question. I don't even want to know. Uh-oh. There are already text messages. Two of them. I'm betting: Kevin and Kevin."

I'm hoping: Josh and Josh. Or Keresey, telling me she's okay.

The first message appears. From Maysie. U 2 BACK TOGETHER? HOPE NO STRIKE

OUTS. TXT ME IN NYC.

"Maysie," I report to Franklin. That girl is relentless. I delete her message, and the next one appears.

SORRY MISSED MTG. CALLED AWAY. RESKED.

I close my eyes, thinking I must be mistaken as I stare at the signature. I hold my phone out to Franklin. "Read this," I say. I can hear my own voice, tentative and hollow.

"I told you I can't read in this cab," Franklin says. He glances at the phone, grimacing, then waves it away. "Just read it out loud to me."

"It says, sorry missed meeting, called away, resked. Like, reschedule. And then . . ."

Franklin slowly swivels his head toward me. "You're kidding."

I press my lips together, staring again at the name of the sender. "Nope, not kidding. It's signed, K Harkins. And it came in overnight while my phone was off."

"Holy . . ."

"Yup," I say, clicking my phone into reply mode. "This is fantastic. This is great. What a relief, you know? I was feeling somehow responsible. I guess we were all overreacting. So mystery solved. She's fine. She's a

238

P.I. after all. They have to disappear from time to time. I'm texting her back." I pause, concentrating briefly on the screen. "Okay, sent. I said we'll be in the office today."

"Wonder if Keresey knows," Franklin says. "And that state cop. Yens."

The cab careens into the departures lane at Hartsfield Airport, me grabbing the strap above my window so I don't crash into Franklin, Franklin bracing himself against his door. We climb out, weak-kneed and grateful for solid ground. If only briefly. I'd rather be in that cab than in the air.

"Want to do curbside check-in?" Franklin asks.

"I'm not that much of a risk taker," I say. "Let's just go in, get coffee and papers, then go to the regular desk agent. I never trust leaving my suitcases outside. It's like asking someone to steal it. Or send it someplace I'm not going."

A whoosh of air as the doors to Terminal A slide open. We check the destinations board. We're on time. For now.

"So the usual plan, right? You guard the stuff, I'll get coffee and papers," Franklin says. "Meet you right here. We have plenty of time."

As Franklin heads off in search of caffeine, I deposit our bags on the floor and plop my purse down on the chair next to me. Inside, I see that lavender ribbon.

Franklin's nowhere in sight. And Luca told me to open the box in the airport. I hold it in the palm of my hand, then with one quick tug on the ribbon, the bow slithers open. I lift the lid. On top of a carefully folded puff of tissue paper, there's a tiny white envelope. With a business card inside. Luca's.

"May every journey's end bring your heart's desire," it says on the back. And it's signed: *L.*

I carefully peel away the metallic oval D-M sticker holding the tissue paper together. Inside is a luggage tag. The signature pale silvery-gray leather, also embossed with the D-M logo. I lift a flap and my business card — maybe the one I gave Luca at the studio — is already inside.

"What's that?" Franklin says. He's peering at the tag, and points to the box and tissue paper on top of my bag. "Where'd you get that?"

"From Luca," I say, holding out the tag. "He gave it to me at dinner. And told me to open it at the airport. It's just a gesture. No big deal. It would have been rude not to take it." I put the box in my suitcase, then unlatch the tiny gold buckle on the tag's

240

strap and wind it through the handle of my new suitcase. I pat it into place, admiring it.

"So I see you've charmed Purse Man," Franklin says, watching me. "Very cozy. How's Josh, by the way?"

"It's a luggage tag," I retort. I tuck Luca's card in my purse. "What could be the harm? Now let's get these babies onto the plane and go home. We've got more important stuff to think about."

"Anyone pack your suitcase for you?" The gate agent is checking my ticket, punching something into his computer, reciting his litany of questions at the same time. He's said this a million times a day. I can't imagine anyone saying yes.

"I wish," I answer with a smile. My suitcase, and Franklin's beside it, is still on the floor in front of me. I read the agent's name tag. "No, Edgar, no one packed my suitcase for me."

"Anyone ask you to carry on anything?" One chubby finger is poised over his keyboard.

Again, why would anyone say yes? Because bad guys, when confronted with the insightful and incisive questioning of a ticket agent, are suddenly intimidated into telling the truth? "No," I reply.

With that, the agent's no longer interested in me. My luggage claim check whirs out from a slot behind the counter. Then another one.

"Oh, excuse me," I say. I gesture to the two suitcases in front of me, and point to Franklin, who's standing behind me. I lift my suitcase onto the scale. "I'm only checking one bag."

"Sorry," the agent says. He folds the second claim check, puts it under the counter and slings my bag onto the conveyor belt behind him. "Next."

I flash Franklin a long-suffering expression that's supposed to convey "these people have no idea and no wonder so much luggage gets lost" as he takes his place in line. Then I give myself a silent scolding. Agents have a difficult job. They're attempting the impossible.

I just hate to fly. And no matter how I work to fight it, I lose. Spiders, no problem. Heights, fine. Snakes. Public speaking. All a breeze. Flying is my only fear. I start my "pretend the fear doesn't exist" exercise.

"We're delayed," Franklin says, interrupting my self-help session. He tucks his ticket flap into the pocket of his navy blazer. "The agent just got the word. Another hour."

"There's a dilemma. Which is worse, flying now or flying later?" I ask. It's still difficult to keep the nerves out of my voice. And yet, I admonish myself to remember, I'm not the only one inconvenienced. I shift back into pretend mode. "No problem. Franko. Let's make the best of it. Let's see if we can get through to the Great Barrington Police on a Sunday afternoon. And I'll check our undercover line."

"You're a fun travel buddy, Charlotte," he says. "Laugh a minute. I was thinking, let's go have a beer and watch baseball. But you're the boss. I'll try the cops. And the GBFD."

We both pull out our cell phones. While Franklin looks up the number for the Great Barrington Fire Department, I dial into the voice mail on our undercover phone line.

"Received, today at 7:42 a.m.," the mechanical voice says. And then I hear a stranger's voice. A man? Maybe a woman. It's difficult to tell. A slow smile spreads across my face as I listen to the new message.

"This is a message for Elsa. You indicated you are interested in making arrangements with us. If you wish to continue, please appear at Baggage Claim area D at the Hartford airport, tonight at 7:00 p.m. . . ."

I listen to the rest of the instructions, then

hand my phone to Franklin. "Bingo, bingo, bingo," I say, doing a little dance move with my hips. "Push 2-2 to listen to this message. I bet I can easily fly to Hartford from Boston and get there in time. And I'll have my suitcase if I need to stay over."

Franklin holds the phone to this ear, his eyes widening as the message plays back.

"It's just after one now," I say. "We have the stop in Baltimore. If our plane's not late again we'll get to Boston by four. If we're lucky, and we sometimes are, there'll be a flight out of Boston and I can get to Hartford just in time." More flying, my favorite. I don't say that.

Franklin has one hand over his ear and has his eyes closed, blocking me out as he focuses on the message and its instructions.

"Don't erase it," I remind him. "This is our ticket to the big story."

"It's risky," Franklin finally says, handing the phone back to me. His face is solemn, downcast. "They could recognize you. I wish we had our hidden camera. Damn. I should go with you, camera or no."

"They don't get Boston TV in Hartford," I remind him. "And even you wouldn't recognize the counterfeit me. Just go back to the station. Put our tape somewhere safe. See if Katie Harkins e-mails. And call Keresey. See if you can find out about that raid. Anything from the fire department PR guy?"

"No answer on his line. The emergency line says they'll page him. It's Sunday. Nobody's anywhere." Franklin consults his watch. "And it's time to go. Look, we can talk about this more on the flight. And remember. Just-call-me-Sally is nowhere to be found, last we heard. We don't want you to end up nowhere, too."

Elsa looks back at me from the Hartford airport's ladies' room bathroom mirror. Of course, the plane from Boston was late. I made it here in time, but now I'm down to the wire. Moving as fast as I could, knowing I had only minutes to make my rendezvous, I slicked back my hair into a high ponytail. Took out my contacts and put on my glasses. A whirlwind visit to a couple of airport shops provided everything else I needed. Some dangly "what did you bring me" earrings and a pink Red Sox cap courtesy of Airport Gifts. From the Minit-Manicures "Retro-Metro" collection, I grabbed a tube of "Purple Rain Pink" lipstick and BeeGees Blue eye shadow. Luckily for my insta-disguise, I already had on plain black slacks and a Levi jacket.

Franklin gave in on my plan, of course,

finally forced to agree this was too good an opportunity to pass up. I had reminded him I'd be in the most public of places. What's more secure than an airport? Even he couldn't argue with that.

I check my image again. Goodbye, Charlie. I check my watch. Hello, someone Elsa.

Across the way, I spot a bank of escalators, red arrows above them pointing to ground transportation, rental cars, USO and Baggage Claim C and D. I know my suitcase from Boston will soon be in Claim Area A. A green arrow indicates that's down the opposite bank of escalators.

Decision. Which way to go? With a wince and a quick prayer to the airport gods, I realize there's not enough time to retrieve my bag and make it back for my rendezvous. I'll have to abandon my suitcase until I'm finished.

From my perch at the top of the steep escalator, I scan the area below as I ride down, using the time to get my bearings. A bank of flickering televisions is mounted on the wall, one showing CNN, another the local news, another the weather. Only a few other people are in this part of the airport, lugging bags and clutching water bottles. No one at all is on the escalator going up.

I mentally run through my instructions.

I'm carrying a bright red I Heart Hartford tote bag, also from the airport gift shop. Tucked inside, but visibly poking out the unzipped top is a copy of the latest *Elle* magazine. It's just seven o'clock, right on time. I know what I'm supposed to do.

At the baggage carousel marked D, only a few straggling bags make their way slowly around the segmented black conveyor belt. They look ignored, like the last of the kids waiting to be chosen for a team. No passengers are waiting to pick them up.

Strips of rubber baffles cover the openings at the beginning and end of the belt. They flap and flutter as the conveyor moves in a sinuous elongated S-shape across the room. I walk to the end of the line, where the belt disappears though more strips of rubber and continues back outside. I'm in the designated place. I wait. I'm alone.

"I can see you." The disembodied voice comes from through the rubber baffles. Someone is outside, behind the wall, in the baggage distribution area. Which is supposed to be off-limits to everyone but airline and airport employees. And TSA.

"Should I be seeing you?" I lean in closer to the voice. Squinting my eyes, trying to catch a glimpse through the black flaps and into the darkness beyond. "Should I come through to where you are? How?"

"Stand back," the voice says. A man. "No more questions."

Glancing around the claim area, I hope no one is watching me talk to the conveyor belt. I consider taking out my cell phone and pretending to have a conversation. No one would notice me then. But it hardly matters. There's not a soul nearby. And maybe the black flaps are hiding me from view, too. That's a comforting thought, disguise or not.

"Put your bag on the conveyor," the voice commands. "Then wait until it comes back to you. Pick it up and look inside."

Following directions, I watch my red bag glide through the baffles and ride out into who knows where. And into who knows whose hands. One of the orphan suitcases follows it. I wait, mesmerized by the mechanical sounds of the moving belt, the slapping of the flaps, the muffled airport public address system intermittently croaking unintelligible instructions, the televisions' constant muted stream of shape-shifting news reports.

Then I see my shopping bag is back on the conveyor. It's now on the other side of the claim area, all the way at the beginning of the belt. It's moving toward me, down one side of the elongated black curve, then up the other, getting closer, inch by inch. I can see the red heart logo. Read the slogan. See the *Elle* magazine still sticking out the top. Every muscle in my body yearns to go grab it. But I've been told to wait. A little warning murmur buzzes through my brain, muttering about unattended bags in airports, did someone ask you to carry anything, did you pack your own bag. I reassure myself. That's not what this is about.

When the bag gets almost to arm's length, I can't stand it. I can see it looks no different than when I placed it on the belt not five minutes ago. When it gets close enough, I snatch it, greedy to see what's inside.

"Ten minutes." I startle, as I hear the voice from behind me. "You have ten minutes to return the bag."

"How do I . . . ?" I begin.

"Get going," the voice commands.

Another scan of the baggage claim area. Sunday evening in Hartford is apparently not the busiest time. For now, it looks like I'm by myself. On this side of the wall, at least.

I head for a bank of chairs, my bag clutched to my chest. Sitting down, I take a deep breath and look inside.

It's just the magazine. I flip the pages,

baffled. And then, there it is. Between the pages, something new has been added.

A triple folded, letter-sized white piece of paper. Nothing that looks even potentially dangerous. It's obviously an order form. A photocopy. A yellow sticky note is attached to the top. In small blocky letters, the words all crammed together, someone has written instructions in magic marker. Fill out. Place in bag. Bag on belt. Then wait. You have ten minutes.

I check my watch, then skim the form, reading as fast as I can. There's a list of descriptions, no brand names, but it's clear what they're offering. It's a shopping list of knockoff bags.

Red-and-camel striped clutch bag, the first line says. That's obviously meant to suggest Burberry. Quilted black patent tote with CC lettering. Chanel, it doesn't say. Brown-and-cream hobo shoulder strap pouch, stripes. A fake Fendi. Black satchel with one red and green stripe, G logo. Gucci. Brown suede tote with three gold balls on drawstring.

I blink, staring at that description. That sounds like it could be the Angelina. A bag that's not even the market yet.

A flood of fear washes over me. This is me, in over my head. As the seconds tick by, I battle the urge to get up and run. I could take the list with me as evidence. Of what? I have six minutes left.

I need to talk with someone. At least brainstorm with Franklin. Problem is, I can't pick up my phone to call him. Whoever is behind the flaps is certainly watching me. I'm on my own. I have to decide on my own. The only person to talk to is myself.

The cons: It's risky. They could already know who I am. They could find out. They could find Franklin. Josh. Penny. I should leave this to Keresey and Lattimer. If the bad guys are burning down houses, no story is worth that.

The pros: No one knows I'm undercover except Franklin. Those purse parties are everywhere. The bad guys, whoever they are, have no idea I was at that particular house. The fire could be a coincidence. An accident. There aren't any other fires. And it's not like I even expect to find Mr. Big. I'm just seeing where the darn bags come from and how they're distributed. They gave me an order form, for heaven's sake. How prosaically unscary can anything get?

"Do it?" I ask myself.

"Do it," I reply.

I check off the boxes for some fake Burberrys, Fendis, three Chanels and four of what I'm theorizing might be copies of Delleton-Marachelle's still unreleased treasure, the Angelina bag. I'll send one of those to Zuzu right away. She'll go bananas.

I enter the number of our undercover credit card. The last entry on the form says, "request delivery date." I pause, my pencil hovering over the blank line. The sooner the better, I think. Day after tomorrow.

Less than a minute to go. The muscles in my neck and back tense and tighten as I walk with all the nonchalance I can muster back to the conveyor belt. I know the person waiting for this is not going to leap out and grab me, that wouldn't make sense. And if security spots me, well, I'm not doing anything wrong. And I'm sure not going to point them to the man behind the curtain. Whoever it is.

The conveyor is still in motion, clanking and whirring, endlessly carrying those remaining suitcases on their circuitous journey. I return to my assigned place at the end of the line and watch the black plastic belt move through the flaps and get swallowed up into the darkness beyond. Hesitating only for a second, I put down the Hartford bag; the *Elle* magazine and completed order form now tucked inside. And I watch them disappear.

A klaxon wail, combination of buzzer and bells and alarms, instantly begins, ringing and echoing across the tile walls of the baggage claim area. A surge of panic races through me, tears well in my eyes. I'm caught. I'm caught. I'm caught. And there's no way to explain it.

It's a setup. Of course it's a setup. A trap. Why didn't I think of this? My thoughts tumble on top of each other, reality revealed with heart-stopping speed. The feds don't know it's me, I realize, they're just grabbing the next stupidly greedy idiot who's signing up to cash in on phony fashion and rip off the purse designers.

The escalator is suddenly full of people. My eyes are so blurry, on the verge of crying, it takes me a moment to grasp who they are.

Passengers.

At that moment, a tumble of bags breaks through the flaps of the conveyor belt. Black wheelies, battered backpacks, corrugated boxes tied with twine, a case of wine. The passengers, alerted to their arriving possessions by the blaring signal, swarm to claim their belongings. I'm so relieved I almost miss what's also on the conveyor. Upright and solitary. Moving along as if it belongs with all the rest.

My red Hartford bag. I race over to grab it, now just one of dozens of weary and anonymous people yanking their property back into safety. I look inside. The magazine is gone. At the bottom of the bag is a beeper.

CHAPTER SEVENTEEN

I'm still punching buttons on the beeper as I race to Baggage Claim A, hoping my suitcase is still there and not already swiped by some treasure-hunting traveler. The black plastic device was already switched on, but there were no messages and no instructions. I clip it, still turned on, to the waistband of my jeans. I guess I'm supposed to wait. And I cannot wait to tell Franklin. But first I'm going to retrieve my suitcase. If it's still there.

Thankful for my flats, I run down the escalator steps. There's a lighted sign indicating my Flight 242 from Boston. Underneath, the luggage carousel is still carrying a collection of suitcases. A few others are disgorging down a chute onto the conveyer below. I spot my black wheelie, with my new silver-gray tag still attached, tumbling end over end as it hits bottom and begins to circle.

"Yes," I say out loud. Score. I trot over toward my quarry, then stop in my tracks. I've spotted something more interesting than my suitcase. There's someone I recognize at the far end of the baggage claim.

Regine.

Tucking myself out of sight behind an information booth, I keep half an eye on my bag as I watch Regine surveying the arriving cargo. She's wearing perfectly tailored jeans again and pointy-toed boots. This time she's in a leather jacket. Her tawny blond hair, just as I remember, falls sleekly around her shoulders. She's already chosen one large black suitcase from the carousel. Not the designer bag that had brought us together in Baltimore. And she's clearly scouting for more.

What the hell is Regine doing picking up suitcases from Flight 242? I'm certain as I can be that she was not on my plane. I didn't see her when I checked my bag at the ticket counter in Boston. I didn't see her in the waiting area. Reluctant-to-fly me was, as always, the last to board. My seat was in the back. I walked past all the other passengers. She wasn't there. But maybe she's meeting someone.

I'm an idiot. Was it me? It certainly was not her voice giving me instructions.

Is she the girl in Luca's photograph? I strain to get a better look at her, comparing her face with my fading memory of the somewhat younger girl in the photo. Possibly, but I can't be sure.

Regine is watching the selection of suitcases move steadily by her, tapping one booted toe. A garishly patterned tapestry satchel with a red ribbon tied on the handle. A little girl's pink plastic Little Mermaid bag. A battered brown leather case, so old-fashioned it doesn't have wheels. My black bag with its iconic and expensive designer tag edges into her line of vision. I see her body language shift, and she leans over, as if to check the tag.

Or take my suitcase.

The puzzle falls into place. Maybe that's why she "practically lives at airports," as I remember she told me in Baltimore. She steals suitcases.

Not this time, honey.

Before she can make a move, I'm beside her. I reach across in front of her, blocking her view and her access. "Excuse me, that's mine," I say, keeping my voice pleasant. No need for a confrontation. I hoist my bag from the belt, and place it protectively behind me, realizing I'm probably over-reacting. After all, lots of suitcases look alike.

"Sorry?" she says. She looks me up and down, as if I'd interrupted her very important train of thought.

Now we'll see if she recognizes me. Not as Charlie McNally, but as the woman she gave the Designer Doubles card to in Baltimore. Today, as Elsa, I look a lot different. But if she says something, so what. I have as much right to be here as she does.

There's no reaction. Nothing. She whirls away, looking annoyed at my intrusion. She's focused on the luggage, not on a middle-aged traveler.

Is she the girl in the photo? Impossible to tell. I open my mouth to ask, then stop. That's a can of worms. What good would it do? And I have to make sure I get a flight back to Boston.

I loop the strap of the I Heart Hartford bag over the extended handle of my suitcase, annoyed. This baggage claim system does not work. That girl could have taken my suitcase. Airports are all about security when the bags go onto the plane, but coming off? You're on your own.

Heading back up the escalator and into the terminal, I'm hyper-aware of the unfamiliar beeper clipped to my waistband. I check it again, flipping up the screen so I can see it as I walk. Still no messages. Still no buzzes or beeps or vibrations. I'm connected to someone now, that's for sure. And I wish I knew who.

My eyes are glued to the screen above me. I've already confirmed there's one last flight to Boston tonight, leaving at ten. Just enough time for me to check my bag again and get to the gate with a few minutes to spare. This is a good thing, because right now I have to watch TV. The local all-news cable channel, all graphics and swirling images, is flashing "Developing Story."

My neck begins to hurt, tilted at a muscle-wrenching angle to see the screen. The sound is muted, too low to hear. But the usually bothersome graphics crawl at the bottom of the screen, coupled with the all-too-understandable video, making it clear what happened. And where it happened. Maddeningly, there's no Who. Or Why. The crawl of words starts again.

"Rescue workers have pulled the body of an unknown woman from the Housatonic River. Police say early evidence shows signs of robbery and foul play. Police are asking the public for help in identifying her. She is in her forties, about five feet two inches tall. Very curly dark red hair, blue jeans and designer T-shirt. If you have information, please call . . ."

As I watch the words go by a third time, my mind is racing. Calculating. Facing reality. No question, this murder victim is just-call-me-Sally. I know it is. Yanking out my cell phone, I hit Franklin's speed dial while trotting toward my last ticket agent of the day. I have so much to tell him. Now this. Wonder if he knows about it? He would have called me. Maybe.

It takes forever for the call to connect and of course there's only one person in front of me. Just as Franklin's voice mail clicks in, it's my turn to cross the yellow line and head to the desk.

The bored-looking agent, possibly a failed bodybuilder from the looks of the biceps under his airline-issue blue polyester shirt, acknowledges me, then glares at my phone. I flap my cell shut, smiling apologetically. I dig for the proper credit card, hoping Kevin doesn't go berserk over having to pay for all these plane tickets. They weren't exactly authorized. I look again at the still-silent beeper. I'm hoping it'll be worth it.

"The 10:00 p.m. flight to Boston?" I say, handing over my card. "One seat? One way? One bag to check."

"There are seats available." The agent taps his computer, talking to me without looking at me. Reciting. "Did anyone pack your bags for you? Anything hazardous or flammable?"

"Nope."

I see him hit the enter button, then watch as my baggage claim check spits out from the printer. And then another one. I purse my lips, remembering. Two baggage claim checks for one bag. This is exactly what happened in Atlanta. But Franklin's not with me this time. I'm clearly alone and I clearly said one suitcase. Maybe it's nothing, but every reporter instinct tells me this is not a coincidence. It's not a mistake. I'm just not sure what it actually is.

"Oh, golly, I only have one bag, David K," I say, reading his name tag as I point to the second claim check. I try to lift my suitcase onto the scale, pretending it's heavy, bestowing the agent-hulk a flirty smile. "Just this one."

"Sorry, ma'am," David says. He reaches down to help little me, then hands me one of the checks. I watch as he peels the slick backing from its matching bar-coded label and bends down to stick the identification tag around the handle of my bag.

It's now or never. I heft my purse onto the edge of the counter, and with a squeak of damsel-in-distress dismay, tip the entire

261

thing onto his workspace.

"I am so sorry, it just fell over," I say, acting flustered and dismayed. I turn to the person waiting in line behind me, apologizing again, then I lean over the counter, scooping up my belongings. And along with them, the second claim check.

David is chasing after some of my pencils and a package of mints that rolled off the desk and are heading toward parts unknown. And that gives me just enough time to compare the numbers on the two checks. The one I'm giving back is just one number higher than the one I'm keeping.

"Oh, thank you," I say. Prettily as can be. I've already replaced the purloined paper right where it was when we started, in plain view, on the agent's desk.

David is signaling the person behind me to step to the front. But I can see him retrieve the claim check and slide it into a drawer. He's not throwing it away. He's keeping it.

This has been a pretty successful trip. And not only because the plane didn't crash. Flying east through the darkness, even stuck in the middle seat between two armrest-hogging businessmen, I had a fairly brilliant idea. I could be way off base, of course. But if I'm right, I'll be able to confirm my theory in the next twenty minutes. If I'm right, our story is an out-of-the-ballpark blockbuster. Still in my Elsa getup, with additional blue eye shadow and pink lipstick applied en route, I wave a thank-you to the flight attendants and head down the jetway. On full speed ahead.

Every bit of fear and worry and exhaustion has disappeared. I'm running on journalism adrenaline, the irresistible combination of lust for a story and the quest for answers. The beeper. Sally. I still have to call Franklin. But now, baggage claim.

I hurry, needing to be one of the first to baggage claim, which I know is all the way across the terminal. As I arrive, the black conveyor belt lurches into motion, and the klaxon alarm signals that suitcases are on the way.

Watching the passengers ignore me, I reassure myself. As Elsa, I'm invisible in Boston. Anonymous. And that works perfectly.

My black wheelie with the silver-gray tag spills over the top of the luggage belt and onto the circular carousel. As it begins its winding journey, I send it a silent promise that I'll come back. Because that's not the only bag I'm waiting for.

Stationing myself at the opening where the luggage first appears, I watch the bags intently as they go by, just like any other traveler. Unlike most other travelers, however, I'm looking for a claim check number. My bag is labeled with ten digits, ending in 4406. But I need a suitcase marked with the number I saw on the second check David K. printed out. And I know that one ends with 4407.

If the airlines compared claim checks before allowing passengers to take bags from the airport, what I think may be the counterfeit bag distribution scheme could never work. But in Boston, as in so many airports, they don't.

The suitcases are appearing more quickly now. One after the other, they fall out the opening and are dumped down the angle of the belt to land on the carousel. My own bag trundles by me, and I know I have to let it continue. If my plan works, I won't be able to carry two suitcases. I need to keep checking.

A huge black wheelie balances, briefly, at the opening of the chute. The tag is perfectly visible. And it ends with 4407.

It tips over the edge. I can't take my eyes off it as it travels the short journey to the carousel. It's right in front of me. With a quick glance confirming no one else has their eye on it and a fleeting prayer to the news gods, I grab the bag by its black handle and wrench it from the carousel.

The second its wheels hit the ground, I whirl away and make a dash for the ladies' room. I look over my shoulder. Anyone see me? Anyone noticing?

No.

I hoist the black bag across the toilet seat. It's heavier than it looks, and so big the wheels almost hit one wall of the tiny metal enclosure while the handle touches the other.

I reach for the zipper. And only then do I see the tiny padlock, holding two zipper pulls together. Of course. It's locked.

Hands on hips, I stare with frustration at the black bag in front of me. I have to open it. Maybe it's not really locked, the unlikely thought pops into my brain. I yank the little silver square, hoping it'll just open. No such luck. I lean against the door of the stall, thinking. If this bag is not being picked up by the passenger who sent it from Atlanta, how would they get a key? What's more perplexing, airline rules now say you can't lock your suitcase, except with a TSA approved lock. And this isn't one of them.

That means . . . I feel my brain churning ahead, struggling to make sense of this.

That means. Someone locked this suitcase after it was put through security. And whoever locked it knew someone would need the key to open it. So where would they put it?

I unzip a flat pocket on the outside of the bag, and slide my hand to the bottom. And I feel something. Small. Metal. I scrabble to get it out. It's the key.

It unclicks the lock instantly. Almost hearing the clock ticking away my safety, I carefully pull open the zipper all the way around the perimeter of the bag. With every inch, I search for something that may be a trap, or a setup to ensure no one has tampered with it, but I can't see anything. And I don't have time to look more closely.

Lifting the top of the bag, I prop the edge up against the stall wall. And stare. It's a bonanza. I've uncovered a fashionista's fantasyland, a jaw-dropping array that looks like the spoils of someone's obsessive-compulsive shopping spree. Three separate piles, stacked so tightly they expanded when I released the constricting zipper. Each pile is a stack of flattened-out, shrink-wrapped packages. Inside each package, what looks like brown fabric. No markings on the plastic. No tags. I tentatively lift a few packages, one by one. They're identical. And there must be — I quickly count, just getting an estimate. Two hundred of them. Two hundred fifty.

With barely a hesitation, I grab one, scrutinizing one side, then the other. A tiny piece of tape holds it closed. Easing the tape away from the plastic flap, a millimeter at a time so I don't tear it, I put my hand inside. I feel suede. I gently, carefully, release the fabric from the plastic, trying to remember how it's folded so I can replace it. As it emerges, I see fringe, and a braided drawstring with three gold balls at each end. I hold it up, mesmerized. I don't have time for this. But I can't believe it.

This looks exactly like the Angelina bag. A purse that's not even on the market yet. A purse that supposedly no one has seen outside of the Delleton-Marachelle inner circle. Real ones will sell for ten thousand dollars each.

I attempt the math. Which involves too many zeroes. But I can easily calculate that if bags of bags like this are crisscrossing the U.S., bringing big bucks to those who foist them off as authentic, or even as cut-rate copies, this is a bonanza. I stare at the faux Angelina. Should I just sneak it into my bag? Take it as evidence?

I yank my ponytail tighter into the scrunchie. No one to discuss this with but myself.

Yes. I'll take it. I'll need it as proof of what appears to be an amazing scheme: that phony claim checks are being used to send extra baggage, carrying counterfeit merchandise, onto airplanes. At the other end of the pipeline, counterfeit passengers just stroll in and pick up the unclaimed suitcases at the baggage carousel. Then they sell the purses inside them for a big profit.

Talk about free shipping.

The FBI — and Katie Harkins — will go crazy. They'll be able to trace airplane passengers, see who else was issued claim checks. And which ticket agents issued them. David K., for one, is clearly involved. And Edgar in Atlanta. And I realize, if anyone traced the numbers, this bag would be assigned to my ticket.

No. It's stealing. What if it isn't what I think it is? Even if it is, I will have taken someone's bag. Not taken, *stolen* someone's bag, albeit briefly. And now I'm contemplating stealing something out of the bag? Taking it with me? I flash a mental replay of that video of the Housatonic River. And then of that burned-out shell of a house on

268

Glendower Street.

Definitely no. I pause, using up even more time that I don't have. Then I yank my purse open and take out my cell phone. I know it's never taken longer to power up. "Come on, come on," I silently mouth the words. "Do it, do it, do it."

I snap one photo of the bag. Then one of the suitcase full of plastic bags. I allow myself a smile, hoping no one's hearing me take photos in the bathroom stall. That would be hard to explain.

One more item to check. And thanks to Zuzu, I know what it is. I zip open a side pocket in the Angelina and slide my fingers down deep inside. I know a real D-M has a tiny metal bead sewn into the right corner seam. In this bag, there's nothing. This is a fake.

Carefully folding up the brown suede, I attempt to recreate the way it was originally, then slide the resealed pouch into the middle of one of the piles. I zip up the suitcase again, leaning my whole weight onto the top to get it to close.

Thread the tiny lock back through the zipper pull. Stash the key in the outside pocket. Slide open the latch to my secret bathroom hideaway. And go.

Question is — will someone be watching

for this bag? And will they see me put it back?

CHAPTER EIGHTEEN

Back at luggage claim, it's as if I'd never been gone. It's still crowded, departure confusion still in full swing. More luggage arriving. Keeping my expression confident and nonchalant, I wheel the bag full of contraband back to the carousel. There I see hundreds of circling bags are still waiting to be collected by hundreds of travel-worn passengers. Most people are in a congested pack, milling around where the bags come out, some pushing those ungainly gray steel rented baggage carts. I make my way to the end of the line where the bags go back outside.

Lifting the black suitcase back onto the carousel, I watch as it gets carried through the black baffles and outside, out of sight and swallowed up into baggage anonymity. If all goes as planned, soon it'll be coming down the chute again.

I can't wait to see what'll happen next.

My own bag is still, thankfully, circling. Grabbing it, I post myself at the exit to the claim area as if I'm waiting for a fellow passenger. And that's exactly what I'm doing. I'm stationed at the only way out. Travelers will have to walk right by me, either heading up the escalators to the parking area, or out the door to buses and cabs. When the person I'm looking for walks by, I'll follow right behind.

I consider calling Franklin, but I'm not sure what I'd tell him. And I may not have time. I fold my red Hartford bag in half and tuck it inside my suitcase, just to be safe. No sense having that on display. Crossing my arms in front of me, I lean back against a pillar. It can't be long now.

The bag of bags is now at the top of the chute again. I watch it hesitate at the top, then get pushed over the side by the luggage behind it. It slides down to the carousel. And then, someone grabs it.

It's a woman, elegant, graying hair cut in a chic bob. Do I remember her from the plane? I don't. She looks like a traveling executive, in her slim tweed skirt, white shirt, hip-length cardigan sweater tied with a soft belt, low-heeled shoes. Her rented baggage cart is already carrying two other suitcases, a large black one and an overstuffed maroon carryall. She sets the contraband case on its wheels, then looks again at its baggage claim check.

Get a cab, I send her a silent plea. If she has a car, there's no way for me to follow her. I'd have to settle for a license plate. If she takes a bus, that has its pros and cons. I pray she's getting a cab. That's got only pros.

The woman shifts the other two bags, and slides the black bag onto the cart's lower shelf. Pausing a moment to retie her belt, she pushes her cart toward the exit. And me.

Turning my back to her, I hoist my purse onto my shoulder as if I'm also on the way out. *Get a cab.* I ESP her another message. *You. Need. A. Cab.*

Yes. She goes past the escalator and through the automatic doors. Above her is an orange arrow with a sign proclaiming This Way to Ground Transportation. And I'm right behind her. Just another tired and harried late-night traveler who wants to get home.

Sliding just behind her in the crowded and lengthening cab line, I figure I can get her cab number, and then, somehow, find out where she told the driver to take her. I have a fleeting "follow that cab" idea, but in Boston that's doomed to failure. We might make it through the sleek new Ted Williams Tunnel, or even the two-lanes-only fifties-era Sumner Tunnel. But as soon as we hit the centuries-old cowpaths that are now paved over and used as Boston city streets, there's no way to follow anyone without being snagged at a light or trapped by a one-way street.

"Where you headed, ma'am?" The stocky red-faced cab dispatcher, a pencil stuck behind each ear, organizes his passengers like a pudgy sheepdog, asking each for a destination, then forming us into docile groups.

"Cab sharing in effect, lookit the posted rules," he announces, waving his clipboard, invoking Logan Airport's time-honored crowd-control method. He dodges out of the way as a brown-and-white Town Taxi almost sideswipes him, sliding into place at the curb with the passenger door swinging open. "Who's for the south shore?" Foh-ah the south show-ah, it sounds like, proving he's a Boston native. "Who's for downtown? Cab sharing in effect."

Three passengers for downtown raise their hands. He shepherds them to a dented Yellow Cab, waiting, engine running, with its trunk already popped. Doors and trunks slam, engines rev, exhaust plumes as my quarry and I move closer to our turn.

"Who's for the western burbs?" The dispatcher scans the line. "Brookline, Newton, Framingham, Natick?"

"Here." Luggage woman raises her hand and the clipboard approaches. "Brookline," the woman says.

Perfect.

I don't delay. "I'm for Newton," I say, wheeling my suitcase closer. "I can share." Newton is the town just past Brookline and I know Madam Suitcase will be dropped off at her destination first. And I, Nancy Drew reincarnated, will be able to see exactly where that is.

"Cab 576." The dispatcher waves both of us to a reasonably safe-looking Red Cab. Here we go. If she recognizes me somehow, or the cabdriver does, well, I guess that won't be a problem. I'll just say I'm coming back from a trip. Like everyone else. But no question, it would be better if I can just stay Elsa.

Thank goodness for text messaging. If I call Franklin on my cell, this person might recognize my voice from television. But I've got to let him know I'm all right. I wait until we motor through gloomy old Sumner Tunnel, where my phone won't work anyway.

As we emerge into the neon and streetlights of Boston's North End, I flip my cell open, holding it up to my window so I can see the numbers. I punch Franklin's speed dial, and with two thumbs, text as best I can. Home. Katie? Fire? FBI? Got big ifno.

Rats. No time to fix spelling errors. Call u L8TR.

We turn onto Storrow Drive, the Charles River reflecting MIT on the right, the lights of Beacon Hill flashing by me on the left. It feels strange, knowing we're going past the turnoff for my own apartment headed to Brookline and points unknown. Stranger still, I'm sitting in the backseat of a cab, right next to someone who's clearly up to her stylish rear end in the counterfeit purse syndicate.

I pretend to yawn, so I can look at her but still keep my hand over my face.

She's now peering through red-rimmed reading glasses as she examines the screen of her cell, a complicated multitasking PDA with a tiny keyboard and green screen. No way for me to read what it says. On her right hand, she's wearing a square-cut emerald, surrounded by diamonds. Very pricey. If it's real. And in her lap, a Louis Vuitton shoulder bag. Very pricey. If it's real. Gucci shoes. This woman has bucks. Or connections.

Unfortunately, she must have told the driver her address while he was loading her stuff in the trunk. So I don't know exactly where we're going. But she said Brookline. And I do know we're almost there.

I look at my cell again. I type another message, quickly, before I can decide not to. "To Josh. Sorry. V V late. Talk 2morrow. Miss U." I pause. That's true. I do miss him.

We're almost at the exit marked Fenway. The border crossing into Brookline is just down Beacon Street and across Park Drive. I stare at my pending text message again. XOXO I add. And before I can reconsider, I hit send.

And then I hear a beeper go off. The one from the airport. The one from the man behind the luggage carousel. The one on my belt.

I startle upright, slapping a hand to my waistband, yanking the beeper off and into my hand. I glance at the woman, panic surging into my chest. *Calm down,* I tell myself. *You got beeped. Everyone gets beeped.* She has no idea how critical this might be. And how, if I'm on the right track, it might be connected to her. I offer an apologetic look, *sorry to disturb you,* but she's already back to her message screen.

I punch the green button. As the message

winds through the ether toward me, our cab crosses the border into Brookline. I stare at the message screen. It's past midnight. They can't expect me to do anything now, can they? And what would it even be? Call someone? Go somewhere? Pick up contraband purses? I still worry it could be a setup.

The tiny rectangular screen on my beeper now shows just one word. TOMORROW.

And then the cab comes to a stop.

I look up, scrambling to get my bearings. I was so involved with my beeper, I missed all the turns. We're in a residential neighborhood, tree-lined, affluent. Well-kept houses, Georgian, Victorian, set back from the street, shapes of elegant landscaping just visible in the glowing streetlights. It's the familiarly prosperous Brookline, but could be any number of streets.

The woman extracts a few bills from her wallet and hands them to the driver. "Have a nice evening," she murmurs over her shoulder at me, perfunctorily polite. She opens her door and gets out. A porch light goes on.

Where are we? I lean forward, and back, and forward again, twisting and straining to see a street sign. Or maybe there's a marking on the house. The fire department requires there be a number; visible, so emergency responders can quickly find their destination. I squint, looking down the impatiens-lined cobblestone walk to her front door. The porch light now illuminates the brass numbers on the white molding. Three. Two. Five.

Three twenty-five — what?

"What street is this?" I ask the cabdriver as he gets back into the front seat. Duh. I must be a bit more tired than I realized. And a bit more freaked out. Out the window, I see the woman entering the house. A silhouette inside is helping her bring in the bags.

"Strathmeyer," he says, putting the car into Drive. "Now where to?"

I hold up the beeper that had given me chills just a few moments ago. "Plans changed," I say. "Now I have to go back to Beacon Hill. Sorry."

"Your dime," the driver replies.

And I'm finally headed for home.

"Where the hell have you been?" Franklin's voice hisses in my ear. Concerned, critical. "I didn't want to call you, didn't want to interrupt anything. But your meeting in Hartford was four fricking hours ago. It's now after midnight. What did y'all think I would do? What did y'all think I would think, Charlotte?"

I close the plastic window between me and the cabdriver, not that he could overhear my phone conversation, being so deeply immersed in his own. Franklin's Mississippi accent signals he's truly stressed. I can envision him pacing the hallway of his South End apartment. Or complaining about me to Stephen.

"Listen, Franko, I'm sorry. I wanted to call you, several times, but I just couldn't manage it." I pause, not sure what to tell him first. "Let me ask you though, did you hear anything about —"

"Where are you now, Charlotte?" Franklin interrupts me.

I look out the cab window. "We're just on Charles Street. Getting ready to turn onto Mt. Vernon. I'll be home in two seconds. Why? Should I just call you from there?"

"Ma'am?" The cabdriver turns around and slides the window between us back open. The cab is still moving. I'm grateful narrow Charles Street is deserted this time of night. Morning. "Cash or charge?"

"Hang on, Franklin. I've gotta pay this guy."

"But, Charlotte, I should warn you . . ."

"Putting down the phone for a sec," I reply. I plop the cell, still on, into my lap and get ready to pay the cabdriver with the last of my cash. Kevin is going to go ballistic over my expense report. Although it's looking like our story might be worth the unpredicted expenditure.

"I'll need a receipt, please," I say to the driver, handing him the money. "Hang on," I say into my lap. I can hear Franklin's voice, buzzing, unintelligible.

We turn the final corner into the narrow turnaround of Mount Vernon Square. I'm suddenly out of energy, so glad to be safely home. I'm tired of pretending to be someone else. Tired of being afraid. Tired of thinking and worrying and planning my next move. Tired of feeling alone. I'll sleep, I'll take a shower, and tomorrow — today — we'll get some answers.

There's my apartment, brownstone in shadow, but illuminated by the old-fashioned streetlights, not burned to the ground as I had secretly feared. And there are the overflowing baskets of scarlet mums on the porch, just as I left them. And next to them, on the front steps is something else. I blink, shaking my head to clear it.

I hear Franklin still buzzing in my lap. I hear the cabdriver pop the trunk, then get out to retrieve my suitcase.

When I look again at my front steps, the

unfamiliar shape is still there. There's a man sitting on the top step. He's leaning back against the wrought iron railing. Across his lap, there's something long and narrow.

I lean back against the seat of the cab, too perplexed to open my own door. Sitting on my front steps is State Police Detective Christopher Yens. And in his lap, a long white box, the shiny slick kind that only comes from flower shops. It's tied with a big white ribbon. The detective is bringing me flowers? He's sitting on my steps, after midnight, in jeans and a brown leather jacket? With — flowers? My brain has finally, formally, crashed.

I put my face in my hands, briefly, and then I hear the back door open. As I look up, the cabdriver, shirttail out and receipt in hand, is staring at me. "This is correct address, yes?" he says.

"Yes. This is correct." I say. It's also weird as hell. I sling my purse over my shoulder and push my way out of the backseat. Never a dull moment. And so much for my sleeping plans.

The cab backs up into the curve of the cul-de-sac and pulls out into Mt. Vernon Street. Leaving me with my new suitcase, my befuddled brain and my unexpected guest.

Detective Yens sets the flower box on the steps and slowly gets to his feet. As he comes toward me, his face is unreadable. "Welcome home, Miz McNally," he says. His voice is pleasant, unchallenging. "I suppose you're wondering . . ." As he approaches, I see his expression change. He takes a step back.

I get it. He's seeing Elsa.

I take off my Red Sox cap, yank off the scrunchie holding my ponytail in place, and push my glasses onto the top of my head.

"Ta dah," I say, keeping my voice down so neighbors don't call the police. Even though they're already here. And I'm wary, playing for time a bit until I understand what's going on. "This better? You're right, I am 'wondering'. If you mean wondering why you're here. So, why?"

"You undercover?" he says, ignoring my question.

"Nope. Just comfortable." No reason to tell him more than he needs to know.

"Your producer Franklin Parrish told me everything," he says.

I look down at my still-open purse, where a glowing light indicates my cell phone is still on. I wonder if Franklin is still there.

"He told you what?" I say to Yens. "And do you always bring flowers when you visit reporters in the middle of the night?"

Yens gestures to my front door. "Shall we chat where it's a bit less public? I expect you might want to put those in water."

I dig for my phone. The connection is still open. "Heellloo, Franklin," I trill. "I'm home. Guess who's here?"

"Mr. Parrish apparently called your news director first," Yens says. He's sitting on one of my taupe-and-navy striped living room wing chairs, elbows on his knees. Leaning toward me. Almost interrogating. "Where were you? He said he couldn't reach you."

"That's what Franklin just told me. But he knew I was out of town," I reply, gesturing to the cell phone on the glass coffee table. I'm perched on the edge of the leather couch, facing the detective. He looks casual, and I'm not too tired to notice, even attractive, but he's all business. Total cop.

Botox is curled up on top of my suitcase, still parked in the entryway, making sure I don't leave again. The white box — I still don't know whether it's flowers — is propped against the door where Yens left it. Maybe he's on his way to a later rendezvous and they're not for me after all.

On the way upstairs, finishing our phone conversation, Franklin had quickly filled me in. He'd been trying to warn me Yens might be at my doorstep. And in reality, he hadn't told Yens everything. Not even close. He'd only revealed I'd gotten a text message from Katie Harkins. He'd gotten a similar message on his e-mail. He'd tried to call me, couldn't get through, and decided to call Kevin.

That, I can handle. "So. Might I ask why you're here in the middle of the night?" I ask.

"Well, after he talked to Mr. Parrish, Mr. O'Bannon called me. As we agreed in our meeting." He looks at me, confirming.

I nod. "Go on."

"So Mr. O'Bannon allowed me . . ." he drags out the phrase, as if the whole journalism thing was too much trouble to bear ". . . he allowed me to talk to Franklin. Who told me about his e-mail and your text message. I told him as far as we knew, Miss Harkins was still missing.

"As a result," Yens says, pointing to the coffee table, "I've come to take your cell phone. We're getting our IT people to put it on a trace. See where the text came from. See if we can find her. I'll return your phone. Soon as I can. We need to find her. I've e-mailed her. Called her. She's not responding to me. She is responding to you." He reaches toward my cell, but I whisk it off the table before he can take it.

Botox leaps up at the sound of my sudden laughter and skitters away down the hall. "I don't think so, Detective. Take my phone? Do you have a warrant? Or a subpoena? Let me ask you, Detective. Are you 'taking' Franklin's computer?"

"Look. I'm not playing games, Miss McNally." The detective's face hardens. "This is serious business. An FBI agent was killed in a raid, just yesterday. In L.A. Our sources say the agency had been tipped off to a warehouse on the south side. By Harkins. The messages you got indicate she was alive, last night at least. If the counterfeiters know where she is, she may be in danger."

"How did the agent get killed? Did they find purses? Any kind of contraband?" A raid 3,000 miles away wouldn't involve Lattimer or Keresey, I figure. But I'm still nervous about my pal. "Let me ask you, Detective. Do you know Agent Keresey Stone? FBI Boston? Was she involved in the raid?"

"The agent killed was a man, that's all I can tell you," Yens replies. He slides his hands down his jeans, then holds out one palm. "Your phone, please."

I'm exhausted and confused, but I know

what I have to do. I shake my head as I get to my feet. "Not going to happen. I get why you want my phone. Off the record? Part of me even wants to give it to you. I do. But you know I can't. Not until you get a subpoena."

Yens stands, too, but makes no move toward the door. His face softens and he seems almost sad. "Is this what they teach you in journalism school? Are there some misguided rules about not helping law enforcement officials when someone's life may be at stake? Maybe more than one person? If your FBI agent friend was in trouble, would you still be on your little get-a-subpoena soapbox?"

"Keresey Stone," I reply, looking at the floor. The pattern in my navy-and-burgundy oriental rug swims a bit as my eyes unexpectedly mist over. This is the dilemma that's haunting me, more and more. The undercover video of the purse party. The fire. The bag of bags. The claim check scheme. Whoever lives at 325 Strathmeyer Road. How do I juggle my responsibility as a reporter, my job, my career, my goals — with my responsibility as a good citizen? Why are they different? And the bigger the story, the bigger the stakes.

I rub my hands over my face, slick back

my shampoo-needy hair and struggle to muster some self-confidence. Choosing my words carefully, I try to explain. To this earnest cop, and even to myself.

"I'm a reporter. I can't make decisions based on my feelings. Yes, in my heart, I'd love to give you that phone. I'm uneasy about Katie Harkins. Like you, I wonder where she is. Wonder if she's safe. But if I break the rules now, hand over information because I want to, what happens when I don't want to? You'll say 'Well, you gave me your phone that time. So now, give me your notes. Your sources. Your raw video.' And eventually I'll have no principles left."

I shrug, searching his face for understanding. "You won't tell me about the FBI raid. You won't tell me about your relationship with Katie Harkins. I understand. It's your job. You do what you've got to do," I say, turning toward the door. I gesture, pointing him the way out. "I'll do the same thing."

Yens arrives at the door first and picks up the white box. He hands it to me with one raised eyebrow. "Apparently someone, at least, thinks you're doing everything right," he says. "But you haven't heard the last from us. I'll be calling your boss in the morning."

I take the box in my arms. "These aren't

from you?"

Yens allows himself a fleeting smile, then lifts a hand in farewell. "They were here when I arrived."

And he's gone.

I stare at the white card. Reading it yet again. The glorious white roses that were inside the box — a dozen, each kept fresh in an individual plastic-topped test tube of water and now in my favorite dark green vase — seem to fill my bedroom with their fragrance. Botox hops up onto the nightstand, almost knocking the airport beeper onto the floor. She pretends not to notice, batting a sleek blade of the bear grass that surrounds the bouquet, then she curls up on my lap, tucking her head through my arm. She's does a convincing cuddle, but I know she's actually trying to block my view of the card. Because it's getting too much attention.

I move the card back into view. "Tomorrow is the anniversary of the day we met," it says. "A year ago today I had never met you. A year ago tomorrow, my life changed. I hope it's changed forever." And it's signed: Josh.

"Our anniversary," I say to Botox, smoothing her calico fur as I test the phrase. Two words, I realize disconcertingly, I've never said together before. At age twenty, I walked out of my marriage to Sweet Baby James before our first year together had even passed.

In lust and inseparable, James and I went to City Hall after knowing each other for about three months. We clung to each other in front of an affable clerk, promised to love and cherish, smiled for the resident rent-a-photographer, then went out for pizza and champagne. I carried cellophane-wrapped flowers purchased at a sidewalk kiosk. I left them at the restaurant. We stayed in bed the entire weekend.

Vows of "till death do us part" aside, clearly James and I each had some misgivings. We never discussed it, but we didn't combine our book collections. Didn't combine our tape cassettes. Didn't have a joint bank account. He paid the rent. I bought the groceries. I wanted a cat. He was allergic. He wanted to go camping. I was allergic. He became more interested in how he looked than how I looked.

After yet another argument about why his six-o'clock dinner was more important than my six-o'clock news, I packed up Gramma's heirloom china, my cassette collection, plus a whole new understanding about sharing life with someone else, and walked out. I've been married to my job ever since. It's demanding, but doesn't demand laundry or dinner.

At age twenty, it's easy to think you know love is the real thing. And it's easy to change when you decide it isn't. Twenty-some years later, I've learned it's difficult to know anything.

"I hope it's changed forever." I read the last line of Josh's card out loud. Do I hope my life has changed?

I do.

But so far, I'm not doing a very good job. While Josh was planning a surprise evening at the theater, I was planning a trip out of town. He sent flowers. I sent a text.

My bedside clock taunts me. It's now past three in the morning. I can't call Josh, no matter how much I want to. He's got classes to teach tomorrow. Today. If Penny's there, she might wake up.

Curling up under the covers, burrowing into my pillow, I'm thinking about "our anniversary." Savoring the words.

Then I think of Luca. He was right. My heart's desire was indeed at the end of the journey.

CHAPTER NINETEEN

Hiding in the hatchback of Franklin's Passat is not the most comfortable place to spend a Monday morning. But someone has to carry a hidden camera up to the door of 325 Strathmeyer Road and try to get video of who we now suspect lives there. It should have been me with the camera, but Franklin and I decided she might recognize me from last night at the airport and in the cab. And we can't take that chance.

So today I, too, have to stay hidden. Luckily for my backseat situation, I'm wearing my black turtleneck sweater, comfortable jeans and flat boots. I have a stash of sugar-free Swedish fish and a latte. My third. I e-mailed Josh to call me at his lunch break. So I'm set. I could camp here for a while without caffeine withdrawal or hunger pangs or missing a call from my sweetheart, but I'm thinking Franklin won't be too long.

"Test, test." I check my connection with

Franklin. I have my phone on, and so does he. I should be able to hear everything he says. And everything she says.

"Gotcha, Roger, ten-four," Franklin answers. He's about halfway to the house. "You okay?"

"Not taking my eyes off you," I answer.

I rearrange myself on the floor, peering out the side window. We parked about half a block away, across the street, and snagged a spot with a perfect view. Our first thought was to have me just sit in the front, pretending to read the paper, pretending to wait for someone. But some nosy neighborhood-watch fanatic would certainly call the cops about an unfamiliar car with a stranger at the wheel lurking in their posh neighborhood. So we practiced my backseat maneuver in a parking spot outside Channel 3. Because of the tinted windows, I can see out of my hidey-hole, but no one can see in. I can almost, but not quite, sit up. My neck is not happy. But it's necessary.

All we need is a name, maybe two. And a photograph. Maybe two.

Franklin's almost to the front walk.

We'd looked up the real estate ownership records on the Registry of Deeds Web site as soon as we arrived at Channel 3 this morning. And what we'd found stopped us both in our tracks.

"Simone — Marshal?" Franklin had said. He held his fingers poised over this keyboard as he read me the results of his search. "Is the owner of 325 Strathmeyer. Does that sound familiar? Bought the place in 2005, a few years ago. For 850 thou."

I swiveled my desk chair, almost knocking over my second latte of the morning, then used my heels to wheel myself closer to his computer. "Marshal? Are you completely kidding me? Do you think someone would be that obvious?"

"Obvio— ?" Franklin frowned as he looked back at his monitor. Then back at me. He tilted his head, wondering. "You think?"

"Ab-so-totally-lutely," I said. "As Penny says, no bout adoubt it."

Franklin waved me off. "Oh, come on. You think everything is a conspiracy."

"That's because lots of things are a conspiracy," I replied. "You think we just got home from talking to purse magnate Sylvie Marachelle and now there's a Simone Marshal involved with this whole thing? Who I followed home from Logan Airport with a stash of phony bags? And the two things aren't connected? I beg you."

I pursed my lips, mentally replaying our visit to Delleton-Marachelle, then pointed to Franklin with a one-finger jab. "Of course. They said there was a sister. Remember? Luca said, 'Sylvie and her sister, something something.' Before the conglomerate bought D-M. When was that, anyway? I bet the sister was the one in that photo on Luca's desk. There's a pretty darn easy way to find out." I waggled a hand, very French. *"Très facile."*

Franklin pulled up a new screen on his computer. "Brookline town list," he said. "Getting it."

"Perfect. If 'Simone Marshal' filled out a town census report, it should also list all the occupants. Let's see if anyone else lives there. Rats," I said, rummaging in my purse. "I can't ever find anything in here."

"No comment," Franklin said over his shoulder. "Your purse is the black hole of Boston. Probably Amelia Earhart is in there."

"You said 'no comment.' So don't comment." I scrounged through the multiple zip pockets of my purse once again, in order, down one side and up the other. Muttering.

I finally find what I'm looking for. Luca's business card, the one from my luggage tag.

And just as I remembered, Luca's private number added in marker.

"You know, Franko? How somehow, sometimes, your instinct just kicks in? It's as if the whole picture suddenly appears. It's probably my extensive experience." I stretch, pantomiming nonchalance. "Ah, yes. And this is why I get the big reporter bucks."

"Why again?" he asked.

"Because I'm going to call Luca," I explained as I punched in the numbers. "See what he says about — oh, here it comes. Damn. The machine."

Franklin turned to me. "Charlotte, wait."

I held up a hand, stopping him.

"Hi, Luca, it's Charlie McNally. In Boston." Like there's another Charlie McNally. Why am I so tongue-tied by this guy? "Sorry to bother you, but I'm wondering if you could tell me . . ." I hesitated. Suddenly alarm bells were beginning to ring in my head. How much should I say? Who knows who might be listening to his messages? The bells got louder. What if he's —

Franklin moved in front of me, waving both hands as if he wanted to have a turn on the phone. I gave him a look, exasperated, and a quick shake of the head. Made me lose my train of thought. I turned my focus back to my call, hoping it hadn't disconnected. "I'm wondering if you could tell me," I continued, "whether Sylvie's sister? The one you told us about?"

Franklin stood, hands on hips, almost glaring at me.

"I wonder if she lives near Boston," I continued, ignoring him. "And could you tell me her name? I'll be on my cell. And thank you again."

I gestured to our wall clock as I hung up the phone. "It's just after nine, maybe they're just not in yet," I said, dismissing my earlier misgivings. "He'll call me back, I guess. He has my number."

"If he's not the mastermind behind the whole thing, Charlotte," Franklin answered. His entire face was a frown. "That's why I was trying to stop you."

I stared at him. Recalculating. Drives me crazy that he might be right. And no use to fight it.

"Yeah." I slumped back in my chair, wrinkled my nose. Because I suddenly saw what might have happened. There's nothing worse than being wrong. I may have just blown our whole story. Now I see the real picture.

"What if — remember Luca was married to Sylvie? And now they're divorced. And she's heir to all the D-M money, right? She's the one with the big bucks. So maybe he's getting revenge. Stealing her designs. And cashing in. Doing the worst possible thing to her he could: taking her ideas and taking the company's good name." I plopped my head into my hands, my remorseful words aimed at my desk.

"I'm an idiot. I might as well have called and said, 'Be careful, we're on your trail.'" I peeked out through my fingers, spotting a ray of hope. "Is here any way to undo a phone message?"

"Sorry, Charlotte. Of course, it's possible you could be right. We'll soon find out, that's for sure. And listen, if Sylvie's sister lived near Boston, wouldn't Luca have mentioned it? Maybe the Marshal-Marachelle thing is wrong."

"Bzzzt." I made the international sound for *incorrect*. Franklin's trying to make me feel better. Impossible. "He certainly would not have told me if she were the key to the knockoff plot. If they were in it together."

"On the other hand, he could be just protecting her privacy. Maybe she's turning her back on her past. Getting an American name. Fitting in." He tapped his keyboard with a dramatic flourish. "Voilà. Here's the town list. Okay, Internet. Show me something good."

And then he went quiet. Staring at the screen.

The air in the room changed. Franklin turned to me, silent. His eyes wide. He had something.

Once again, I scooted my chair closer to him. And for a moment, I was silent, too. And then Franklin read the town list entry out loud, his voice heavy with disbelief.

"The owner is listed as Simone Marshal, age 48, occupation, homemaker. Under other occupants, it lists Reggie Webber, age 22, student."

"*Sacre* frigging *bleu,*" I said. "Excuse me. But Reggie? That's Regine, if I'm not mistaken. And I'm not. Reggie is Regine, and she's Simone Marachelle's daughter. Whatever that means. But who's 'Webber'?"

"I'm hitting print," Franklin said, clicking his mouse. "And if we're going to get their pictures, I think we should go. If we knock on the door now and they're not home, we can try again. But if they leave for good, we're screwed."

"Because they were alerted by my phone call, you mean. Because Luca instantly called them. And then everyone shredded everything. And we've — I've — ruined our story."

Franklin's forehead furrowed, and he smoothed his already impeccable khaki pants as he stood to leave. "I hate to say it," he said, his voice full of reluctant apology. "But maybe."

Finished with my fast-forward replay of the entire morning, I watch Franklin head up the flower-lined front walk of 325 Strathmeyer Road from my backseat hideout. Our snazzy Sony HC-43 camera is hidden in his L.L. Bean monogrammed briefcase and he looks for all the world like a prep-school alum in khakis, old school tie and suede designer jacket who's searching for his long-lost buddy. Our fervent hope is that Simone Marshal not only answers the door, but also buys our story.

We have to verify her name to make sure the person who arrived last night is "Simone Marshal," alias Simone Marachelle, and not a visitor. Or a renter. Or, the idea creeps unpleasantly into my consciousness, some random person whose name is Simone Marshal.

No. I shake off my own second-guessing. Someone who arrived at that house carried in at least one suitcase full of fake bags. And I'm convinced all three she picked up were contraband.

We have to get her photo to confirm who she is. And I'm considering — it might be time to tell Keresey. I eye the beeper that's now clipped inside my purse.

I wish I were going to the door. But I'm a team player. And I know how to take turns. I'm still clinging to a faint hope that Luca's not the mastermind. That I didn't get carried away by my own overconfidence and spill the beans.

My cell phone is on and so is Franklin's. I don't want to miss anything. State law says we can't record audio, so her voice won't be on the tape. In the worst possible scenario, if Franklin needs help . . . well, I'd just have to risk getting recognized.

"I see you," I say. "We found a perfect parking spot. You rolling? The lens in the right position? I can't wait to see her. Make sure you don't block my view when she opens the door."

"*If* she opens the door," Franklin answers. "And shush. Let's go radio silence. I don't want anyone to see me chatting with Mr. Suede Jacket."

"Radio silence?" I can't help laughing. He's always so earnest. "You're so . . ." Then I stop. He's right.

Stretching out my legs behind me, I prop my chin on my hands and don't take my eyes away from Franklin. He walks up the three cobblestone steps, past the terracotta urns of elaborately topiaried ivy, and pushes a black button by the doorjamb. The bell. He turns to me for half a second, then turns back to the door.

Nothing.

Here's where undercover works gets sticky. Your goal as a journalist is to get answers without the subject realizing it's happening. But the only way to be convincing is to do what you would do if you actually were the person you're pretending to be. Franklin the "old school chum," guilelessly hunting for a friend, would simply ring the doorbell again.

Franklin the producer would start wondering if there were a way to see if anyone is actually home without ringing the buzzer again. I see him scan the second-floor windows. Looking for open screens, blowing curtains. He's listening for noise from a television. He turns back to me again. But I know he can't see me.

He lifts the lid of the rectangular mailbox beside the door. Checking for mail. And any names that might be on the mail. In plain sight, of course, so he doesn't have to commit a federal offense by touching someone else's mail. I see him point to the box, then shake his head. Dramatically, to make sure I see it. The box is empty.

"Just ring the buzzer again," I say to myself. "No big deal. A real person on the trail of a friend would just ring again."

Franklin pushes the button.

I nod. Good move.

A beat. Another beat.

And the door opens.

"Yes?"

I hear the voice, barely, through Franklin's phone. A woman. But even squinting, I can't make out her face, She's two steps back from the light, still in the interior shadows.

"I'm so sorry to bother you," Franklin begins the spiel we'd devised. "I'm looking for Steve Rosenfeld?"

Binoculars. I need binoculars. I cup my hands around my eyes, and press them to the window, somehow thinking this might create a binocular effect. It fails.

"I'm sorry?" The woman has moved even farther back into the house.

Franklin adjusts the bag on his shoulder and I know he's anxious about getting the shot. I am, too, because if she keeps backing up, I'm never going to be able to see her. I can hear Franklin using his most courteous dinner-guest voice as he explains what he's doing.

". . . and this is the last address I have," he says. "Your last name is not Rosenfeld?"

If this woman is totally unsuspecting or hasn't had her coffee, this is where she might offer her real name.

"No," she says. "They were the previous owners."

We know this from the Registry of Deeds records. Which if she's the current owner, she clearly knows. Which is why we used the name.

"Ah," Franklin says. "That's so disappointing. When did you buy it from them? When did they leave?"

Good move.

I strain to hear. Both for her answer and for a French accent. I can see Franklin is listening. But I can't hear a thing.

And then the door closes.

"Let me see, let me see." I'm clamoring for the tape before Franklin's even all the way into the driver's seat. "Did she tell you her name? Was it Marshal? Did she have a French accent? I couldn't see her at all, can you believe it? And I could barely hear a thing."

The door slams. Franklin loops the handle of the camera bag over his head and onto the passenger seat. I reach over to grab it.

"Can we just get out of here, Charlotte?" He sounds relieved that the pretense, and his performance, is over. "And then we'll pull over and look at the video. And you can get out of there."

"Okay, fine. My body is one big cramp. But what about her name?" I'll wait for her pictures, but not for her name.

"Let me see. She has gray hair, in a pageboy, just like you described," Franklin says. "Flashy ring, expensive shoes. Gucci, if I know my logos. And I do."

"Franklin B. Parrish, you tell me right now. Is she Sylvie's sister?"

"There was mail on a side table, addressed to Simone Marshal. She picked it up, and looked through it. She had on a necklace with a diamond initial. The initial is M."

I purse my lips. Trying to convince myself that's persuasive. And I need to be supportive of Franklin. He did the best he could. "Well, I guess that's pretty good," I say. "And we'll be able to use the video at some point, anyway, to get an identification. The pictures are really the most important thing."

From my vantage point, still stuffed into the hatchback, I see Franklin's face in the rearview mirror. His eyes are twinkling.

"Oh, you're asking her name?" he says, all innocence. "Why didn't y'all say so, ma'am? She sounded a lot like Catherine Deneuve, but she told me her name is Simone Marshal."

Franklin's driving so I can't punch him, but that means Simone is French. And his description sounds like she was the same person who picked up the bags in the airport.

"It makes you wonder about the other people you see in airports, you know?" I say. I'm now on my back, looking at the ceiling, trying to uncrick my neck and wishing for a seat belt. "You figure everyone at baggage claim was on the plane, and yet, how would you know? But who knows how many times the same person might show up there, pretending to be a passenger. I just noticed Regine because she gave me that card. I might have seen her a million times before."

"Everyone's anonymous in airports. Just focused on the suitcases," Franklin says. "That's why the counterfeit passenger scheme works."

"That's why they call it organized crime," I say. "We know the crime. We just don't know who organized it."

I feel the car make a wide turn, and brace myself on the back of the front seat so I don't get plastered against it. The car moves forward, then back, then forward. We're parking.

"Here's Beacon Street," Franklin says. "Let's get you out of there."

There's a click of a lock, then the hatchback pops open. My eyes squint as blue sky and sunlight replace the gloom of my camouflage position. I twist my legs around and slide to the ground, my knees protesting with every move. My neck will never be the same and I've got polka dots of hatchback lint sprinkled over my black sweater. But there's only one thing I care about.

"Let's see that video, undercover man," I say, holding out a hand to take the camera.

Franklin's sitting on a low stone wall lining the lawn in front of a Beacon Street brownstone. He's zipped open his bag, and he's flipping the switches that change the Sony from camera mode into viewing mode. He holds up a hand to stop me. "Hang on, Charlotte. I'm getting it."

"Push Rewind," I instruct, unnecessarily. I can see he's already doing that. I can also see he looks perplexed.

"Is it not working? Is the screen just blue?" I persist. "That means you haven't pushed the right buttons. Let me see. Let me do it," I say, sitting down next to him. I stretch my legs out across the sidewalk and lean in close to Franklin, peering with him at the tiny screen. It's not blue.

It's shoes.

"Maybe it's just . . ." he begins.

"Yeah." Not good. Not good. I'm doing my best to stay calm, but tell that to my racing heart and clenching lungs. Years of experience recognizes what's about to happen, but I still try to ignore what I fear is the inevitable.

"You took a lot of video," I say. I'm riveted to the screen. "All we need is one shot. Literally, one frame of her face. We can freeze it in the edit booth. Let's not panic."

Franklin's face is grim as he hands me the camera. "I can't stand it. You have to watch the rest of it. Just tell me what you see. I might have to throw up." He puts his elbows on his knees, face in his hands. His glasses are pushed to the top of his head. "Just tell me."

A woman navigating a double-baby stroller approaches, eyeing us quizzically. We probably do look out of place. Two yuppies sitting on a wall along one of Boston's main streets staring at a video camera, an open hatchback in front of them. One of the yups clearly upset.

The nonstop traffic on Beacon Street, a din of honking horns, clattering trolleys and the occasional siren, adds an urban soundtrack to our increasingly depressing silent movie. I've rewound all the way to the beginning.

"Okay, starting from the top," I say. "There's got to be something. I see you walking to the door. I see the front walk, I see the door. Shrubs. Swish pan to me. Back to the door. The mailbox. Empty. The door opens. Darkness. The camera jiggles." I remember watching this moment as it happened, Franklin nervously adjusting his bag. That's where this all went from genius idea to disaster. "Then I see . . . feet. Shoes, actually. Like you said, Gucci shoes."

The video keeps rolling. I keep narrating. I keep hoping. But the picture doesn't get any better. Or different. It doesn't tilt up for one fraction of a second.

We got nothing.

"Franko?" I say.

"Don't even tell me," he replies.

I puff out a sigh. I wish I didn't have to tell him. All of our planning. All of our strategizing. Our one big chance. And we have nothing to show for it. Not one glimpse of her face is caught on camera.

CHAPTER TWENTY

"It's okay, we'll just move to plan B." I reassure Franklin for about the millionth time. We're on the way back to the station, me comfortably in the front seat now.

Franklin's seething.

"What is plan B?" He hits the turn signal with a little more force than usual. "I can't believe I blew it. We don't have her picture. Without it we can't confirm she's Marachelle, not Marshal. And your Mr. Suave in Atlanta has probably already warned her we're on the case. We're not having the best of days, partner."

We ride in silence for a while. I'm thinking about our rapidly disappearing story. We'll have to tell Kevin and Susannah we've got all kinds of leads, and plenty of ideas, but so far no way to prove any of it. And our November deadline is uncomfortably looming.

"Did you hear from Katie Harkins?" I ask.

"Nope."

"Did you call her? Leave a message?"

"Yup."

More silence. Franklin's the first to reassure me when I screw up. But he has a hard time handling his own failures. He flips on the radio, then instantly turns it off again. That means he's thinking.

We pull up to a stoplight. He turns to me, eyes narrowed.

"Did he ever call you back, by the way?" he says. "Luca?"

I give Franklin a quick finger point, then plow through my tote bag. "Good thought. I turned my phone off as soon as you got to the car."

My phone powers up. And there's the trill that means message waiting. "I'll put it on speaker if it's him," I say, pushing buttons to retrieve the message. "The call must have come in while you and I were —"

"Don't remind me," Franklin interrupts.

It's from Luca.

"Listen, it's Luca," I say.

There's a buzz of static as I rewind to start the message from the beginning again.

"How nice to hear from you, Charlie." Luca's voice, with that continental accent, comes crackling through my phone's tinny speaker. "About Sylvie's sister? Her name is

Simone, but . . ."

"Whoa," I mouth the word, and look at Franklin, my eyes widening. Franklin nods, looking almost happy again.

". . . but where she lives I'm afraid I can't tell you."

I frown. "Why not?" I say over the voice.

"Shh." Franklin hisses.

"I can't tell you because — I don't really know. She and her sister are —" Luca pauses. "Estranged. After Delleton-Marachelle was acquired by ITC, they had a falling-out. Simone never wanted to sell. She said she was embarrassed Sylvie would allow her father's respected name to be 'usurped by philistines who also made potato chips and canned soup.' Sylvie won't even discuss her sister now. Where she went? Where she lives? I'm not sure anyone here knows."

As Luca says goodbye, my mind is racing, trying to place this provocative piece into the increasingly complicated puzzle.

"If he's telling the truth, that means he knows nothing about the airport baggage scheme. And of course, he doesn't know that we know where Simone Marshal is."

"If," Franklin replies. "And that's a big if. It would also be a pretty great way of throwing us off the track. If he knew she was in

Brookline that would be the last thing he'd mention."

"What is the deal with this traffic?" I say. "There's not a baseball game here, right? Maysie's in New York." I look out the window into Kenmore Square, the tangled intersection that's home to Fenway Park and constantly teeming with Boston University students, Red Sox fans and confused tourists trying to navigate rental cars. Not one vehicle is moving. And every driver is honking.

Josh is still in class now, but I don't want to miss his lunchtime call. I'd prefer to have that conversation in private, instead of code-talking in the car with Franklin pretending not to listen. I've got to get back to the station.

I snap on the radio. "Let's see if there's a traffic report, at least."

"—atonic River," a plummy-voiced radio announcer is saying. "Again, state police say they now know the identity of the woman, apparently a victim of foul play, whose body was found in the Housatonic River yesterday. Stay tuned to this station for more details. And now, weather in Boston is . . ."

I turn down the volume. And pick up my phone. "I've got the assignment desk on speed dial," I say.

"Channel 3. May I —" a voice on the other end begins.

"Listen, it's Charlie McNally," I interrupt, hoping it's someone who will recognize my name. "Do me a quick favor, okay? I'm stuck in traffic."

"Sure, I —"

"Go to the wires. Look up the regional stories. Got it?" I turn to Franklin. "I'm putting this on speaker."

The traffic begins to inch forward. There's only silence from the phone.

"Hello? Charlie? Okay, the Associated Press is up on my computer screen," the voice says. "This is Kelly, by the way. Now what?"

"Okay, Kel, do an edit-find. Search for Housatonic. Read me the story about the body found in the river. The most current one. It should be in breaking news. Is there a victim's name yet?"

Silence again.

"Got it," we hear. "Okay, let me read it fast . . . Massachusetts State Police . . . dut dut dut . . . body . . . dut dut dut . . . Housatonic River, foul play . . . police say no leads . . . okay, here's the name. It says, 'Police say the victim is Sarah . . .' " Kelly pauses. "Gar-sin-ka-vich? G-a-r-c-i-n-k-e-v-i-c-h. Of Great Barrington, Mass. Then it says Sarah whatever worked as a ticket agent at the Hartford airport. Her fellow workers are planning a memorial service later this week. 'She was a valued employee, and a staunch union member,' says airport workers' union president James L. Webber. 'We have lost a colleague and a friend.' And that's it. Want to hear it again?"

"No, thanks," Franklin and I answer at the same time.

"Bye," I add, clicking off our connection.

I prop both my booted feet up on the Passat's dashboard, then whisk them down after a warning glare from Franklin. "That's it. I'm done. My brain is officially full," I announce.

And then my airport beeper goes off.

"You are not going to Logan Airport by yourself to pick up phony purses," Kevin says. He's barricaded behind his I'm-the-big-exec desk, arms folded across his chest. The door to his office is closed, but every nosy snoop in the newsroom monitored Franklin and me going in. "Tonight at nine or any other time. Forget the beeper message. As your news director, I forbid it."

He unbuttons his double-breasted jacket, smooths his elegant paisley silk tie, then re-buttons his jacket. His desk is littered with printouts of budget spreadsheets, copies of last night's ratings, and two piles of DVDs in clear plastic cases. I figure they're all video resumés from small-market newbies, any of whom would eagerly take my place for half my salary.

And there may be a job opening after I tell Kevin the rest of our news. Franklin and I have decided to come clean. If Sarah Garcinkevich is just-call-me-Sally, and no doubt in my mind she is, this is bigger than we can handle. We might have video of a murder victim, who she was with, and where she was the day before she was killed. Our jobs are certainly at stake. But we agreed we have to tell.

Franklin and I are side by side on the long, low couch in Kevin's office. I imagine the two of us already look like guilty ten-year-olds. This may be our last visit to the principal's office before we get kicked out of school.

"Well, Kevin," I say, glancing at Franklin. Here we go. "There's actually more to this. You know the body the police found in the Housatonic River?"

I lean forward and spill the whole story. First the baggage-claim scheme. Then Simone Marshal. This morning's camera fiasco. That's the easy part.

It's suddenly very hot in Kevin's office. My turtleneck is a cashmere toaster oven. My hands clench in nervous fists. I take a deep breath and jump.

I describe my disguise in the Plucky Chicken, and the purse party, and meeting Sally at the mall.

"I know we should have told you," I finish, "but I took a hidden camera to the party. Before you gave us permission. It was all my idea. Franklin wasn't there."

"But I —" Franklin interrupts.

I know he's trying to share the blame. But he shouldn't.

"Nope, it was all me," I insist. I hold out my hands, palms up, trying to explain. "But now, see, if just-call-me-Sally is the body in the river, and she was an airline ticket agent, that means she was probably in on the baggage scheme. And remember? She told me she was branching out on her own?"

"Charlie and I decided," Franklin says deliberately, "she was simply taking the purses that were supposed to be shipped to other airports. Swiping an occasional bag for her own use. Instead of putting them on planes as she was supposed to, she just handed them off to a few trusted comrades."

"And who could prove that something hadn't happened on the other end?" I add.

"They could have been stolen instead of picked up. It would look like just another case of lost luggage. And it's not like the counterfeiters could have reported the theft."

"It's just our theory," Franklin says. "But it makes sense. She redirected them and sold them. Along with the ones she was assigned to sell."

"And the brains of the operation was James Webber, the union boss. He could easily have recruited the airline workers who were in on it. When he found out she was scamming him, he had her killed to send them all a message."

"It's just our theory," Franklin says again.

The Channel 3 theme announcing the noon news comes through the almost-muted speakers behind Kevin's desk. He picks up his TV remote, and turns up the volume, staring at the four state-of-the-art flat-screen monitors attached to the wall beside him. A different station's noon news is on each one, the sound up only on Channel 3. Our anchors introduce a story about some traffic disaster, showing video of earth-movers and broken windshields and gesticulating angry drivers and people in suits. Kevin seems absorbed by it.

Franklin and I quickly exchange baffled

glances. He's watching the news? I lace my fingers together in my lap. All we can do is wait. All he can do is fire us. Susannah can choose my replacement.

Kevin holds up his remote again, killing the audio.

"We'll deal with your hidden-camera escapade later," Kevin says. He spins the remote on the flat surface of his desk. And spins it again. When it stops, he picks it up and points it at me. "But for now, you just bring me that tape. And any copies you have. We're giving it to the police. I'm calling Detective Yens. And you're calling your pals at the FBI."

I don't know what to say. And apparently Franklin doesn't, either.

Kevin shakes his head, and suddenly, just for an instant, it looks like he's attempting to hide a smile.

"You two are too much," he says. "But you were right about the story, I must admit. So I'll work on the staties. You work on the feds. Today. As in, instantly. And then we'll get this thing on television. Now — get out of here."

"Happy Anniversary to you, too," I say. Anyone who walks by me as I'm on my cell phone with Josh probably thinks I won the lottery or something. I know my smile must be amped to jackpot level. At least.

"I'm out in the hall, by the elevator. We're on the way to the FBI and Franklin will be here any minute. But I'm so glad I didn't miss your call, sweetheart. Like I said in the message, the roses are perfect. You're perfect."

I look around. The coast is clear. "And I can't wait to make you just as happy as you make me," I whisper.

"That sounds like a possibility," Josh replies. His voice is guarded. Ultra-business. In the background, I hear the unmistakable sounds of silverware and children's voices. He's got cafeteria duty. "Let me ask you though, do you provide in-home delivery? And would I be able to set up a specific appointment if I ordered your top-of-the-line full-service package?"

"Ah, the full-service package is extremely elaborate and quite special," I reply, playing along. I tuck myself into a corner for more privacy and lean my forehead against the wall. "In fact, sir, I can't remember a situation where we have actually provided that level of accommodations. But I'm sure, in this particular case, you will be able to have whatever you'd like."

"Then I think we have a deal," Josh says.

"Could you hold for one moment?" I hear Josh discussing something with whoever is with him in the cafeteria, hear him say the words "cable television installation," and "appointment."

"Sir?" I interrupt. "If you'd like to sign up for what we call our super-deluxe package, which includes extra personal features never before offered, you'll have to make an appointment right now. I think I could fit you in . . ." I hesitate, and a tiny blush begins as I hear my unintended double meaning. But on the other hand, it actually is exactly what I mean. "I think I could fit you in later this evening."

"Charlotte? You ready? What the heck are you doing?"

Franklin's tapping me on the shoulder.

"Oh, hello, Franklin," I say into the phone, reentering the real world. "Hang on, it's Josh. Josh? You there? Call me later, okay? I think I can help you hook up, just the way you'd hoped, sir. And it will be tonight."

Franklin looks perplexed as I click the phone closed. "Huh?" he says.

"Josh is getting cable," I say. "The total package. Apparently he just can't wait any longer."

CHAPTER
TWENTY-ONE

Special Agent Marren Lattimer's office is now a combination art gallery and gadget shop. All of the framed photos he had leaning against the wall are now arrayed ceiling to floor behind him and beside him. His government-issue block of a wooden desk is strewn with stainless steel, leather and plastic gizmos. What looks like a row of toy guns. A cigarette box? One of those games with the clacking metal balls. A Rubik's Cube. A couple of cell phones in different sizes.

"Are you a collector?" I ask, as Franklin and I take our places in the brown vinyl leather chairs across from the FBI Chief. I see Franklin eyeing the Cube. "Or are those high-tech secret weapons, like in James Bond?"

I feel Franklin shift in his chair and even attempt to give me a surreptitious kick to shut me up. I know he thinks I'm not being deferential enough. After all, this guy's the honcho of the FBI. But I don't like turning over our research and our results to law enforcement. I know Kevin insisted, but I still think it's crossing the line. And moreover, Mr. FBI should be grateful we're here. We've accomplished what his team couldn't.

Luckily Keresey arrives, interrupting my nervous chatter. Today she's Ralph Lauren chic in jeans and a black turtleneck.

"Guess you got the clothing memo, Charlie," she says, eyeing my duplicate getup. She perches on a wooden sideboard against the wall, showing her sleek black boots under her narrow jeans. "You and I could be, what, sisters? If you had a badge. So, what's up? Hey, Franklin. Hey, Chief."

"Agent Stone." Lattimer's all business. Not interested in girl talk. He looks at his watch. "Miss McNally? You asked to meet with us?"

"I know you're busy," I say, to acknowledge I've noticed his patronizing watch move. "But at our initial meeting you said you were interested in cracking the distribution system. For counterfeit purses."

Lattimer nods. "Correct."

"And you said, at that time, at least, you hadn't made any progress."

"What's your point, Miss McNally?" Lattimer says. His computer beeps, and he turns to look at his monitor, clicking his mouse. "Keep talking. I'm listening."

Well. That's rude.

"My point, Agent Lattimer, is that Franklin and I *have* made progress."

"Progress in what?" Lattimer doesn't take his eyes off his monitor.

I mentally count to ten, quickly. And get to about five. "Progress. In cracking the distribution system."

Keresey stands, and walks to a spot behind Lattimer. He looks up at her, then, slowly, swivels his chair back toward me.

"Say again?"

"I said. We know how the phony bags are transported and disseminated."

"We think we know," Franklin puts in. "It's our theory."

Lattimer and Keresey exchange another look. Keresey looks distressed. And I realize — maybe she's worried I've accomplished what she couldn't. Which might not be good for her career. Lattimer looks skeptical.

"Well, that certainly takes a load off my mind," he says, finally looking at me. His voice is bitterly dismissive. "If you'll just outline your findings, I'm sure my agents will be grateful."

What a jerk. I stand up, ready to bolt.

Then sit down again. This isn't my play. Nevertheless, I don't have to be sneered at, even by the FBI.

"I'm not here because I want to be," I say. I keep my tone chilly. "I'm here because our news director asked us to talk with you. Believe me, sir, I'd be just as happy to leave this investigation in your very capable hands. And we'll just put our story on the air. You can hear about it then."

I'm pushing this, I know. So I wait. He wants our info, he can ask for it. No matter what Kevin says.

Lattimer picks up his Rubik's Cube, twisting the multicolored squares. "I assume, Ms. McNally," he says, staring at his toy, "you didn't come to my office to turn over your notes to the feds. So . . . what are we talking about here?" With each phrase he snaps another color into place.

"My news director has instructed me to tell you what we found," I say. "But only if you'll agree to give us an exclusive on the story. Exclusive on the takedown. Exclusive on the aftermath. Exclusive on the arrests."

Lattimer snaps another color into line. "I gather we're about to hear an 'or else'?"

"If you want to put it that way, fine. Here's the way I'd put it. In an unprecedented move for the benefit of public safety, and one which I must admit I'm not convinced is acceptable, we're willing to give you raw information. In exchange for some access." I cross my arms across my chest and lean back in my uncomfortable chair. "Your call."

I'm halfway hoping he says no. Then we will have at least tried, and then we can do this on our own. But I'm just an employee. And would prefer to stay employed.

"Chief? May I say something?" Keresey is frowning, and fingers the necklace cord that holds her badge around her neck.

Lattimer raises a hand, giving permission.

"No offense, Charlie. And I know we've worked together in the past. But not like this, Chief." Keresey shakes her head, and her frown deepens as she turns to her boss. "Making deals with the news. That never works. Always some snafu. Something goes wrong. We need to handle this ourselves. In-house."

For several moments, the only sound is the mechanism of the cube. And then all the colors fall into place. Lattimer looks up, showing off proof of his achievement. "Generally, I'd agree with Agent Stone. But the agency does have some history of, shall we say, agreements in principle with the media. In this case, it appears Miss McNally and her colleague believe they have something valuable."

"But —"

"Agent Stone, you're overruled. Let's hear what these two have to say." Lattimer sets his elbows on the desk, then tents his fingers. One raised eyebrow telegraphs *I dare you.* "Miss McNally?"

I pause, knowing this is an irrevocable step into journalism quicksand. A step I'd rather not take. But I have no choice.

"We know it's happening in Boston, and in Hartford and in Baltimore," I begin. I outline our discovery of the duplicate claim checks and my confirmation of the system in a stall of the Logan Airport ladies' room. I reveal my visit to the purse party, noting that Kevin had taken our video of Sally-who-I'm-sure-is-Sarah to Detective Yens, then my meeting at the Hartford baggage claim with the red bag, and the retrieval of the beeper.

"I can't let you take it, but I can let you see what it says," I say, showing him the beeper.

I push the button, and the message lights up. I hold it so the agents can see. FLIGHT 1017. ATL. LOGAN. MON. CC NUMBER 2 COME.

"So we figure they'll send the claim check

number later," Franklin says. "And that flight arrives at 9:00 p.m."

"Tonight," Keresey says.

"Which means we have to move fast." Lattimer looks at his watch. He points to Keresey, then me. "You two. You're both going to the airport."

"And me," Franklin says. "I can shoot the video."

"Negative. No video." Lattimer picks up his cube. "Here's our M.O. Agent Stone will wear —"

"But the video's part of the deal," I interrupt. "We're television. If we don't have video, it didn't happen."

"We're the Federal Bureau of Investigation, Miss McNally. And we're in charge now. And if you two are capable of doing what I tell you, you'll get your exclusive. But not on tape. Understood?"

What I understand is, I'm screwed. And trapped. And I've just given away all our leverage. Which is why trading info for access is always, always a bad idea. I'm silent. Fuming. Franklin, too.

"As I was saying," Lattimer continues. "We'll accompany you to Logan Airport. I'll be stationed on the balcony overlooking the claim area. Out of sight, but keeping you under surveillance. Agent Stone will wear the same clothing you used as — Elsa? She and I will be in radio contact. You two look enough alike to begin with. She'll shadow you. If there's a snafu, she'll move in to take your place. Or take them down."

"Chief, may I interrupt you here? Why not just let me do the pickup? They'll never know the difference. And if something happens, I can handle it. There's no basis for putting Charlie out there."

Lattimer is shaking his head, clearly ready to reject her idea.

"And what's more," Keresey continues, "if I do the pickup, the bags will never be out of federal custody. The chain of evidence will be stronger. We don't want to risk losing our case based on some legal technicality."

"Duly noted. Thank you for your input, Agent Stone." Lattimer, dismissive, turns back to me. "Miss McNally, you'll do the pickup as I outlined. You hand over the bags you collect. We'll use the claim-tag routing numbers to trace the issuing ticket clerk and convince that person to give us the principal players. All we need. Chain of custody is not a consideration. We'll be there. We'll witness the exchange."

"All the more reason for me to shoot it," Franklin persists.

"But what if it goes wrong?" Keresey, both palms flat on Lattimer's desk, leans toward her boss, pushing. "What if this move puts Charlie in danger? Should we check it out with the director in D.C.?"

"You're over the line, Agent Stone," Lattimer replies. "I'm in command of this operation. If these guys have someone staking out the exchange, they'll expect to see Miss McNally. And, if she's willing . . . ?

I nod.

". . . it's Miss McNally they'll get. And we'll proceed as planned."

"Nice purse," I say to Keresey, pointing to the black shoulder bag on the front seat. She's driving our nondescript unmarked car, procured from the FBI motor pool. "Is it loaded?"

"Government issue," Keresey replies, accelerating up the winding ramp into Logan Airport's central parking. "Assigned to me fully equipped with one loaded Smith & Wesson. Marren's going to give me a radio set to airport emergency frequency. Under the seat, there's another bag just like it for you, too. Put on your Elsa makeup, then you can stash your own purse in the trunk. You won't need anything else from it."

"Is mine fully loaded? Gun and radio? I'm

still quite the hotshot, you know, after your lessons." I point my forefingers and shoot some parked cars, making the appropriate noises.

"In your dreams," Keresey says. "Your bag is empty. Counterfeit, you might say. But we have to match. And remember, that course was just at the firing range. I'll take care of the bad guys. You stick with your pad and pencil, sister."

Even now, we actually do look like sisters. We're both still in jeans and boots, our hair down, wearing Audrey Hepburn–sized sunglasses. While I hide in the ladies' room, she'll soon be shopping for the accessories that will transform us into identical twins.

"Where's Franklin, by the way?" Keresey asks, pulling into a parking space.

I shrug. "Maybe home with Stephen. Sulking."

That's not true. I hate to mislead Keresey, but we're not missing these shots. If it's not on video, it didn't happen. I figure Kevin will approve.

"Listen, now that we're alone," I say, changing the subject. "I didn't want to say anything in front of Lattimer, but we heard from Katie Harkins."

Keresey clicks the car into Park, and turns to me, her eyes wide with surprise. Or fear.

Or questions.

"I didn't say anything in front of Lattimer, because thinking back to that day on the bridge, I didn't remember whether you had told us he knew you were asking about her," I continue. "But I got a text message from her. Yesterday."

"We got a message from her, too," Keresey replies, her face grim. "Early Saturday, Lattimer said. What did yours say?"

"Just that she wanted to reschedule our meeting. So where is she? What's up with her? I thought she was the big insider? What did she say to you?"

"Off the record?"

Whatever. We'll figure the rules out later. Now I just want to know.

"Sure."

"She was apologizing. Said she got burned by a source. Katie Harkins is the one who tipped us to the L.A. warehouse, said we had to move in that day. But it was a bust. One of our agents was killed."

I know this. From Yens. Who told me he heard it from sources. This Katie Harkins thing is haunting me. She's the piece that doesn't fit.

"You ever think maybe she's in on it?" I say. "Like, she's leading you guys to the wrong places? On purpose?"

"Sorry. Classified," Keresey says.

A thought slams through my brain. Maybe Simone Marshal uses yet another name. I struggle to see whether that would make sense, but Keresey is talking. And I realize it's time for us to go.

Keresey slings her purse over her shoulder, and opens her car door. "Just to confirm we're on the same page. We'll go in separately. You find a spot to wait. Check the board, confirm the plane's arrival time. I'll get sweatshirts, hats, whatever else looks good. Meet me in the ladies' room, departure level by the Legal Sea Foods restaurant, fifteen minutes before the flight comes in. You got the Hartford bag?"

"And the beeper." I pat my belt. "Because we need that claim check number."

"Right." Keresey says. She opens the trunk for my tote bag. "Are you all set? Ready for this? It'll go down exactly as it should. Just follow my lead."

Of course the plane is late. Thunderstorms in Atlanta make a nine-o'clock arrival wishful thinking. The red lights across from the listing for Flight 1017 from Atlanta are flashing "delayed." Estimated time of arrival, 9:45 p.m. I have more than an hour to wait.

I know exactly how I need to spend it. First, calling Amy to feed Botox. Then, announcing my own delays and rearranging my own arrival time. Josh had texted me he had a Bexter Board of Directors meeting, was dropping Penny at Victoria's, and invited me to a late-night anniversary celebration. Now I know our celebration is going to have to be just a bit later. And I know I'm going to have to handle this just a bit delicately.

My cell phone is in my purse. In Keresey's trunk. Time to hit the pay phone.

"Hey, sweetheart," I say, as Josh answers. "Happy Anniversary, second notice. Guess where I am."

I quickly fill him in on the strategy. Lattimer, Franklin, Keresey. Ladies' room.

"This could be it," I say. "Exactly the proof we hoped for. The clincher."

I pause, hands clamped over my ears to keep out the airport noise, resting both elbows on the scuffed white plastic of the phone-booth counter. Waiting to hear my future.

Through a second of silence, I feel a hesitation. A tension.

Then I hear that Josh-chuckle. "Charlie Mac, I love you. All of you. And you know? That means I love how much you love your job. And that means I'll be here. Keeping the champagne cold."

"And yourself hot," I add. I'm attempting to sound seductive. Sexy and suggestive.

We both burst out laughing as soon as the words came out of my mouth.

"Love you," he says. "Stay safe. Come home soon."

"Love you, too," I whisper. I hang up the phone, holding the receiver just a second longer than necessary. Keeping our connection.

With luck, I'll be sipping champagne in just a few hours.

The plane is now scheduled to land at 10:50 p.m., one of the last commercial arrivals of the night. This should all be over by 11:10 p.m. As predicted, I got beeped, and what looks like a baggage claim number appeared. And now, finally, after reading the entire *Boston Globe* front to back, I'm heading for the Logan Airport ladies' room. On my way to become Elsa for the last time.

I glance up to the mezzanine where Lattimer probably has the entire baggage claim area under surveillance. I don't see him, but I guess I shouldn't expect to. I don't see Franklin, either. Also a good thing. He and our Sony HC-43 are going to meet me back at the station. He's getting the whole thing on tape. Two can play this game.

"Lattimer will kill us," Franklin had said as we headed back to our office after our meeting with the agents. "But who cares. He reneged, completely backpedaled on what clearly was an agreement to allow us to shoot video of the baggage-claim rendezvous. I vote we go for it."

"Shoot now, answer questions later," I'd agreed. "Who's he to tell us what to do?"

"Well, he's the FBI, I guess," Franklin said.

"Yeah, well, we pay his salary. Think you can hide? And still get the shots?"

"It's only a question of whether I'm a sky cap. Or passenger. Or perhaps I'll be a gray-haired minister in my Dad's old collar and jacket. Let me figure it out. I'll get the shots this time for sure," Franklin said, nodding confidently. "No more feet."

He's still not over the Strathmeyer Road fiasco. But what happens in about twenty minutes will be the best video we could hope for.

I yank open the ladies'-room door, smiling, expectations high. A frazzled-looking mom with a baby draped across her shoulder hurries an empty stroller past me out into the corridor. The door closes, muffling the late-night sounds of the airport clatter and cleaning crews.

Once inside, it's all hum and glare. Porcelain. Mirrors. White-and-gray tiled walls, white-and-gray tiled floors. The fluorescent ceiling lights turn every reflection haunted and harsh. A bedraggled-looking woman fusses with her hair, frowning. Another stands, impatiently rubbing her hands under a laboring automatic dryer. I see the towel holder is empty.

Following instructions, I go all the way to the back where a second row of sinks and mirrors lines the rear wall. This part of the bathroom is empty. Perfect.

I rip a section of coarse brown paper toweling from a wide roll someone deposited on the ledge of the sink, twist the faucet, and hold the towel under a stream of tepid water. The only temperature available. I attempt to wipe off my makeup, but the plain water doesn't make a dent. It doesn't matter. Streaky make-up is totally Elsa. We're not going for glamour.

I add her trademark blue eye shadow, her favorite pinky-pink lipstick, then look down at my watch. Keresey should be here. And when I look back into the mirror, there are two of us.

"Here's your sweatshirt and here's your hat," Keresey says. She, too, has blue eyelids and bubblegum-pink lips and a ponytail. She's wearing a gray Red Sox hoodie with "Ortiz" on the back and a navy blue baseball cap with the Sox "B" emblem on the front. Her purse — still, I assume, fully loaded — is slung across her chest, messenger style.

My hoodie is identical. My bag, although holding only makeup, looks identical. My hat is red.

"No more blue larges," Keresey explains.

I yank the sweatshirt over my head, redo my ponytail, then add the cap. We eye each other in the mirror. And both of us smile.

Then Keresey frowns.

She looks around the deserted bathroom, then points me to an open stall door. "Come with me," she says.

With a final check to confirm we don't have company, she draws me into the handicapped stall and latches the door behind us. She perches on the edge of the toilet seat, propping her running shoes on the wall.

"Only one pair of feet will show," she says, her voice low. "Stand by the sink. And listen. But don't answer. If anyone hears voices, they'll assume someone is on the phone."

I look at her, trying to gauge her expression. Something's up. "What?" I mouth the word.

"I know the SAC thinks it's better for you to pick up the bag," she says, her voice so soft I struggle to hear. "But I know he's wrong. I think it's too dangerous. I don't want you anywhere around that baggage claim. You'll go behind the last bank of chairs, right by those three potted palm containers. Lattimer knows that's my position. He won't be able to tell it's you. And I'll do the pickup."

I hold up a hand, stopping her. I unlatch the door, and look out. No one.

"The place is empty," I hiss. I close the door and turn on the water in the sink, full blast. "And no way, Keresey. I'm not afraid. Lattimer is watching. You'll be there. It's a public place. And, K, you'll get nailed. You can't unilaterally change your boss's plan. You can't put your career on the line."

Keresey shakes her head, undeterred. "This operation is snake bit. Raids fail. Our sources are wrong. What if it happens this time? I can't risk anything happening to you. And I still insist this could blow up because of a chain-of-custody violation. And that's unacceptable. Trust me on this, Charlie. I need to get that suitcase myself. Then we'll meet back here as we discussed, and secure the evidence. End of discussion."

"But Lattimer will —"

"I checked with Lattimer before I came here, when he gave me the radio. He's seen me in this blue cap. Give me your red one." She holds out her hand. "And the Hartford bag. And give me that beeper with the claim check number. Now."

The *Boston Globe* newspaper someone left on the chair beside me is now positioned in front of my face. The three potted plants are behind me. I'm sitting in a far corner of baggage claim. As instructed, I'm hiding. But I'm worried. I don't see Keresey yet. She may honestly be protecting me, I suppose. But picking up a suitcase at an airport baggage claim is about as safe as any activity could be. So why did she insist on doing it?

'I need to get that suitcase myself,' she'd said. Why? And why did she insist on taking the beeper? She knew the claim check number. Of course, the bad guys will expect me to have it and it might clinch Keresey's disguise.

What's haunting me is that the beeper is my only proof of the setup. We should have shot some videotape of it, but we just didn't think of it. I'd never have predicted someone would take it from me. Even someone I'm pretty sure is on my side. If something happens to the beeper — what, I don't know, but something — we could never prove any of this happened. I don't have the order form. I only have a business card Regine gave me at the Baltimore airport. That's about as weak as evidence gets.

"Passengers on Flight 1017," the static-slurred announcement blares over the public address system, cutting through the silence, "may claim their luggage at Area A."

I close my eyes briefly in silent entreaty. Keresey will get the suitcase. Lattimer will never know. Franklin will get the shots. We'll get our story.

Carefully, slowly, tentatively, I peer out from behind my newspaper. The baggage claim area is filling with slow-moving passengers, dragging carry-on bags, coats slung over their shoulders. I position the newspaper back in front of my face.

I bite my lip, calculating the dangers of revealing my whereabouts versus my unrelenting desire to catch the action as it unfolds. No one will notice me, I convince myself. I risk another look, moving my newspaper barrier, cautiously, to one side.

I don't see Keresey. There's an extra-large black wheelie, two huge cardboard boxes and three smaller battered-looking bags still available on the conveyor. My bet is on the big black one. And if I were doing this, I'd have already grabbed whichever suitcase has a claim check with the number that's on the beeper and headed for the hills.

Now the place is almost empty. *Where is she?*

A woman in a denim jacket claims two of the small black bags, wheeling them toward the exit. A Harvard sweatshirt takes another. The skycaps heft the cardboard boxes onto a waiting cart, and an elegantly suited businessman hands them some money and pushes the cart away. The skycaps head for the staff-only door, one punching buttons on the lock pad beside it. Only the black bag remains on the conveyor belt, gliding slowly along the wall toward the fluttering black rubber flaps that lead outside. And no one here to claim it.

Keresey will be here any second. She has to be. There's only one bag left.

And then, a tall man in a dark suit, raincoat over his arm, trots across the claim area, and grabs the bag. He hefts it off the belt and wheels it away. I almost leap from my chair. *That's ours!* I want to yell. Did he take our suitcase? Who is he? Does Keresey see him? Do I need to stop him?

Out from behind the rubber flaps that lead

outside, another suitcase is added to the line. A massively huge black one. Wheels. A Delleton-Marachelle luggage tag, just like mine, is looped through the handle. And taped beside it, the thin white sticker with the baggage claim number.

And suddenly, I'm looking at myself. Red baseball cap, hoodie, purse casually over one shoulder.

Keresey is alone, walking confidently toward baggage claim. In five seconds, she'll have the black bag. The last one to come off the plane.

I cover my face again, my heart racing, every muscle clenched, holding my newspaper so tightly the pages are crumpling in my fists. I don't dare put it down. I don't dare show my face. If Lattimer sees me, he has to think it's Keresey. Even Franklin may think I'm Keresey.

I can't look.

I have to look.

I peer around the corner of the paper. And Keresey is gone.

CHAPTER
TWENTY-TWO

Her purse is on the floor. The bag is still on the conveyor belt. The staff-only door is closed and the skycaps have disappeared.

"Keresey?" I say out loud. Where the hell is she? Why is her purse on the floor? I whirl, looking up to the mezzanine. Over to the exit. Beside the escalator. Where's Lattimer? Where's Franklin?

It's just me.

I race to the conveyor belt and grab Keresey's purse, slinging it over my shoulder. I'm panicked, my brain on fast forward, trying to understand what's happened. Nothing makes sense.

"Keresey?" I call out, louder. But I get no answer. And I realize something must be very, very wrong. Where did she go? And why?

The staff-only door. Where the two baggage guys went. I yank on the handle. It's locked. The only way out is —

I leap onto the conveyor belt, just before the spot where the rubber flaps still flutter, and take one wobbly step until I reach the opening. Grabbing the steel railing above it, I swing my legs through the flaps, and drop down to the other side.

This is where the bags come out. When I got the beeper in Hartford, this is where the mysterious voice came from. I blink, getting my bearings. There's no one here now.

Two huge — and empty — motorized luggage carts stand on the cement alley that's the baggage handler's roadway from the arriving airplanes to baggage claim. There are no walls out here, but a corrugated metal roof runs above me, down the length of the building. It's a checkerboard of lights — pin spots illuminating some of the path into pools of brightness, other parts left almost impenetrably dark.

What am I supposed to do now? My tote bag with my phone is in Keresey's trunk. I wasn't supposed to need it. I struggle to hold down my panic. Should I go back inside and find the police? Where the hell is Lattimer? Every moment that passes, Keresey may be deeper in danger.

I look to my right. Darkness. And a flat expanse that must lead to the tarmac and the runways beyond.

I look to my left. In a patch of light, I see
something red. A few quick steps and I'm
there. It's my Hartford bag. Keresey's gone
this way. Or more likely, been taken this
way. But why?

I have to find her. We traded places. This
is what she would have done for me.

I race down the path, running on tiptoe,
hugging the side of the building, my fingers
scraping along the bricks. At the end of the
covered alleyway is an expanse of asphalt
leading to buildings beyond. Two hundred
yards ahead, splotchy, eerie light glows from
an airplane hangar. Flickering green neon
letters spell out General Aviation.

Closer, I see something on the ground.
Straining all my senses, I hear nothing. I see
no one. I race toward a pool of shadow. It's
a red baseball cap. I look up. And silhou-
etted in the raw light showing through the
opening of the cavernous airplane hangar, I
see Keresey's unmistakable shape. She's not
alone. Two other shapes — who? — are
dragging her by the arms across the floor.

Keeping myself in the shadows, holding
my breath, I dash across the pavement
toward the hangar. It takes just seconds. I
flatten myself against a dark outside wall,
two stories, no, three stories high. I peer
around the corner into the building.

In the center of the hangar, under a huge bank of glaring megawatt spotlights, is a sleek white prop plane, a single-engine Cessna, nose pointed toward the tarmac.

And, crumpled on the cement floor, is Keresey. Limp and motionless. I clutch the door frame for support as my stomach lurches, throwing me off balance. Is she . . . dead? I watch, paralyzed. Mesmerized. I see her chest rise, then fall. She's breathing. Struggling for equilibrium, struggling for calm, I plaster myself against the outside wall again. Trying try to figure out what the hell to do.

I need one more look inside. I have to see what they're doing. And then I'll go for help.

The muscles in my neck and back tense as I lean forward, infinitesimally, toward the opening, barely daring to move.

Now, in the light, I can clearly see the two men. And I recognize them. The blue-uniformed skycaps from baggage claim. Muttering to each other, they're ignoring the still-motionless Keresey. Both are focused on the plane, its propeller motionless, its wheels still chocked with yellow blocks.

One of them, shorter, with buzz-cut hair and padded ear protectors around his neck, walks along the fuselage, then examines something under the right wing. The taller

347

one unlatches the cockpit door, grabs a strap, and pulls his rangy body up into the pilot's seat. I can see their shirts have embroidered patches on the arms — Local 376. Airline workers' union. James Webber's rank and file.

I not only recognize these guys, I recognize what they're doing. This is a preflight check. What if they're going to take Keresey away? What will happen when they find out she's not me?

If I leave to get help, they could be gone, airborne, before anyone can get here to stop them.

I lean back against my wall again, staring, unseeing, toward the terminal. I'm baffled. And enraged. And terrified. And bewildered. Lattimer must have seen this go down. Franklin, too. Where on earth are they? This is not how this was supposed to work. I'm alone. And faced with an impossible dilemma.

I can't go in. They'd overpower me, too.

I can't leave. They'll take Keresey away and disappear.

What's more — it was supposed to have been me picking up that bag. If Keresey hadn't insisted, it would have been me on the floor. It would have been me in mortal danger.

And suddenly, overwhelmingly, that makes me mad as hell. And I know how I can win. Keresey pretended to be me. So I'll pretend to be Keresey.

I have her gun. And her radio. And I know how to use them both. The realization hits me so hard my eyes sting with tears. Channeling my new alter ego, I know I have to become as steely and hard as any federal agent. Now. What would Keresey do?

I see both men are focused on the plane. Before I can stop myself, I press my back against the wall and ease around the corner. I'm inside the hangar, keeping myself hidden by the shadows. I wait, assessing. No one notices me.

I crouch down behind a baggage cart, one of a dozen — some full of suitcases, some empty — lined up in front of me along the wall. Slowly, one click at a time, I pull back the zipper on Keresey's purse, holding one hand over the opening to muffle the noise. It's so quiet I fear even the clicks of a plastic zipper coil might give me away. After an eternity, the bag is open. And there are my secret weapons. The radio. The gun. Feeling a rush of power and impending triumph, I settle in, making sure I'm concealed behind the hulking baggage cart. I don't have to make a move yet. And the longer I wait, the more likely Lattimer will finally arrive and end this whole disaster.

Tall Guy climbs out of the cockpit and walks to one of the baggage carts.

"Hey. Nolan," he calls to Short Guy. His voice echoes through the hangar, alien and hollow. "Let's get this done."

Nolan yanks a black suitcase from a cart on the other side of the hangar. It's huge, almost a trunk. "Jesus Christ, Eddie," he hisses. "Get over here. I need a hand with this sucker."

Together, the men drag the trunk across the floor, the scraping of metal on cement reverberating across the room. They reach Keresey. And stop. Nolan clicks two latches on the side. The top flips open and they both look inside. What's in there? Is that where they're going to put Keresey?

"Eddie, you done?" Nolan says. "She ready to go? He told us fifteen minutes."

"Roger that. Preflight checks out. Just need to confirm the fuel shutoff. Check the fuel mix. Start the engine." Eddie points to the Cessna, and both men head in that direction. "Unchock the wheels, yo. Let's do this. Then we're good to go as soon as it's time."

It's clear whatever I'm going to do has got to be done soon. Gun first? Or radio?

I glance into my purse. And instantly my plan disintegrates. Even in the gloom and shadows, I can see my secret weapons are duds. I've got a radio, all right. But it's a dead chunk of metal and plastic. No lights flash, no speaker buzzes. It's been turned off.

And I have a gun. That's good. But it's not loaded. That's bad. The magazine lies in the bottom of the bag, taunting me.

If I turn on the radio, the static and squawk will instantly telegraph where I am. If I slam the magazine into the Smith & Wesson, the sound will be a dead giveaway. I'm trapped by the silence. Where the hell is Lattimer?

And then I see Keresey move.

She stretches one leg, slowly. She shifts one arm from across her face. I can see her eyes. They're open. And blinking.

Eddie's in the cockpit, in the pilot's seat. Nolan's by the open passenger door, back to me, looking into the plane. No one is paying attention to Keresey but me. She's up on one elbow. And she must comprehend what's happened. And maybe what's about to happen.

There's a whine and a rattle, then the propeller begins to whirl into motion. And that's all the noise I need.

I slam the magazine into place. Ratchet ammo into the chamber, just like Keresey taught me. The clatter of the propeller fills the room, racketing against the metal walls and rattling the metal girders across the ceiling. I spring from behind the luggage cart and roar into the dim light, my adrenaline powering into the red zone. I'm almost screaming.

"Federal agent!" I yell. Both hands are wrapped around the weapon, just as Keresey taught me. The forefinger of my right hand flat against the barrel. My feet wide apart, braced, the gun aimed straight at Tall Guy. I hope. "Freeze! Freeze! Freeze! You're done! You're done!"

Nolan turns away from the plane, mouth open, his face twisted in surprise, then rage. He slams the cockpit door closed.

Short Guy cuts the engine, the propellers slacken, then stop. In a split second, Nolan's reaching behind his back. He takes a step away from the plane, then two.

"Charlie! Shoot! Now! Aim for body mass, like I taught you!" Keresey's yelling as she tucks her elbows and rolls toward me. She scrabbles to her feet, still yelling. "Now, now, now!"

"FBI! Freeze! And both of you — back off!" Marren Lattimer's voice bellows through the hangar. "Do it!"

Holding the biggest and loveliest gun I've ever seen, Lattimer strides across the floor, leather jacket, running shoes, badge around his neck, brandishing his weapon at Nolan. "I said do it! Back off. Do it! Show me your hands, asshole. Then put both hands on the plane."

Nolan retreats, hesitating, wary, walking backward, hands outstretched. They're empty.

I'm in love with Marren Lattimer.

Lattimer gestures with his weapon, hurrying him. Nolan turns, slowly, keeping his eyes focused on Lattimer. Finally he puts his hands, palms flat, on the fuselage. Eddie, still in the cockpit, is twisted in his seat, watching out the window.

Did I say I'm in love with Marren Lattimer? I can't believe he's here. My hands are shaking, still clenched on Keresey's gun. My eyes swim with tears. I don't have to shoot someone. I wasn't sure I could and I'm tremblingly grateful I don't have to find out. I'm only a reporter. I think for a living. And I think I want to get the hell out of here.

Keresey puts her arm across my shoulders, backing me away, as I lower the gun. "It's over now, Charlie," she murmurs. "You did great, sister. But why didn't you radio for help?"

"Your radio was off. The gun wasn't loaded. Are you okay?" I ask, my voice low. My heart is still racing. Every nerve is on fire. I know she's right, it's over, we're safe, the cavalry has arrived, but tell that to my wobbling knees.

"I'm good." She gives a weak smile and steadies herself on the pole of the wheeled metal luggage cart beside us. Sinking to the floor of the cart, she sits, stretching her neck and shoulders, one arm still wrapped around the pole. "Really. I'm good."

Lattimer is approaching, his gun still aimed at Nolan. Lattimer's smiling, but I figure Keresey's in deep trouble. If I had done the pickup, as Lattimer ordered, she could have moved right in to nail these slimes. She'd have loaded her gun. And turned the radio on.

"I'll take that now, Charlie," Lattimer says. His voice is reassuring, even friendly, as he holds out a hand for the gun. He glances at Keresey, then back at me. His eyes narrow. "We don't want civilians doing our job."

"Right," I say, with as much smile as I can muster. I still have both hands on the gun. And I'm thinking — it's Keresey's. Why isn't she getting it back? Maybe this proves she's in trouble. Maybe I can still protect her. "But Keresey was only trying to —"

"Now," Lattimer says. He cocks his head at the Cessna. "This is not the time."

True. I glance up at the plane. Short guy still plastered to the fuselage. Tall guy in the cockpit, watching through the tiny side window. I guess you don't try anything when the feds have got you cornered with major artillery.

I feel Keresey move behind me, then she steps between me and Lattimer. "I'll take my own weapon back, Lattimer," she says. Her voice is ice. Demanding. She reaches her hand behind her, waggling her fingers. "Let's have it, Charlie. My purse with the radio, too."

"Don't do it, Charlie," Lattimer says. "Give me that gun. Now. 'No' is not an option."

"Wha— ?" I look at Lattimer, then Keresey, then Lattimer. I take a step away from Keresey. My fingers curl around the gun again. Aren't we all on the same team?

"Charlie. Give. Me. My. Weapon," Keresey demands. "Listen. Lattimer's in on this. Why do you think he's more worried about that gun than about the assholes with the plane? They're his assholes. That plane is full of bags. I watched them load it. Give me the gun."

"Bullshit, Stone. This is Keresey's show, Charlie. She's in on this. She set you up. She tried to keep you away from the pickup. That was all to lure you out here. She's clearly not hurt. Her gun wasn't even loaded. Her radio wasn't on. Wonder why? Helping you was the last thing she cared about. You were going into that trunk. Give me that gun. I'll take her — and her moron crew — into federal custody."

One of these two is a fraud. One of these two is a counterfeit cop. One of them set me up. The other can save me.

"Bullshit, Lattimer," Keresey sneers back at him. "You turned off the radio and unloaded the gun before you gave them to me. Why do you think he wanted you to do the pickup, Charlie? He wanted you dead. And that's exactly what was going to happen. If you give him that gun now, we're both done. He'll kill us. Leave us here. Like the people he's already had killed. We'd be victims in another failed raid."

She holds out her hand, imploring. "The gun, Charlie. Let me use it. And this whole charade will be over."

How do I tell who's the real thing? How do I recognize the fake? The gun in my hand is the balance of power.

If I'm wrong, I'm probably dead.

Keresey edges closer to me. Almost pushing me away from Lattimer. "How did you know we were here, Lattimer? In this hangar? Did you get a call from your pal Katie Harkins?" Her voice is sarcastic, sinister, mocking. "Charlie, ever ask yourself why no one has ever seen that woman? No one but Lattimer here. That's because she doesn't exist. Lattimer made her up."

"Listen, hotshot," Lattimer says. "If you and your hotshot buddies —"

With a flash of memory and a stomach-lurching realization, my brain shifts into overdrive. How would he know the radio was off? The gun was unloaded? And in an instant, I realize that anonymous phone call, threatening me, was from Lattimer. That voice called me "hotshot," talked about my "hotshot buddy." The clicks were his infantile Rubik's Cube.

My turn to fake.

Smiling, I look down at the weapon as if my decision has been made. "I guess I understand what you're saying now, Lattimer."

His shoulders relax. He glances at the plane.

I hand the gun to Keresey.

And I dive for the floor. With a blaze of light and a blast that ricochets through the shadowy recesses of the hangar, Keresey fires once, twice, and Lattimer slams to the ground. His gun is still in his hand. He's silent. Motionless. He's dead. Or he's pretending.

Lifting my head, I watch Keresey walk toward him. She's taking one cautious step at a time. Her arms are still outstretched, the gun braced in front of her. Pointed at her boss.

Suddenly, the whine of the plane's engine starts again. Nolan grabs the door handle and swings himself into the cockpit. The noise of the prop muffles whatever he's screaming at the pilot and the wheels of the Cessna slowly begin to move.

"Keresey!" I yell, scrambling to my feet. "They're going!

"I hear it! Get that radio!" Keresey commands. Her voice is strident. She's still heading, cautiously, toward Lattimer. He hasn't moved. But I know that means nothing. He could be faking.

The clatter of the prop revs louder and louder, the whine of the engine speeds to a roar. Keresey's voice rises, powering over the increasingly ear-splitting clamor. "Call in a mayday! Red button! Whatever freq's open! We can't let them get off the ground. Tell them it's a code double alpha. Double Alpha. Got that?"

The plane's wheels continue rolling, slowly, deliberately, across the hangar floor, the nose of the plane headed into the vast darkness of the tarmac. The noise is now deafening, the metal walls reverberating. I can see the two blue uniforms in the cockpit, headphones on, adjusting control switches above the windshield.

"Got that!" I flip a silver toggle to ON, and the slim black radio crackles to life with a burst of static and a high-pitched beep, green lights flashing. "Mayday. Mayday!" I push the red button, trying to keep my voice calm. Hoping they can hear me over the engine noise. Hoping I'm actually getting through to someone. "This is a code Double Alpha. General Aviation Hangar!"

There's a crackle as I release the button, and then more static. The plane is halfway to the door.

"Roger that." A voice comes back. Calm. "We copy your Mayday. Please specify which Gen Av hangar. Over."

Dammit. Dammit. I have no idea which hangar. And the plane is still moving. It's almost too loud to think. All I know is . . . "Behind Baggage Claim A!" I yell into the radio. "A white Cessna. Headed for takeoff! Code Double Alpha!" Which I hope means — stop the darn plane, there are bad guys on it.

"Lattimer's clear," Keresey yells. He's still on the ground, facedown on the cement, arms behind his back. Keresey's clicking him into handcuffs — his own? She's tucked his weapon into the back of her Levi's.

"Over here," I call back to her. "Help me with this!"

I race behind one of the wheeled baggage carts, trying to whirl it around. It's enormous, and cumbersome, thick-gauged chains along each side clanking in protest as I maneuver it across the floor and aim it at the Cessna. One hand on each side of the cart, shoulder high, I try to push the ungainly metal carrier — like a grocery cart on growth hormones — pressing forward, straining, one step at a time. I'm too slow. The cart is too big. I can't possibly get there in time.

"Keresey!" I call again. "Hurry! This needs both of us!"

Keresey falls in beside me, still holding her gun. She takes the left side, and I take the right. "Now!" I yell. This is our last chance. Whoever I just radioed to help us may not be able to find us in time. The plane will take off. The guys will get away. With the evidence.

"Push it, push it, push it," I scream. "Into the propeller! This will work! Do it!"

We move forward together, shoulders bent and legs extended, trying to aim our ungainly weapon where it'll do the most good. Suddenly, we feel the wheels align. The cart picks up speed, seeming to acquire a momentum and will of its own.

"Don't get too close to the prop!" Keresey screams as we power the cart, faster, toward the moving Cessna. "We have to let it go!"

"On my count!" I yell. Slamming every muscle in my body against the cart, I know this is our final play. I hate airplanes. "Three two one — go!"

Both of us are yelling, something, anything, as together we heave the cart directly into the path of the propeller, both of us stumbling backward as we let go. Keresey trips, and I grab her, catching her, and then, in an instant, we see it's going to work. Perfectly. The cart is headed straight for its spinning target. We're both breathing hard, panting, gasping. And then we realize what's going to happen next.

"Take cover!" Keresey yells. "Now, now, now!" She grabs my arm, dragging me along with her. We run, together, and dive behind another massive baggage cart. My elbow clangs on one of the metal rails and I feel one knee of my jeans rip on the rough cement floor. "Cover your head!" she commands. "Stay low! If it's a direct hit —"

Whatever she says next is lost in a shriek of splintering metal, a scream of mechanical rage. I lift my head, just enough to peer over the thick wood-and-metal baggage cart we're using as a shield. The spinning propeller chokes and staggers, twisted into an angry tangle by the lumbering metal missile we launched. The crippled Cessna lurches forward, one wing tipping, scraping along the floor with an ear-shattering metallic screech, red-orange and white-hot sparks spitting ceiling high. The baggage cart is thrown into the air, its chains caught on the prop blades, then it crashes to the ground, wood splitting, chains popping, shards of rubble and wreckage jettisoned across the hangar.

And then in seconds, although it doesn't seem possible, it's even noisier. The screaming wail of sirens, one, then another, then another, signals — finally — Keresey and I are no longer in this alone.

I would have thought nothing could ever

surprise me again. But sitting in the squad room of the State Police airport headquarters, an institutionally neutral-on-neutral array of battered office furniture and paper-piled metal desks tucked into the rear of Logan Airport terminal C, I can't take my eyes off FBI Special Agent Keresey Stone. And I'm surprised.

It's not only because she slammed her own boss into his handcuffs and supervised the grim-faced posse of feds who took him away. It's not only because, as she's just explained to an equally grim-faced U.S. Attorney, she got a buddy in the Bureau's "facial rec" section to do an Internet photo scan and found the photos of the purported Katie Harkins on a Web site of some small-town photographer. That's when she realized Lattimer had created an imaginary informant — a fictional nonperson he was using to sidetrack law enforcement focus and set FBI raids up for certain defeat.

It's also because I can't see her face, which is buried in Detective Christopher Yens's uniformed chest. And her still-hoodied body is being cradled in his arms. And it does not look like interagency cooperation. It looks like love. Well, lust.

"Sweetheart, you're sure you're okay?" Yens asks. He smooths Keresey's hair, more tenderly than I could have predicted, lifting one strand away from her forehead, then carefully putting it into place.

Whatever Yens was saying is lost in a kiss so passionate I only allow myself to watch the beginning. The big finish, which doesn't appear to be imminent, I'll let them handle on their own. And I'll grill Miss Keresey about this later. Married to Uncle Sam indeed.

Since the police operator has finally connected my phone call, I turn away from this law-enforcement love affair and focus on Franklin. Who apparently hit the video jackpot.

"So, Franko, you got it? All of it?" I ask, rolling a rickety chair up to a paper-littered desk. "You're the best. What's the video look like? How'd you know to —"

"Hello, to you, too, Charlotte," Franklin says. "You're on speaker phone here. I'm in the newsroom. With Kevin. With Susannah. Toni DuShane just left. And she says, legally, we're fine."

"Good to go," Kevin's voice interrupts. "Public place. Hidden camera, video only. And wait until you see the —"

"I totally got it all," Franklin puts in. "First you, I mean Keresey, going for the suitcase. Then the two union goons dragging her through the door. That took about one second. Clearly they'd held the suitcase back, kept it for last, had this all arranged. And then Keresey, I mean you, making that Batgirl move through the conveyor belt entrance. Of course I thought it was Keresey going after you. So I figured you were fine. And she'd call for help."

"But where were you?" I ask. "I looked for you."

"Pink shirt, tan cap. Positioned just close enough to the Dunkin' Donuts kiosk to look like an employee. It was closed, of course, but a guy who looks like a minimum wager standing next to a coffee shop? Invisible."

Keresey and Yens have untangled themselves from each other, although they're still holding hands, and are listening to me. She points to an orange button on the phone.

"Good one," I say to Franklin, giving Keresey a thumbs-up. I hit the button and the squad room is filled with the buzz of the newsroom. "But how about Lattimer?"

"Well, that's when I knew things were not, shall we say, what they seemed?" Franklin replies through the speaker. "He ran to the luggage claim, grabbed the suitcase, then bolted. But not in your direction. I followed him of course, out the door. He threw the bag onto a curbside check-in rack, then took off. And I lost him. And that's when I called the cops."

"And I guess we found him," Keresey says, leaning toward the phone. "He knew exactly what was supposed to go down."

"And we found the bag," Yens puts in. "Full of phony Delleton-Marachelles. Now sealed tight in the evidence room. And a whole battalion of state cops are on their way to 325 Strathmeyer Road."

"Yoo hoo," Susannah's voice trills through the speaker. "Let's schedule an airtime for this, shall we? I'm off to California for a meeting. But 'It's In The Bag' — seems to be in the bag."

CHAPTER
TWENTY-THREE

"Happy Anniversary, Brenda Starr." Josh yanks the sheet back up over his knees. And mine. I'm not sure we'll ever find all the clothing that's strewn across the floor, fallen behind the mattress, pushed down between the sheet and the puffy chocolate-and-caramel striped comforter of Josh's classically sleek cherrywood bed. Propped up on pillows against the slatted headboard, we're the definition of disheveled. It's almost four in the morning. We're wide-awake.

Glass clinks on metal as the ice cubes settle in the silver champagne bucket on the nightstand. I settle in myself, burrowing into my pillow and curving into Josh's shoulder, remembering. Savoring. Wanting.

"Would you like a little more?" Josh asks. I can feel him adjust his body, turning ever so slightly, his skin sliding against mine.

"Oh, I couldn't possibly . . ." I begin. And then I hear the slosh as Josh pulls the dark green bottle of Moët White Label from its icy cooler. Ah. He meant more champagne. "Well, if you insist."

Josh turns toward me, legs outstretched, propping himself on one elbow. He holds his glass for a toast. "To you, my sweetheart. And to your big story. And to the perhaps the wildest evening of your life."

I'm blushing.

"Charlie McNally. I meant at the airport," Josh says, clinking my glass. "But I still can't get my brain around this. You're telling me Lattimer was behind it? And Katie Harkins doesn't exist?"

"Yup. Nope," I say, closing my eyes to savor the crisp chill of the champagne. But Josh is right. Wild. I turn to face him, mirroring his propped-on-elbow position. "Keresey was suspicious, she said, since usually CIs whose tips don't pan out are dumped. And apparently the State Police counterfeit squad was also getting bogus info from 'Katie.' That's how Keresey met Yens. And remind me to tell you the scoop about that."

I take another bubbly sip. "Anyway, when Keresey asked Yens about her, turns out, he'd been suspicious, too. He'd never seen her. Neither had she. So they wanted to know if Franko and I had, and, of course, we hadn't. When Ker pushed Lattimer for more info, that's when he gave her those photos. Supposed to be proof she existed. Ker gave copies to Yens. They each checked with me and Franko. The 'missing persons' thing was just their cover story. To pump us for what we knew.

"But here's what clinched it — Keresey's agent pal found the photos on the Web. The woman was some photographer's model. Public domain. 'Katie Harkins' is the handiwork of Lattimer's imagination. A fake."

Josh drains his glass, then sits up, cross-legged, and pours us each some more. His hair is a salt-and-pepper haystack. His chest is still tanned from his Cape Cod summer. I curl one hand around his ankle. I can't resist touching him.

"So if Harkins was . . ." he pauses, tilting his glass, thinking. "And the information was phony . . . that means . . . Lattimer had his own agent killed? Hurt?"

"Yes, or had his confederates do the job," I say. "It was all a . . . a diversion. He did everything by e-mail and voice mail. He just made up all the information. Then he'd redirect all the bureau's attention into the phony raids. And meanwhile, the real counterfeiters would be shipping and distributing. And out of the line of fire. I just hope they can prove it."

"Twisted," Josh says. He puts his glass back on the nightstand.

"Lucrative," I answer. "Very, very lucrative. We're talking multi, multi, millions."

Josh leans toward me, one lock of hair falling across his forehead. He takes my glass, deliberately, and puts it aside. There's a look in his eyes, strong. Soft. Only he smells like this. Only he tastes like this.

And the phone rings. "Let the voice mail get it," he says, leaning closer. I can feel his warmth. Or maybe it's my own.

The phone rings again. "Forget it," Josh whispers. "I'm making other plans."

Then Penny's little voice warbles from the answering machine. "Daddy-o?" she says. "I woke up because I had a bad dream, and Mom said I could —"

With an apologetic sag of his shoulders, Josh picks up the phone. I tuck myself beside him. I can wait. I listen to Josh's comforting words, something about Dickens her stuffed dog, and *Harriet the Spy,* and Halloween candy. I'm floating, almost sleeping, when I hear him hang up.

And then he starts dialing.

"What, honey?" I say. I don't even open my eyes. "Who are you calling?"

"I'm just erasing that whole conversation,"

he says. "You know. I picked up while she was leaving a message, so the whole thing is there. Saved. All recorded."

Something shifts in the back of my mind. Now my eyes are open. Wide-open. I sit up, staring at the wall, my hands laced across the top of my head.

"Charlie?"

I turn to Josh. "Hand me the phone, okay?"

Josh looks baffled.

But I know I've just clinched the case against Lattimer. And I have to call Keresey. "That anonymous phone call? The one I'm convinced was from Lattimer? It's still on my phone. It happened just like you and Penny. I answered during the message. But I never erased it. And that means it was saved. And that means it's all still there. And that means Lattimer's going down."

Josh reaches toward the phone. And then hits the light switch, dissolving the room into darkness.

"Tomorrow," he says.

And lusciously, gradually, in the soft expanse of Josh's bed I realize he's right. Tomorrow will be fine. Because right now I'm not Elsa. I'm not Keresey. Luckily, happily, deliriously I'm Charlie McNally. And I think I'm beginning to recognize the real thing.

"Hurry!"

"I'm hurrying," I yell back at Franklin. "You don't have to tell me to hurry."

We're clattering down the two flights of stairs from our office into the newsroom.

"The video's supposed to feed by microwave from FBI headquarters," Franklin says. "The receive techs are ready to roll on it. It should be coming in any second now."

"Should be?" I can hear my voice, taut and nervous.

I'm sleep-deprived, wearing jeans and a backup black wool jacket I grabbed from my news-emergency stash. My hair is a *Glamour* "don't." But we've got breaking news and it can't wait. It's 10:54 a.m. There's a local news break scheduled for 10:58 a.m. Plenty of time to get it on the air. If we hurry.

I grab the banister, swinging myself down to the next flight. Franklin's right behind me.

"Producer's Jessica!" I point to the punked-out blonde at the on-call producer's desk. "Franko, tell her the scoop. I don't need prompter. I'll wing it. I need a minute-thirty. Two minutes, tops. I'm heading for the anchor desk. And make sure that video is rolling."

"We have bars and tone from the fibbies HQ," a voice calls from the glass-walled video-receive room. "Exterior FBI. No heads."

I careen into the anchor desk chair, click on my microphone and plug in my earpiece. If we only have video of the FBI headquarters and no people, that'll still work. The clock says 10:57 a.m.

"One minute to air, Charlie." I hear Jessica, now in the control room, through my earpiece. "Franklin's in here with me. We'll roll the video live. Just narrate what you see. Great job, kiddo."

The in-house monitor flashes from black into the familiar gray stone edifice of the FBI headquarters. The massive metal front doors, embossed with menacingly clawed bald eagles, remain closed. I organize my thoughts, knowing I have only two minutes to tell this whole story.

"Fifteen seconds," Jessica says.

My fifteen-seconds-to-air routine never changes. I slide my tongue across my front teeth, removing any stray red smudges. I give my hair one last — and today, futile — fluff into place. I pat my lapel to reassure myself the tiny microphone is where it should be. "I'm a pro," I chant silently. My pre-air mantra. "Bring it on."

In my ear, I hear the brass and synthesizer anthem that means breaking news. In my on-air monitor, blue and silver graphics tilt and whirl, commanding viewers' attention. Jessica's voice buzzes her final instructions.

"Two. One. And go."

"This is Charlie McNally in the Channel 3 newsroom with breaking news. On your screen now, live pictures of the headquarters of the Federal Bureau of Investigation. Only on Channel 3, this exclusive story. We have learned federal officials say they have solved the murder of Sarah Garcinkevich, age 44, of Great Barrington, whose body was found in the Housatonic River last week.

"In developments that are sending shock waves through government agencies, as well as the world of high fashion:

"Now in custody for murder and international counterfeiting and potentially a host of other charges is airline union boss James Webber.

"The identity of his co-conspirator creates another scandal in FBI history — we have learned it is Boston's FBI Special Agent in Charge Marren Lattimer. He is also now in federal custody, and sources say each suspect is in negotiations to turn state's evidence against the other.

"Law enforcement officials are still keeping details confidential. But I can tell you the evidence against Lattimer includes an answering machine recording of the now-disgraced special agent making a sinister and threatening phone call.

"What's more, we have learned federal agents have descended on Logan Airport, as well as several other airports across the country. Baggage claim areas are in lockdown, and several baggage agents, members of the airline union, are being taken into custody.

"Bottom line, what some call the 'victimless crime' of counterfeit designer purses has turned deadly. Channel 3 news and government officials have cracked an ugly conspiracy of murder, money and make-believe couture.

"We'll have much more on this megabucks international counterfeiting conspiracy in my exclusive report . . ." I pause, just a fraction of a second. And the perfect title comes to mind. " 'The Real Thing,' next week at 11:00 p.m. on Channel 3 news. I'm Charlie McNally reporting."

I hear the news theme in the background. I'm done.

So much for Susannah's hypercute "It's in the Bag" brand. She's out of town and word is she's on a job interview. We've got a big story, a new title, and one week to get it on the air. Cake. I unclick my microphone, and think about a nap.

Jessica's voice buzzes through my earpiece.

"Great job, C. You rock," Jessica says. "Who's the guy in Kevin's office, by the way? He's hot."

I twist in my chair, looking past the reporters' desks, then the producers' desks, and past the expanse of the assignment desk. I can only see a corner of Kevin's office, but the door is open. And in the visitor's chair is a lanky figure. All attitude. Elegance. I don't even need to see his face.

"He's French," I say into my microphone.

Close up, Luca Chartiers looks more sleep-deprived than I do. He must have taken the first plane out of Atlanta, and his pale gray pinstriped suit and starched white shirt seem to be all that's holding him up. He stands and takes my hand briefly, solemnly, seeming to tread cautiously through unfamiliar territory.

"I'm not sure the company will survive this," he says. "But had it continued, we would certainly have perished. Zuzu and I will do our best. But I wanted to come

thank you in person. Without you, we . . ."
He shakes his head slowly and drops back
into his chair.

"Survive?" This is the rest of the puzzle,
that's for sure. And I'm betting it's centered
on Strathmeyer Road. Why else could he be
here?

"Was Simone Marshal really Simone Marachelle? And Reggie Webber her daughter?
And why were they — ?"

Kevin interrupts, holding up a video cassette. "FBI just sent us this statement," he
says. "Mr. Chartiers here has seen it. Sylvie
Marachelle is in custody in Atlanta. Simone
Marachelle and Regine are in lockup here
in Boston."

Kevin pauses, then slides the cassette into
his playback machine and pushes the green
button. "Well, it's best if you hear it for
yourself. Listen."

I hear the tape click into place and the
whir as the video begins to roll. Luca
Chartiers studies the floor, his hands, the
ceiling, his eyes anywhere but on the flickering television monitor.

At the sound of Simone Marshal — Marachelle's — voice, we turn to the screen.

"You bastards have no right," she says,
her voice rising. "I have done nothing
wrong. The designs are mine. Mine! My

377

sister and I are the victims. The victims!"

It's the woman from the cab, no doubt about that. She's all points, narrowed eyes, hollow cheeks, hair gelled and slick to her head. She's wearing some sort of close-fitting black sweater, and still manages to look chic, even in custody. Her tone is bitter, menacing, and she's spitting each word at the camera, and at whoever is doing the questioning.

Keresey's voice is next. "Simone Marachelle Marshal Webber," she pronounces. She's all business, sounding formal and detached. "You are under arrest for the theft of proprietary designs from the firm Delleton-Marachelle. You are additionally charged with organizing the illegal manufacture of —"

"It is not 'theft,' " Simone tosses her head, defiant. Her voice goes shrill and insistent. "They are our designs, Sylvie's and mine. How can we steal our own designs? Why should we allow that . . . that . . ."

She leans forward into the camera, so close her face goes suddenly out of focus. The camera adjusts, clicking her into a clear close-up.

"That company is the criminal, not I. Not my sister. Not my daughter. We were only taking what is rightfully ours. We are not —

indentured servants to that, that, manufacturer of potato chips. The Marachelles —"

"Sylvie. Stop. That's enough." A cuff-link-sleeved hand appears from offscreen, and goes to Sylvie's shoulder. A male voice continues from offscreen. "That's all my client has to say, Agent Stone. We're done here."

The screen frizzes into buzzing black-and-white snow. Kevin pushes eject. The truth is recorded and inescapable.

Luca's face is spiritless, flat. He's still staring at the now-blank monitor. I remember his across-the-dinner-table cosmopolitan twinkle at La Caleche, the pride flashing in his eyes as he discussed his designs. Now he's drained and disillusioned as a soldier in defeat. Sabotaged by his own colleagues. And his ex-wife.

"So they were just pretending to be estranged?" I ask. I think I understand the rest of the story. "Sylvie and Simone were actually conspiring to —"

"They believed their legacy had been stolen," Luca says, interrupting my theory. "That it was their duty to take it back. And take the profits for themselves. The sisters knew where to get the bags manufactured, of course. So they invented a quarrel. Sylvie left and changed her name. It was all part of the ruse. The groundwork for the scheme. When Simone married Webber, they had a ready-made pipeline."

Luca sighs.

"And Regine." His voice is quiet. "She is Simone's daughter. The father — I do not know. Quite the family affair."

"Quite the setup," Kevin puts in. "Access, production, and distribution."

"And profits," Franklin says. He's standing in the open doorway, holding a legal-sized sheet of paper. "I just talked to Christopher Yens. Here's the return on the search warrant, fully executed last night in Brookline. His guys found thousands of fake bags hidden in the house on Strathmeyer Road. Ready for parties. Ready for the street. Ready to rake in the big bucks."

"The counterfeits came from insiders at the authentic purse company itself," I say slowly. "Some of the very people who pretended to be victims. Wow. That's major league."

"Sylvie and Simone were getting the profits from both ends," Luca confirms. "From all of us at D-M, and then from their own scheme."

I look at Luca, then Kevin. Remembering why we started this in the first place. Our story. "You'll agree to be interviewed for our story, won't you?" I ask. "On camera? Before you leave today?"

Luca nods. "I am here until this evening."

I plop onto Kevin's couch, scouting his desk for a notebook or something to write on. I grab a pad of yellow stickies and take the sleek fountain pen from the marble holder, looking at the news director for permission. "Let's make a list of what we still need. First, this only solves the origin of the Delleton-Marachelle copies. So there's much more out there. But "The Real Thing" — can just be the D-M story."

I bite my lower lip, thinking. There's something else. "How did Lattimer get involved, anyway?"

"Keresey told me that," Franklin says. "Apparently he confessed that Sylvie seduced him, back when he was assigned to the Atlanta bureau. He was sick of government paychecks and she promised him a gold mine. He's trying to make it all her idea, of course. But that's why Zuzu acted so hinky when we mentioned Katie Harkins. She'd never heard of her."

The bleat of the intercom on Kevin's desk interrupts. "Mr. O'Bannon? Mr. Char . . ." the tentative voice pauses. "The cab is here."

Luca gathers his briefcase and shakes hands with Franklin, then me. "I'll be at the

Copley Plaza Hotel. One journey ends, another begins," he says with an uncertain smile. "I must try to remember that."

We watch Luca and Kevin cross the newsroom, heading for the front door.

"I'll get a photographer," Franklin says, turning toward the assignment desk. "See how fast we can get to the Copley. Maybe we can get Keresey on cam today, too."

"Franko." I stand, stopping him.

"What? I've got to —"

The rest of his question is muffled by my quick hug.

"Thank you, Franko. You did great. As Mom always says, be careful what you wish for. We wanted a biggie. And we sure got it. And I almost got it in the head."

"The world of make-believe fashion is not a pretty place," Franklin agrees. "The bags were phony, but the danger was certainly real."

"Lattimer tried to tell us it was terrorists," I say, remembering that day in Lattimer's office. "And I guess he was right. They took the law into their own hands. They stole millions of dollars from legitimate businesses. They killed whoever was in their way. Sounds like terrorists to me."

Of course the doorbell rings, right during

the good part. Right in the midst of the eleven-o'clock news. Right at the part of our story where Franklin's undercover video shows me vaulting through the luggage claim, then reveals a furtive Marren Lattimer snaking the black suitcase from the conveyor belt.

I snuggle in closer to Josh, my legs on top of his, our wool-socked feet entwined on the leather ottoman in front of us.

"I'm not budging from this couch," I say, hitting the pause button on my TiVo remote. I punch another button. "And now, I'm rewinding. That's the glory of digital recording. You can watch our perfectly perfect story again, uninterrupted, from the beginning."

The doorbell rings again. Botox leaps from my lap and scampers off to hide in one of her secret cat hangouts.

Josh takes the remote from me with a laugh, and points to the door. "See who it is," he says. "It might be, just a wild guess, here. Maybe the pizza we ordered from Late Night Sam's? Or I suppose it could be the Attorney General with some sort of medal of honor. A reward for your first-night-of-the-November-book scoop. Either way, a good thing."

"Oh, yeah, the pizza," I say, disentangling

myself, briefly, from Josh's arms. "Of course."

I pad to the doorway and click the speaker button on the intercom.

"Yes?" I say. Pepperoni, mushrooms and extra mozzarella. Just what I need.

"Velocity Delivery Service," a voice says. "You lost a suitcase? The airlines found it. We have it here for you. We just need a signature."

EPILOGUE

"Please make sure your seat backs and tray-tables are in the full upright position, and . . ."

Josh unlaces his fingers from mine and unclasps his seat belt. Flipping up the two armrests between us for takeoff, he shifts from his aisle seat into the middle seat next to me, and clicks on his seat belt again.

"You okay, sweetheart?" he asks. He threads his arm through mine, taking my hand again. He leans close to my ear. "This will all be worth it, I promise. You're a good sport, sitting at another gate, keeping your eyes closed when we boarded. I told the agent it was a surprise."

"You sure we can't just drive, wherever it is you're taking me?" I reply. I'm only half joking. When Josh showed off our plane tickets, I couldn't decide whether to be thrilled or terrified. "Mystery destination" he'd said. All he'd tell me was I needed a bathing suit, flip-flops and sunscreen. And since it's almost December, I guess driving is out of the question.

I cinch my seat belt tighter. And pretend. "I'm dandy, really," I say. I can feel my smile is forced. "I'm just swell."

The flight attendant walks toward us, counting whatever it is they count, and touching each of the overhead compartments. She smiles down at us. "The weather in Miami is beautiful," she says as she passes.

I look at Josh. Miami? Maybe the flight attendant just let the cat out of the bag. Curiosity trumps fear, if only briefly.

He raises a palm, twinkling at me. "Not a chance. Connecting flight. And I told the crew about my little surprise."

"I tried to get Penny to spill it," I admit, checking my seat belt again. Maybe if we talk about something else, I'll be distracted. "You know how secrets drive me crazy. But she insisted she didn't know."

"She doesn't," Josh says. "She's expecting a postcard from us."

So much for that idea. I'm not distracted. I'm freaking. Even my darling Josh can't make my fear disappear. Even a secret romantic trip to a sunny destination won't work.

I still hate flying. I lean my forehead against the plastic window, looking out as the last of the bags are loaded onto the 757. At least there's my suitcase, the new one, still recognizable by the D-M baggage tag Luca gave me. What did he write on that note? May every journey end with your heart's desire? My heart's desire is to get off this plane.

The baggage handlers back away from the plane, then chug off in their empty cart. The cart, at least, brings a brief smile to my face. My secret weapon. And the clear victor in the cart versus Cessna battle. Guess they had to replace the cart that got mangled. And the plane. Which reminds me of plane crashes. Which reminds me of the lump in my stomach.

"It always feels like I may never come back," I say, still facing outside. I can feel Josh looking at me, but I'm so apprehensive I can't face him. "Like I'm taking off into somewhere unknown. Alone. Leaving my . . . security, you know?"

Josh's roar of laughter surprises me. "This is the woman who faced down two thugs and a psychopath FBI agent armed with a .44 Magnum? The woman who risked her life for a friend? Yes, darling, I can see how much you crave security."

He leans close and kisses my cheek, then turns my face toward his with one finger. "And you think flying is dangerous?"

The engines begin that whine, the wheels begin to move. I can feel my chest clench and I have to remember to breathe. For a moment, I can pretend it's the plane parked next to us that's actually underway. But it's us.

Focus on Josh. Focus on Josh. Focus on Josh. And from the look on his face, he's focusing on me, too.

"We're together," he says. "You're not alone. Not in flying, not in your life."

I look at him, so earnest and genuine. Devoted. Hilarious. Patient. Maybe, just maybe. A wisp of a thought dances through my mind, so ephemeral it almost escapes. My contract with Channel 3 expires next June. Maybe I should . . . consider . . .

"You're not leaving. You're arriving," Josh continues. "And you need to know your journey is toward a new destination. Not away from an old one. You see? When you take off, that's a beginning. Not an ending."

"Well, folks, we are next in line for takeoff on runway L115." A voice crackles over the loudspeaker, almost understandable. "ETA in Miami is two and a half hours, with connecting flights to —" the announcement pauses, and I can hear some unintelligible voices in the background. "More on that later," the voice turns exaggeratedly jovial. "But we're told the weather is clear and sunny at all final destinations."

The plane slowly taxies down the tarmac, gradually picking up speed. And for an instant, I have a glimmer of what Josh means. I've done the same job for more than twenty years. Had the same life for more than twenty years. I love it, of course. And I'm happy. But if I don't allow myself to take off, how will I ever get anywhere new? And maybe that's how you know the real thing. If you're willing to leave the ground. Let go. Fly.

"As I was trying to tell you, before our captain so rudely interrupted," Josh says. "I think I know your problem, Miss McNally. I think it's time for you to stop flying solo."

"Well, yes, it is better with you here," I say, and this time my smile is genuine. I curl both my arms around his, getting as close to him as I can despite the padded armrest between us for takeoff. "And you know, maybe I should think about —"

Josh reaches into the pouch on the seat back in front of him. And pulls out a little blue box.

A small, square, robin's-egg-blue box tied

with a white satin ribbon.

"No more flying solo," he says again. And he hands me the package.

The roar of the engines fills the cabin, the gravity and velocity and speed pressing my head into the back of my seat. I feel the massive airplane, with me and Josh strapped inside, leave the ground and soar into the gray November sky, heading for a destination I still don't know.

What do I know? I know what's in this little box. And I know what I'll say after I open it.

And where Josh and I will go after that? Well, we'll have to take off first. And find out the rest when we arrive.

ABOUT THE AUTHOR

Award-winning investigative reporter *Hank Phillippi Ryan* is on the air at Boston's NBC affiliate. Her work has resulted in new laws, people sent to prison, homes removed from foreclosure and millions of dollars in restitution. Along with her twenty-six Emmy and ten Edward R. Murrow Awards, Hank has won dozens of other regional, national and international journalism honors for her hard-hitting investigations. Hank began her television career reporting and anchoring the news in Indianapolis and Atlanta. She's also worked as a proofreader, a radio reporter, a legislative aide in the United States Senate and — in a two-year stint as editorial assistant at *Rolling Stone* magazine — helped organize presidential campaign coverage for Hunter S. Thompson. She and her husband live just outside Boston.

www.HankPhillippiRyan.com

The employees of Thorndike Press hope you have enjoyed this Large Print book. All our Thorndike, Wheeler, and Kennebec Large Print titles are designed for easy reading, and all our books are made to last. Other Thorndike Press Large Print books are available at your library, through selected bookstores, or directly from us.

For information about titles, please call:
(800) 223-1244

or visit our Web site at:
http://gale.cengage.com/thorndike

To share your comments, please write:
Publisher
Thorndike Press
295 Kennedy Memorial Drive
Waterville, ME 04901